MOB

ALL OUR TOMORROWS

Recent Titles by Pamela Oldfield from Severn House

The Heron Saga
BETROTHED
THE GILDED LAND
LOWERING SKIES
THE BRIGHT DAWNING

RIDING THE STORM

ALL OUR TOMORROWS

Pamela Oldfield

This first world edition published in Great Britain 2001 by
SEVERN HOUSE PUBLISHERS LTD of
9–15 High Street, Sutton, Surrey SM1 1DF.
This first world edition published in the USA 2001 by
SEVERN HOUSE PUBLISHERS INC. of
595 Madison Avenue, New York, NY 10022.

British Library Cataloguing in Publication Data

Oldfield, Pamela, 1934–
    All our tomorrows
    1. Love stories
    I. Title
    823.9'14 [F]

ISBN 0–7278–5680–4

Typeset by Palimpsest Book Production Limited,
Polmont, Stirlingshire, Scotland.
Printed and bound in Great Britain by
MPG Books Ltd, Bodmin, Cornwall.

One

"**D**o it!" she told herself. "Do it *now*!"

Forcing a confident smile, Moyna Ellyard pushed open the door to The Linen Store, startled as usual by the loud clanging from the bell. With her head held high she walked through the shop, a tin of fairy cakes clutched to her chest, past a middle-aged assistant measuring blue silk.

"Good morning, Mrs Ellyard."

Moyna smiled at her. She never could remember their names. Cook or Crane? She passed the other assistant, an older woman wrapping tea towels for a customer, folding brown paper and tying string with practised ease. She glanced up at Moyna.

"Good morning, Mrs Ellyard."

"Good morning."

Past the manager, stationed as usual at the cashier's till. They didn't have a cashier, just the two assistants, the manager and a cleaning woman.

"Good morning, Mrs Ellyard." He was small and wiry with suspiciously black hair.

"Good morning, Mr Dunn. I hope you're well."

"Oh yes, thank you. And yourself?"

"Very well."

He leaned forward and lowered his voice. "I'm sorry we

1

couldn't run the promotion you suggested. I tried but your husband was adamant. You understand, I'm sure."

"I do, but thank you for trying."

George had refused even to consider her idea for the mid-summer sale, as she had known he would. She glanced round the store in search of Miss Wheatley. There was no sign of her, but she might be in the stockroom. Frustrated, Moyna started up the stairs. At the top of the stairs she turned right and went straight into the office. The small room looked even smaller, furnished as it was with two metal filing cabinets, a small table for the crockery, tea caddy and gas ring, and a large desk which supported a typewriter, ledgers and numerous wire mesh trays for correspondence. A couple of chairs took up any space which remained.

George glanced up from his ledger. "Is it too much to expect you to knock?"

Setting the cake tin on the table, Moyna swallowed. Do it, she urged herself. Ask about her. She drew a long breath to steady her nerves while George ran a pencil down the page in front of him, muttering soundlessly ás he added figures in his head. For a moment or two Moyna watched him, trying to see him through the eyes of another woman. She saw a man in his late forties who had once been attractive, with a sturdy frame and curly hair. Now he was balding, a little overweight and had a nose that was gradually reddening with the over-liberal intake of after-dinner port. But he was still "hale and hearty", as he frequently told her. Fit as a fiddle. In jolly good shape. He was proud of his health and had no patience with her frequent headaches and occasional bilious attacks.

Crossing the room, Moyna took a plate from the cupboard, covered it with a doily and arranged the cakes.

He looked up. "Oh dear. No icing today?"

Ignoring the mild sarcasm she said, "You know I try to vary them."

"I don't know why you bother, dear. I don't think they're appreciated."

"I'm sure they are, George." She kept her tone light. "A little Saturday treat. And it gives me a chance to show my face. Meet them. Say hello."

George shrugged. Moyna filled the kettle, settled it on the gas ring and lit the gas. Fighting back irritation she began to set out the cups and saucers. The women would come upstairs one at a time for their mid-morning break. Ten minutes. No more. Moyna had promised herself that today she would meet the wonderful Miss Wheatley face to face – but where was she? In the toilet perhaps. And when she *had* met her, what then? Would she know whether or not she was right to suspect George of infidelity? Or if not an actual infidelity, then the desire for one.

George closed the ledger with a sigh and rubbed his eyes. "I didn't sleep well," he said. "I was wide awake for hours." Idly he swivelled in the ancient leather chair from which he refused to be parted. Moyna glanced round the office. Shabby, untidy and fusty from lack of air.

"Shall I open the window?" Her hand was already on the catch.

"If I want it open, I'll open it myself." The familiar note of asperity crept once more into his voice. "I do wish you wouldn't meddle, Moyna. The Linen Store is *my* responsibility. *My* area of expertise."

"But I just thought—"

"Please don't, dear. I don't interfere with the laundry or the cooking."

Moyna was surprised to feel a spurt of anger instead of the familiar hurt. She spooned tea from the caddy into the teapot without replying. The kettle whistled and she turned off the gas and filled the teapot. As she did so she fought off a deepening despair. Once she had loved this man, but for years he had kept her at a distance.

She turned to face him. "Don't you love me any more, George?" The blunt words shocked her. It wasn't the question she had come to ask. She felt in her heart that he didn't love her although she didn't know why. He certainly kept up a pretence of loving her and for years she had told herself that was enough. Now fear gripped her.

"What sort of question is that?" Her husband was staring at her in astonishment. "What on earth possessed you to burst in here with a damn fool question like that?" A dull colour flooded his face. "I think the best thing you can do is to go home."

Tearing her gaze from his face she studied her clasped hands. Her determination wavered dangerously.

"Moyna! Did you hear me?"

"But the cakes . . ."

"Oh for God's sake! They can eat a few cakes without your supervision. Go home! We'll talk later."

His expression was thunderous but she still hadn't asked him the real question. She drew a quick breath. "Where is Miss Wheatley, George? Why can't I meet her?"

"Why the sudden interest in Miss Wheatley?"

"I'm curious, that's all, and I think I should meet her. You introduced me to the others."

I need to look into her eyes, she added wordlessly, to see if my suspicions are correct.

"Miss Wheatley doesn't come in on Saturdays. She helps her widowed mother run their boarding house. It's a busy time for them. Look, Moyna, you're not yourself. Go home and have a bit of a rest."

His voice had softened marginally, she noticed. Guilt, perhaps, or remorse.

"Miss Wheatley . . . What's she like?" she persevered. "Is she satisfactory?"

"Of course she is. I wouldn't keep her on if she were not. I've told you before. She's quite charming, willing to learn, eager to please. The customers like her, the staff like her

– and so do I. Now do, please, get along home, Moyna, before Miss Crane comes up."

So Miss Wheatley was "quite charming". A paragon in fact. Moyna struggled to remain calm. It would never do to let George know how frightened she felt. "I'm beginning to think that Saturday is not a good day for the cakes," she told him with a smile. "Too busy. Next week I'll come in on a different day." And then I might get to see Miss Wheatley, she thought, because I shan't tell you in advance.

George's expression changed. "That's not a good idea. Saturday is the only day . . . I'll allow it."

Her heart hammered a warning. Don't lose your temper, Moyna. "What will you do then, George, if I come in on Thursday? Throw me out? Won't that look rather strange?"

"Do try not to be ridiculous."

For a moment they glared at one another. Moyna was aware that they were on the verge of a confrontation but knew that George had the most to lose by an embarrassing scene. He needed the respect of his staff and wouldn't want to be heard quarrelling with his wife.

There were footsteps on the stairs.

"Well, I must get on," George told her briskly. "I'll be home for lunch as usual." He resumed his seat and returned to his figures, denying by his change of tone that anything out of the ordinary had happened.

After a moment's indecision Moyna left the office without a word, passing the older of the two assistants coming up. Of course. This one was Miss Crane.

"Goodbye, Miss Crane. Have a nice weekend."

The grey-haired one was Mrs Cook – and Miss Wheatley was still a phantom who, in George's eyes, could do no wrong. But was it any more than that?

At the bottom of the stairs she saw the older assistant heading towards her, a bundle of aprons in her hands.

The powdered face crumpled in a smile. "Did I see the cake tin?"

"You did, Mrs Cook. Fairy cakes." Smile back, she told herself.

"Oh, how scrumptious! You do spoil us! And how's that boy of yours? Young Frank . . . Quite the young man now, I expect."

"Very grown up. Yes. Just turned eighteen."

She gave Mrs Cook a nod and then hurried towards the shop door. The manager darted from behind the counter and opened it for her.

"Thank you, Mr Dunn."

"We are always pleased to see you, Mrs Ellyard."

Too upset to go home, Moyna walked to the sea front and found an empty deckchair. Leaning back she breathed deeply with her eyes closed. So this Miss Wheatley was "quite charming". And what else? Eager to please? What did that mean exactly, she wondered. She tried once again to imagine this paragon. Blonde curls, big blue eyes with fluttering lashes, a trim body . . .

"Oh don't be ridiculous!" she muttered, attempting to drive the image from her mind. What would a woman like that see in George? She certainly wouldn't see what Moyna had seen all those years ago. Then George had been a young man with a wonderful way with words. He could charm the birds from the trees, as Moyna's mother had said, half in love with him herself. In those far-off days George Ellyard had been a great companion with a sense of fun.

"So what went wrong?" It was a question she had asked many times.

Recovering a little of her composure, she stood up and began to walk down to the water's edge, making her way past a large moated sandcastle on which a young boy and his father were working.

The man looked up. "A des res!" he explained, half apologetically.

Moyna smiled. "All mod cons, I hope."

The boy sat back on his haunches and squinted up at her. "A giant lives in this castle."

A yard away his mother glanced up from her magazine. "He's giant mad!"

Moyna nodded, her throat tight, envying the little family. Once she had sat on these same sands with George and Frank, but now their son was growing away from them. He was currently in France on a walking holiday with his friend Douggie. What did Frank think of their marriage, she wondered, with a cold feeling in her stomach. He must notice the atmosphere; must be aware that something was wrong. And yet he gave no sign. Perhaps he thought that all marriages were loveless. She hoped not. She hoped he would eventually find a woman with whom he could be happy.

The September sun was still comfortingly warm and she wished she could take off her shoes and stockings and paddle. Hardly the done thing, though, for a thirty-eight-year-old woman. George would certainly not approve.

Frank used to love watching the ships and spent many a happy afternoon with the binoculars George had bought him for his tenth birthday. Shading her eyes, Moyna scanned the sea. A few local boats fished close to shore but further out there was a cargo vessel low in the water. Carrying coal, perhaps. To her left three girls surrounded a man selling toffee apples, their young voices shrill with excitement. At the water's edge an elderly man was rolling up his trouser legs and to her right a young man with a towel round his waist struggled beneath it to remove his wet swimming costume.

George had said they would talk and that was a start. But not over the midday meal, she decided. She had two nice fillets of plaice and she didn't want to waste them. She would make sure that they enjoyed their dinner. Her mother always claimed that the way to a man's heart was through his stomach – although it hadn't worked with George, she thought ruefully. They would talk this evening.

She climbed the steps to the promenade, still wondering if she had done the right thing by challenging George about his feeling towards her.

"Why on earth did you say that?" she muttered, and recalled the expression on George's face. At least she had managed to surprise him so maybe it was for the best. If he no longer cared for her they need no longer pretend, but she had no idea where it would lead. What mattered was that *she* had taken the initiative and George would be wondering. She imagined him sipping his tea and nibbling a fairy cake as he tried to chat normally with Miss Crane. On second thoughts he would most likely decline the cake.

"Let him wonder!" She leaned over the rail watching the seagulls, listening to the soft roar of the waves, breathing in the familiar scent of drying seaweed and warm sand. She whispered, "Good for you, Moyna. You're doing well!" and lifted her head and smiled.

"Beautiful! *Beautiful!* That's what I like to see. A happy smiling face!"

Startled, Moyna turned to see a beach photographer hurrying towards her, a boater at a jaunty angle on his untidy curls, his camera poised. Moyna opened her mouth to say "No" but closed it again.

He said, "One more for luck."

Feeling reckless, Moyna nodded. His easy banter soon had her smiling in earnest and before she knew what was happening he had taken several more photographs. He made a note of her name and address and promised delivery in three days' time.

"Oh! I don't know," Moyna began. "My husband—"

"Don't tell me!" He raised his eyebrows. "Why don't

husbands want a lovely snap of their lovely wives? Beats me. The thing is – will he be in when the post comes?"

"No–o, I suppose not."

"There you are then, my love. Keep it a secret if that's the way you want it. Tuck it away in a drawer under your nighties!" He rolled his eyes suggestively as he held out a hand for the money. A minute later the deal was done and Moyna was about to thank him when his interest was suddenly aroused by a large matron carrying a Pekinese.

"Beautiful. *Beautiful*," he enthused, darting towards her. "That's what I like to see. A lovely lady with a lovely little dog!"

Moyna watched the woman brighten. Men! But she was pleased that she had had her photograph taken. Why shouldn't she have a snapshot of herself looking pretty and *happy*? It was only a small extravagance and the photographer was right, she needn't tell George. She would keep the snap in her shoe box. It held an assortment of past treasures – photos of herself as a child, letters from a school friend, glossy beribboned birthday cards and a small raffia cross given to her in Sunday school on Palm Sunday.

Crossing the road, she dodged a tram as her mind returned to the coming confrontation. If George did still love her, let him say so – and let him prove it. She couldn't remember when he had last bought her flowers. If he didn't love her – she swallowed hard. How much would she care? Did she still love *him*? Probably not, she thought, and was chilled by the idea. If he were in love with Miss Wheatley . . . She quickened her steps.

By the time she arrived home a little of her new-found courage had deserted her and as she let herself in at the front door she was quaking inside. Tonight she and George would talk and because of that talk her life would change. For better or for worse.

*   *   *

9

"We're celebrating tonight!" cried Ginnie as she raced up the stairs in search of her mother. "Guess what?"

She found her in the front bedroom known as the Primrose Room. Her mother, tugging sheets from the bed, looked up in exasperation.

"For heaven's sake, Ginnie! Must you go shouting round the place like some kind of hoyden? Haven't I—"

"Tonight's the night!" Ginnie tossed a bottle of wine into the middle of the mattress.

"Celebrating what, exactly?" Iris demanded, picking up the bottle. "Wine? We don't drink wine."

"We do tonight!" Ginnie threw herself into the middle of the bed and lay laughing up at her mother. She adopted a deeper voice and said, "I've decided, Miss Wheatley, that you have settled in well here and show great promise. I shall therefore raise your wages, beginning next month!" She sat up. "I've got a rise, Mum!"

"Don't call me Mum!"

Ginnie rolled her eyes in mock despair. "Mummy, then. Half a crown a week more. I can't believe it." Hurling herself from the bed she retrieved the wine and set it on the chest of drawers. Then she tossed her jacket on to a nearby chair, snatched up a clean sheet from the pile and moved to face her mother across the bed.

Iris Wheatley had the same abundant red hair as her daughter and neither had been tempted by the prevailing fashion for short waves. Iris's smooth hair was drawn up into a french pleat. Ginnie's curls were tied back with a navy-blue ribbon. Ginnie had long since decided that her mother's eyes were hazel while her own were a wonderful emerald colour, although this made her feel a little disloyal.

Together they shook out the sheet and laid it carefully across the bed.

"You don't look very pleased," Ginnie grumbled, disappointed by her mother's reaction.

"But you don't work Saturdays. When did he tell you about this rise?"

Ginnie hoped she wasn't blushing. "An hour ago. I just popped in – to tell Miss Crane something." Better not to admit that curiosity had driven her into The Linen Store. She had hoped to meet Mr Ellyard's wife but had missed her by about five minutes. "I promised to take Miss Crane a magazine. We'd talked about a recipe for quince jam and—" She shrugged lightly. "Well, that's when he told me about the money. He saw me in the shop and said I was to go up to his office so I did."

"And didn't the others wonder?"

"No. Why should they? I don't wonder if he wants to talk to Mrs Cook or . . . Anyway, what does it matter? I've got another half crown a week! You might at least pretend to be pleased."

"Of course I'm pleased! It's wonderful, Ginnie." Iris smiled. "Really I am."

"I show great promise, so there!" Ginnie laughed, reaching for a clean pillowslip. "He'll be making me manageress before long, I shouldn't wonder! I shall be rich before you know it! We'll do all the things you want to do with this place. New curtains with matching bedspreads. A carpet for the hall. You can get rid of the old washstands and we'll have a handbasin in each bedroom." These visions, she knew, would distract her mother's attention.

Iris brightened, patting the pillows into place. "I've had this wonderful idea for the rooms." She shook out the top sheet. "We'll name them after famous stars – but only if they've appeared in Margate. We might have to get their permission, but why should they mind? They should be flattered. This could be the Gertrude Lawrence room, next door could be Jessie Matthews . . ."

"Or Jack Buchanan!"

"Jack Buchanan? Name one after a man?" Iris hesitated.

"Well, I suppose we could. I was thinking more . . ." They smoothed the sheet and folded in the corners. "We could have a framed photograph of each person on the wall—"

"A *signed* photograph!"

"—And playbills – or sheet music if she – or he – is a singer."

Ginnie struck a pose, one arm extended. "Who-o-o stole my heart away? Who-o-o made me dream all day . . ." It was her mother's favourite song.

Iris grinned. "Exactly. So what do you think?"

"It's a smashing idea."

They added blankets to the bed and threw over the primrose-yellow eiderdown.

Ginnie's mind was still working on the idea. "We could play the gramophone during the evening meal – just songs from the musicals!"

Iris's face had lit up at the prospect and Ginnie saw her chance. "But I'm not to tell the others about the half-crown in case they're jealous." She gave her mother a sideways glance and added, "I think Mr Ellyard has taken a shine to me."

Iris straightened up instantly. "Taken a shine to you? I should hope he hasn't! A young woman like you. Why, Mr Ellyard's old enough to be – *and* he's a married man, for heaven's sake! Just because he gives you a rise you don't have to go thinking that he's smitten."

Ginnie laughed. "I'm his favourite, Mum. I can tell. He fiddled with one of my curls when no one was watching."

"He did *what*?" Now she had all her mother's attention. "What's got into the man?"

"Nothing's got into him. He's just fascinated by my hair. Honestly Mum, I feel a bit sorry for him. He's so . . . so dull."

"George Ellyard *dull*? Surely not."

"What makes you say that?"

Iris looked flustered. "I mean . . . he doesn't strike me as dull. Quiet perhaps. Or earnest."

"Earnest *is* dull!" She thought about him. "I might send him a Valentine card next year. Just to see his face! Brighten his day."

Her mother had one hand to her heart and was breathing quickly. "Mr Ellyard is your *employer*, Ginnie. Just because he's given you a rise you've no call to go pestering the man. Valentine indeed!" She narrowed her eyes. "I hope you've done nothing to encourage him, Ginnie, because if you have you'll be sorry. Because I shall go down to the store and ask to see him. I'll give him a piece of my mind. You should never have gone there in the first place. I was never happy about it." She paused to take another breath. "He's no business having favourites."

"*Mum*! For goodness sake! He likes me, that's all."

"You're just an employee, remember. And you'd better keep very quiet about the rise. Miss Crane and the other one might get jealous and women can be very spiteful. I don't mean to spoil your big moment—"

"Don't you?" Ginnie gave her a withering look. "Then why are you being so horrid?"

"I don't mean to but—"

They were saved by the front door bell.

Iris said, "That'll be Mrs Loame, forgotten her key again. You'd better let her in."

"No, *you* let her in. I'll bring down the washing." Her mouth a thin line, Ginnie bent to gather up the bedlinen. She caught sight of the wine bottle and was tempted to empty it into the slop bucket by way of retaliation. Her mother hated waste. After a moment or two, however, common sense prevailed. Ginnie rolled the bedlinen into a bundle, picked up the bottle and turned at the door to look back at the room. The Gertrude Lawrence room. It was a brilliant idea. But not for the room in its present state. Like all

13

the rooms, it was shabby. Shabby enough, apparently, to deter many of the guests from making a return visit. The wallpaper had faded, the paintwork had discoloured and the rugs were almost threadbare. Her mother blamed Margate for their declining fortunes. "The town's not what it was" was her favourite lament. Her uncle blamed it on the film shows. "Cinemas will be the death of theatres," he insisted whenever he could find someone who would listen.

Ginnie sighed, her anger fading quickly as it always did where Iris was concerned. She adored her mother and woe betide anyone who criticised her in Ginnie's hearing, but at eighteen Ginnie considered herself an adult and able to look after herself. Closing the door behind her, she made her way downstairs to find her mother in conversation with their only permanent resident. Mrs Loame was an elderly lady of means who had moved into Ocean View nearly six years earlier and with any luck would end her days with them. They had no idea how old she was but Ginnie hoped she would live to be a hundred.

Mrs Loame turned, patting her thinning hair with a fragile hand which was weighed down with rings. "Oh, there you are, Ginnie dear. I was just telling your mother that the Walls man won't be calling this evening. He's had a rather nasty accident, poor fellow. A collision with a baker's van. He was thrown from his bicycle at the corner of Princes Street. He wasn't seriously hurt but the ice creams and cones ended up all over the pavement!"

"He could have been killed," said Iris. "Oh well, no ice cream for tonight. I'll have to make a fruit jelly instead. We've got three in from Bromley tonight. A Mr and Mrs Hatton and their daughter. Staying for five days. They were at The Carlton for the first two days but didn't like the beds." She couldn't resist a smile. "Lumpy as hell! That's how the father described them. Mind you, when did you ever hear a good word about The Carlton?"

"It's an ill wind . . ." said Ginnie.

"Ginnie's had a rise at work," Iris told Mrs Loame. "Her employer said she was a hard worker and very promising . . ."

Mrs Loame beamed. "Ginnie dear, how splendid."

"Half a crown extra a week!" Ginnie held up the bottle of wine. "So we're celebrating tonight."

"I should think so too. A rise. What fun."

Back in the kitchen, her ill humour forgotten, Ginnie donned an apron and made a start on the vegetables while her mother made a very large beef and onion pie. The kitchen was one of Ginnie's favourite rooms. Large and airy with a vast cooking range and a gas cooker, it was always cosy in winter though difficult to keep cool in summer. The large Welsh dresser occupied one wall and an array of saucepans covered another. A third wall had a hatch which opened into the dining room and the fourth boasted two large windows. Now, watching her mother, Ginnie bided her time. The matter of Mr Ellyard's behaviour, she knew, was not yet exhausted.

At last Iris said, "Your Mr Ellyard – what kind of man is he? A bit of a womaniser, would you say?"

"Oh no! Quite the opposite. Miss Crane and Mrs Cook don't like him very much. They think he's grumpy. He's not really but he *is* . . ." She searched for the right word to describe her employer. "Not grumpy exactly, but gruff. He comes across as a bit of a sobersides but—"

"A sobersides? Really, Ginnie! I've seen him once or twice in the shop and he struck me as pleasant enough."

Ginnie raised her eyebrows. "I'm beginning to think you fancy him yourself!"

"Don't be ridiculous."

"His heart's in the right place, I grant you that, but the old biddies—"

"Ginnie Wheatley!" Iris wagged a finger at her daughter.

"Old biddies indeed. Show a little respect for your elders, please!" She pushed the pie into the oven and stared distractedly around the kitchen. "So he has got a heart and it's in the right place. Which brings us to Mrs Ellyard." She began to roll the pastry scraps into a ball. "What's she like?"

"I haven't seen her yet. She brings cakes in on a Saturday for the morning tea break but I'm never there. Miss Crane says she's rather quiet. 'Put upon', is how she described her."

"Pretty?"

"She didn't say, but I expect so."

"Are they happy together?"

Ginnie stared at her. "Happy? How should I know?"

"I thought the others might gossip. You know."

Ginnie grinned. "If she likes dull, earnest men she should be deliriously happy!"

Her mother tutted at this flippancy but then her gaze landed on the dresser. "Oh, I forgot to tell you – your uncle Michael left you a couple of comps for the show tonight."

Ginnie brightened. Complimentary tickets were always welcome.

Iris went on, "He had three pairs to give away so they're not doing too well. If you want to nip away early that's fine with me. I can wash up. You can take Laura with you."

Michael Wheatley, Ginnie's uncle, worked as assistant stage manager at the Theatre Royal and a lot of complimentary tickets meant box office sales were slow. If the theatre closed again he'd be out of work.

Ginnie frowned. "But what about our celebration? The wine?" she asked.

Iris smiled. "It'll keep, love. We'll celebrate tomorrow."

"We could go together – slide in a bit late."

Her mother shook her head. "I'm not in the mood, if you must know. Just clear the tables and then get off. It doesn't start until eight and it's always a few minutes late."

As Ginnie leaped towards the door to tell Dora the good news, Iris held up a finger. "And no more talk about Valentine cards. I mean it. I don't want any daughter of mine fluttering her eyelashes at a married man. Now you promise."

Dramatically, Ginnie crossed herself. "Cross my heart and hope to die!"

Once outside she allowed herself a broad grin as she hurried across the road to her friend's house. "I'll send him a birthday card instead!"

An hour later, as the police constable made his way up the front steps, he straightened his tunic and took a deep breath. This was a test, he told himself. If he could deal with this he would make a good policeman. He fixed his eyes on the front door and tried again to remember the little speech he had memorised. Reaching the door he was faced with a new quandary. The knocker or the bell? He chose the latter and waited.

The door was opened by a middle-aged woman.

She said, "Oh my Lord!" and a hand went to her heart in anticipation.

"I'm Constable Budd, Mrs Ellyard. I'm afraid I have . . ."

She was shaking her head. "I'm Mrs Locke, the daily. I'll call – oh, here she is."

From behind her a younger woman appeared. She was well dressed and her short dark hair was fashionably waved.

"Who is it?" she asked, then caught sight of the uniform. Her large eyes darkened as she caught her breath.

It was just the way they had described it, he thought. A policeman on your doorstep is never going to be good news. Unless you need one, of course.

"Mrs Ellyard?"

"Moyna Ellyard – yes."

"I wonder if I could speak to you privately, madam?"

"Of course. Please come in."

She led the way to a sitting room and they both sat down. He removed his helmet and held it in his hands.

"I'm afraid it's your husband," he said. Damn. He'd got it wrong already. Supposed to start with "I'm afraid I have bad news."

"George? Why – what's happened?"

She was fiddling with the pearls at her neck. A rather nice neck, actually. Slim. He liked tall women.

"I'm afraid it's bad news. There's been a bit of an accident."

Still hovering behind her employer, the daily woman gasped.

He continued, "He was taken to hospital, madam." That was better. Break it gently, one fact at a time. He relaxed a little, feeling more in control.

"George? Oh no! You must be mistaken." She glanced at the daily woman as though for confirmation. "He's on his way back to his shop. We've just had our lunch."

"I'm afraid it is him, Mrs Ellyard. He was found—"

"Found?"

"He was found by the postman lying on the pavement—"

She stood up. "I must go to him."

He rose to his feet. "I'm afraid . . . that is, there's really no hurry, madam."

"What d'you mean? Is he unconscious?"

"Well, yes, in a way." He never would be conscious again. "I regret to tell you that your husband is . . . he's dead." Watching her face, he saw a slow realisation dawn.

She sat down heavily, staring up at him. "George is *dead?*"

He nodded. "Found unconscious on the pavement, madam. Dead on arrival they say."

"You're sure it *is* George? I mean he was fine. On his way back to work. I can't believe it."

"Probably a heart attack. I'd like to offer my condolences."

Ten minutes later Moyna sipped the tea Mrs Locke had made for them and waited for the panic to subside. At the moment it was overwhelming, making it hard for her to breathe and causing her heart to beat at a terrifying pace, leaving no room for grief. She and Mrs Locke sat on opposite sides of the table, staring at each other in shocked disbelief.

As the silence lengthened, Moyna felt obliged to break it. She said, "I think . . . at least . . ." She saw Mrs Locke waiting for the rest of the sentence but had no idea what she wanted to say. Speechlessly, she shook her head.

Stunned by the suddenness of the disaster, Moyna still trembled as she tried to come to terms with the knowledge that her husband was dead. "People don't have heart attacks at that age, do they?"

Mrs Locke frowned. "Not Mr Ellyard. All that cricket he played . . . and the evening walks on the beach. Never missed, come rain, come shine. Can't believe he's gone. I just *can't*."

"Neither can I." Moyna put down the cup. "I'll have to tell Frank, poor lamb. He'll be broken-hearted. That's if I can reach him in France. They're walking. He could be anywhere. And what on earth can I say to him?" She could think of no way to soften the blow. His father was dead. "And the people at the The Linen Store. Oh dear! Mr Dunn will be dreadfully upset."

Mrs Locke dabbed at her eyes. "That poor lad! Ruin his holiday, this will. Ruin his *life*, most likely."

"Oh, don't say that!" Moyna felt fresh tears on her cheeks and pressed a damp handkerchief to her eyes. She could imagine her son returning to the hotel to be greeted by the news of his father's death. She could see his face, puckered into despair, could hear his voice shaking with grief. The walking holiday would have to be cut short. She would send a telegram. Oh God. There was so much to think about.

"You'll want him back here for the funeral."

"The funeral!" She forced herself to confront the idea. George had always hated funerals, had avoided them whenever possible. This one he couldn't avoid. Poor George.

She said, "I have to go to the hospital to . . . to identify his . . . him." She couldn't bear the word "body". The man lying in the hospital was George. She tried to imagine him as he had been when she last saw him. Hale and hearty, a little hurried but no more than usual. They had eaten their meal, each pretending that everything was normal, carefully avoiding any mention of Miss Wheatley or the talk they would have later. Now they would never discuss her. She sighed. He had left with the usual peck on the side of her face, his head already filled with the afternoon's business. George Ellyard. The man she had loved for eighteen years; the man who had tried to love her in return. At least in the beginning. He had given her their son and had provided for them all. George Ellyard, a respected member of the church and one-time chairman of the businessmen's club. George Ellyard, owner of The Linen Store and useful allrounder with Margate's reserve cricket team.

His familiar image failed to materialise. Instead Moyna saw him silent and still, covered by a white sheet. Could he really be dead? It seemed so improbable.

With an effort, she levered herself to her feet. She was vaguely aware that the full impact of the tragedy was yet to come, so she must do all she could while she was still functioning. "Ring for a taxi, please, Mrs Locke."

"Should I come with you?"

Moyna hesitated. "Thank you, but I think I can manage." Manage what exactly, she wondered dazedly. Manage the rest of her life alone? She sighed. At least she was financially secure. The shop would continue under Mr Dunn's supervision and Frank would attend the College of Music as planned. And her own life? She would doubtlessly resume her normal activities at some stage – her painting class, the duty visits to George's mother in her home in Hastings. Thank goodness the poor soul was in no state to understand what had happened to her son.

Pulling on her coat, Moyna caught sight of her face in the hallstand mirror and was shocked. She looked pale and drawn, her eyes haunted. Years older.

"I can't do this, George!" she whispered. But her frightened face reflected the simple truth – somehow she had to do it. There was no one else. If she had that kind of strength within her, now was the time to discover it.

The Linen Store was located in Northdown Road. The original name had been retained but it was now a misnomer. It sold more than linens. The right-hand window was filled with a display of materials and a number of dress patterns. Two mannequins suitably draped with fabrics and lace eyed each other blankly across the window space. The left-hand window contained mounds of cushions, draped curtains and bedspreads.

Moyna stepped out of the taxi and hurried inside. It was now nearly closing time but the shop was still busy. Mrs Cook was holding up a length of sprigged cotton for the approval of a stout lady in black. Mourning, thought Moyna with a shudder and blinked back a further rush of tears. Fortunately Miss Crane was discussing curtain material with a customer and didn't register her arrival. A woman with two small boys was carrying one while dragging the other away from a pile of cushions. A younger woman waited at the counter with a bath towel. Stanley Dunn was no longer guarding the till. No doubt he was upstairs in the office.

As Moyna hurried through the shop towards the stairs she avoided the eyes of the two assistants. Mr Dunn could break the news to them later, choosing a suitable moment. She knocked on the door of the office, was invited in and offered a seat. It crossed her mind that this holy-of-holies was going to be *her* office from now on. She stared slowly round at the muddle of filing cabinets, samples of cloth and unopened boxes. The large desk was entirely hidden by a confusion of bills, papers and envelopes and she wondered, not for the first time, how George, who was so tidy at home, could be so untidy here. A recent offer to tidy up had been greeted by him with undisguised horror.

Stanley Dunn looked surprised to see her back so soon. He pushed his glasses up to the bridge of his nose and blinked his small brown eyes. George had been quite clear about his manager. "Dunn may look like a startled blackbird," he had told her, "but he's surprisingly shrewd."

"This is an unexpected pleasure—" He stopped, obviously alerted by her expression. "My dear Mrs Ellyard? Is something wrong?"

Moyna sat a little straighter in her chair. "I'm afraid it is. I've got terrible news. Mr Ellyard has died. On his way back to work. I can hardly believe it myself but the police came . . ."

His mouth had fallen open and he stared at her wide-eyed.

"They think it was a heart attack." The words came out in a rush. "I'm on my way to the hospital to . . ." Her voice failed her and she brushed away tears with the back of one hand as she fumbled in her bag for a handkerchief.

"But that – that's incredible! A heart attack?" His small hands fluttered helplessly. "Oh, this is quite dreadful, Mrs Ellyard. A calamity. What can I say? It's impossible – that is, I know it *isn't* impossible but . . ."

His confusion steadied her and she drew a deep breath. "I wanted to tell you personally. You need have no fears for your position, Mr Dunn. My husband thought very highly of you. Of all of you. Things will continue as before. At least, hardly as before, but you know what I mean." She saw relief flicker in his eyes. Unemployment in Margate was high and another position like his present one would be hard to come by. "I'd be grateful if you would tell the staff."

Stanley Dunn lowered his head into his hands and mumbled something. She assumed it was thanks. Possibly a prayer.

He looked up. "Mr Ellyard promised the new assistant a rise just this morning. Another half crown a week. Am I to let that stand?"

The question startled Moyna. She had never been consulted about the workings of the business and for a moment she hesitated, surprised by the sense of control it gave her. But why was Dunn asking? Was it because he didn't think the young woman merited a rise? Fleetingly the unkind thought crossed her mind that she had it in her power to say "No" but her natural sense of fair play triumphed and she nodded.

"Whatever my husband said must stand. He must have thought her satisfactory." It occurred to her suddenly that now she would never have that important talk with George. Nor would she know how much Miss Wheatley meant to him. They had both lost George Ellyard.

She stood up on leaden legs. "I have to go to the hospital now to . . . for identification purposes."

Stanley Dunn nodded. "If there's anything I can do . . ."

She swallowed hard, shaking her head silently. George was gone. There was nothing anyone could do but bury him with flowers, well-chosen words and a hymn or two of praise.

Two

Four days later Moyna adjusted her hat with trembling hands. George was being buried today. In less than an hour he would be under the ground. It still seemed impossible. Please, she prayed, let me get through the day without breaking down. She pulled down the black veil and was surprised to see that black suited her. George hated black and she had never worn it but now, satisfied with her appearance, she went in search of her mother. The older woman was muttering to herself in front of the hallstand mirror. Emily Grant was very like her daughter, but with increasing age grew thinner, which did not suit her. Years of criticism of the world in general had given her a dissatisfied expression.

Emily said, "I knew this hat was a mistake but you would insist. Strong-willed. That's what your father called you. He thought that a husband would tame you but he was wrong."

Moyna had heard it all before. "You look very nice, Mother . . . Oh, the car from Berridges is here."

"It won't stay on. I should have bought the felt. Thank heavens there's no real wind today. I need another hat pin."

"I'm sorry, Mother, but they're waiting for us. I don't want to be late."

Emily tutted but gave in. Arthritis had recently affected her legs and she clung to Moyna's arm with a martyred air as they made their way to the front door. Outside, however, the sight of the well-polished car cheered her. "At least they've sent something decent. When your father died the car was splashed with mud. Disgraceful. I told them so in no uncertain—"

"It was pouring with rain. It wasn't their fault. Let's go, shall we." Moyna settled her mother in the back seat then moved round the car to join her. The car edged forward at a respectful pace, following the hearse which also gleamed. George would have approved, she thought. At least it was a fine day. There would be no bedraggled group round the grave.

"Frank should be here." Emily stared straight ahead. "It's not right. A son ought to be at his father's funeral."

"I know he should, but what can I do?" Moyna smoothed her skirt down. George hated her to show her legs, but getting into cars was so awkward. "They don't know exactly where he is, Mother. He may not even *know* yet. He'll come as soon as he can, poor lamb." She fussed with her stockings.

"I never really liked him, you know. George, I mean. There was something about him. Of course your father wouldn't have it. Men stick together."

"Mother!" Moyna stared into the grim face. "You thought him a 'very good catch'. They were your very words to Father, so don't try to deny it."

"I may have liked him at the beginning, but not later. He changed – even before the wedding. It was the baby that did it. You should have refused to let him near you until the ring was on your finger. Oh yes, I can count, Moyna. I knew exactly what was happening."

Moyna was startled. "Why didn't you say something?"

"Because your father didn't know and I thought it best to

25

go along with the pretence, but I kept my eyes and ears open. Once he knew the child was on the way George changed. You know what they say – marry in haste, repent at leisure." Her lips trembled.

Moyna tried to think of something to say but her mother went on inexorably. "I've never said a word against the man, but now he's gone it doesn't matter."

"It matters to me, Mother!"

"Something changed in him. Don't ask me what it was, but something happened. When you were first engaged he was nice enough, I grant you that. Cheerful and well meaning. I said to your father, 'She'll be fine with him.' We were both pleased. Oh, I'm not saying he wasn't a good provider because he was. A bit mean at times, perhaps, but—"

"Mean? I admit he was careful but—"

"Oh yes. I caught him out one day. Keeping a measly bit of coal on the fire until you and I took Frank out in his pram. I popped back for my gloves and there he was stoking up the fire. For himself."

"That's not a crime – if the fire was getting low."

"Don't make excuses for him. He knew and I knew. He looked very guilty. I said to your father—"

Moyna cast a nervous glance at the driver. Presumably they overheard a lot of conversations like this. Family squabbles. No doubt the drivers compared notes while the service was taking place, having a laugh at the mourners' expense. She lowered her voice. "Frank and I never went without. That's all that matters." It didn't help that she was right, Moyna reflected, but she would never admit it. "And it's not right to bear grudges. It must have been years ago."

Emily turned her head and stared through the window. "Mind you, you were never in debt, that I know of. That counts for a lot. But he did change and you know it."

26

Moyna sat back in her seat, willing herself to stay silent, but eventually she said, "Perhaps it was the responsibility. A wife and young child . . ." If only she could believe that.

"I never did believe in long engagements. I thought at the time that a year would have been enough but you settled on two years. Ah, here we are at last. I hate funerals and this one will be no exception."

Moments later Moyna entered the church and saw the young woman almost immediately. Was that Miss Wheatley? Could it be anyone else? Young with beautiful red hair, she was sitting alone at the back of the church wearing a black jacket that fitted badly around the neck. They made eye contact briefly and Moyna could see the red-rimmed eyes beneath the small veil which decorated a black straw hat. So she had been crying. Do young women cry over the death of middle-aged employers, she wondered, and quickly suppressed the doubt as unworthy. If it was the assistant then the tears were a mark of respect and George would have liked that.

"Who on earth's that?" Emily's voice caused a few heads to turn in their direction.

"I don't know, Mother. Please keep your voice down."

"It's bad luck – strangers at a funeral." Emily stumbled, her grip tightening on Moyna's arm. "At least she knows her place."

They were each handed a copy of the service and a hymn book and muttered their thanks. As they passed down the aisle Moyna was aware of murmuring voices, rustling papers and an occasional cough. The air was scented with flowers and wax polish and the organist was improvising softly in the background. Moyna smiled at various friends and acquaintances and at others whom she did not recognise. There were members of the cricket club and a few business associates. Stanley Dunn sat with a woman Moyna took to be his wife. Presumably Miss Crane and Mrs Cook had

been left to hold the fort at the shop. Perhaps she should
have suggested that The Linen Store closed for the day but
it hadn't occurred to her until now.

Moyna and Emily took their places in the front row and sat
down. Emily, unable to kneel, covered her eyes and bent her
head. Moyna knelt, averting her eyes from the coffin which
contained the body. Try as she would, she had been unable
to drive from her memory the sight of his face in death, the
expression resigned and peaceful. She wondered now how
they had achieved such serenity but didn't want to know.

Emily nudged her. "I thought you ordered carnations.
They've sent chrysanths."

"It doesn't matter. George wasn't interested in flowers."
With an effort she tried to pray but suitable phrases escaped
her.

The churck clock struck the quarter. Fifteen minutes late.
Settling her hat more securely upon her short dark waves,
Moyna sighed. George had hated it when she returned from
the hairdresser with stylishly short hair.

"Aren't you a bit old for that?" he had asked. "And the
fringe doesn't suit you."

George had had a knack of wrong-footing her, she
reflected, but then made a renewed effort with her prayers.
Please God, let his soul rest in peace. *Please* let me think
only kind thoughts. She resumed her place on the pew.

Her mother leaned towards her. "It's chilly in here. You'd
think they'd at least start on time. George might not be in a
hurry but I am. I'm starving."

"You should have had a bigger breakfast," Moyna told
her. "I did warn you that we'd be late eating."

A cold September sun streamed in through the stained-
glass windows. It brightened the interior of the church but
did nothing to warm it. Her mother was right. Frank should
have been with them, but she had done all she could. The
telegram breaking the news of George's death had obviously

been delivered to their hotel, but if the two lads were in another area there was no sure way it could reach them.

The organ pealed suddenly and a crocodile of choirboys made its way to the stalls in front of the altar. They looked angelic but Moyna was not deceived. Frank had been a chorister and his accounts of their exploits had enlivened many a Sunday teatime. George had pretended to be shocked but secretly she and George had found the tales amusing. Now they passed her, eyes to the front, newly washed hair gleaming, their voices sweet and high. The vicar followed, resplendent and inspiring in his vestments, and the service finally began.

At about this time, in his office in the police station, Sergeant Evans was standing by the window, bellowing into the telephone.

"No I don't understand," he said. "I ordered the stuff weeks ago – the usual requisition . . . Of course I used the correct form, you idiot. I always use the correct form. D'you think I don't know my job after nearly eleven years in the force . . . It's called efficiency, in case you've never come across the word! No, next week will *not* do . . . And *I* suggest you get off your backside and send it round *today*! . . . Exactly! Now *do* it!"

Constable Budd appeared in the doorway with a sheet of paper in his hand, but the sergeant waved him away.

"But Sarge, I think you should look at this. It's the coroner's report on that sudden death."

Sergeant Evans put his hand over the mouth of the telephone and hissed, "Get out, Budd. Can't you see I'm busy?"

Bravely, the young constable stood his ground. "I think this might be serious, Sarge." He waved the paper. "Very serious. It's a copy of—"

The sergeant snatched the paper from him, threw it on to

his desk and waved Constable Budd outside the room. He
continued to harangue the man on the other end of the line.
"What's your name? . . . *Your name!* Are you deaf as well
as daft? . . . Finley? Right then, Finley, you get my stuff here
pronto or I'll have your guts for garters. Understand?"

He hung up the telephone and gave a long, exasperated
whistle. "Ruddy incompetents!" he muttered to the empty
room. "Couldn't organise a piss-up in a brewery! I don't
know where they find them, I really don't." He picked
up his mug and drank what remained of his tea. "Cold!
As always!"

He snatched up the sheet of paper which the constable
had brought in and glanced at it. As he read it his face
paled and all the bravado vanished as he sat down heavily.
After a moment he said, "Oh God!" He stared blindly ahead,
stricken into silence, then jumped to his feet. Rushing out of
the office into the reception area he cornered the constable
and waved the paper in front of his face.

"Sarge, I told you it was—"

"This is dated three days ago! Three ruddy days ago!
Where the hell's it been all this time? For heaven's sake,
Budd!" He clapped a hand to his head and stared wildly
round. "Where was it?"

"On the floor, Sarge, behind the—"

"On the *floor*?! Goddammit, man! You know what this
means?"

"Someone must have dropped it but it wasn't—"

"I don't mean that! I mean the report. Bruising to the
face and ribs. It wasn't a heart attack." He referred to the
report. "Considerable bruising! We are talking violence.
Assault. Punches and a good kicking. So what should we
have started, Budd?"

"An investigation, Sarge."

"Exactly. And we haven't done so. The man was attacked
in broad daylight in a street in the heart of Margate and we've

done sod all to find the perpetrator." He closed his eyes then opened them again in shock. "We must stop the funeral! Get the file, Budd, and find out if we were notified of the date." He caught sight of his constable's expression. "What? Oh, God! Don't tell me!"

Constable Budd nodded. "We were, Sarge. It started an hour ago. He'll be well buried by now!"

Outside the church a sombre group of mourners gathered round the open grave while behind them the choirboys, divested of their robes and responsibilities, scurried cheerfully along the path on their way home. Stanley Dunn had asked to say a few words and he spoke now. Moyna listened, trying not to stare at Miss Wheatley who she now saw was clutching a single red rose. Moyna's heart thudded. Did that signify anything or was she being paranoid?

" . . . always well-intentioned . . . considerate and understanding . . . a worldly man, not perfect but none of us are . . . a kind heart beneath a rather brusque exterior . . ."

Moyna kept her eyes on him. Poor chap. No doubt wondering what would become of the shop and his livelihood. She hadn't had much time to think about it, but she anticipated few changes. As the vicar spoke the final blessing a strengthening breeze ruffled his untidy white hair and the women clutched their hats. The sun was now hidden by tall cedars and Moyna shivered in the cool air.

"Goodbye George," she whispered. "Forgive me if you can for failing somehow to come up to your expectations." And I'll forgive you, she thought, for never caring enough.

It was at that moment that Moyna noticed the young woman again. She had stepped forward. Her lips moved silently and, with all eyes on her, she dropped the rose on to the coffin.

Back at the house, all was bustle. Moyna had engaged

caterers to provide what they had described as "a simple but satisfying cold collation" and ham, cold beef and salmon were laid out on the table in the dining room. Mrs Locke, wearing a black dress beneath her usual pinafore, was in her element, fluttering among the guests with a tray of sherry glasses. Several smaller tables had appeared and these were covered with white cloths and decent bone-handled cutlery. Folding chairs were also provided. At least George would have approved of this, Moyna comforted herself, and her spirits rose a little.

About thirty people were soon crowded round the tables, being served by two waitresses complete with white aprons and lace caps. Moyna's appetite had deserted her but she stood to one side replying to the various condolences. The bank manager promised help in times of trouble. The couple from next door pressed her hands and reminded her that she and George would eventually be reunited in Heaven. Moyna sipped her sherry and smiled wanly. When they had all gone home she would be alone with the solicitor and George's will. Not that she was worried. George had always kept her informed of the state of the business, which was never less than satisfactory or more than adequate. The Linen Store would come to her and she would leave it to Frank. If he had made a career for himself in the world of music he could sell it.

Her mother appeared beside her. The sherry appeared to be having a beneficial effect and she smiled as she touched Moyna's arm. "You must eat something, dear. Do come and sit down."

"I will in just a moment." Moyna sighed. "I'm so sorry Frank didn't get here in time. I had thought when we'd finished the food we might move into the sitting room and listen to Frank playing the piano. *Sheep May Safely Graze*, perhaps. George loved that."

Emily looked doubtful. "D'you think he would? You know how shy he is."

"But he wants to be a concert pianist, Mother! He's got to start somewhere."

"Does he, Moyna? Does he really want to be the focus of hundreds of people's attention? Wasn't that George's idea? He's always been so ambitious for the boy. Just because he enjoys playing it doesn't follow that he wants to perform in public. I sometimes regret giving him those lessons."

Surprised, Moyna thought about it. Had it really been Frank's idea or had George pushed him into it? They had talked for so long about Frank's musical career that she couldn't remember how it had all started. As a child, Frank had been happiest in the shop and had spent many happy hours there, playing with the cotton reels and being petted by the assistants. She smiled at the memory of her young son earnestly measuring cushions and scribbling meaningless symbols on a sheet of paper. George had assumed he would eventually take over the shop but when his grandmother had offered to pay for "a few piano lessons" he had shown an immediate flair for the instrument, delighting his music teacher with his progress. Now, aged eighteen, he was about to embark on a three-year course at the Royal College of Music.

"I'll talk to him about it," she said, and it came to her suddenly that from now on decisions would rest with her. Responsibility was something new and she hoped she was ready for it. She was about to elaborate when, from the corner of her eye, she saw the solicitor hurrying towards her.

"Can't stand the man!" Emily muttered and withdrew to her seat at the table.

Mr Levy was a plump little man – in his late forties, Moyna guessed. If she hadn't known better she would have thought he looked nervous.

33

"Mrs Ellyard, I wonder if we could talk privately in about twenty minutes," he said in a low voice. "I know your guests will still be here but I have another meeting and the service was a little late starting . . ."

"Of course. I don't think I'll be missed for ten minutes or so. We could talk in George's study."

"Ten minutes?" He swallowed hard. "I – I really think we should allow a little longer. The will is not . . . Well, shall we say, not entirely straightforward. That is, not quite what we expected. Oh dear . . . I'm so sorry, Mrs Ellyard. This isn't at all easy."

As Moyna stared into the solicitor's unhappy face she was aware of a deep coldness somewhere inside her. He was nervous and that could only mean bad news.

In the police station, panic had taken hold. Sergeant Evans was once again shouting into his telephone. "Do I have to spell it out for you?" he demanded, his face red with anxiety and frustration. "This is a possible murder investigation – at the very least a robbery with violence. Yes, manslaughter. No, we didn't know sooner. If we had we'd have moved on it. How could we? The report has only just reached us . . . How do I know why it took so long?" He rolled his eyes and crossed his fingers. "We need to do a door-to-door and quickly before all the witnesses disappear – that's if there ever were any witnesses . . ."

And please God there were, he thought. If this was murder it was his big chance. Margate had its normal complement of drunk and disorderlies, a few burglaries and now and then a domestic quarrel, but a murder was rare. He had won a commendation for tackling an arsonist single-handed, but a murder! He had never been so fortunate. And now, by some freak of chance, this one was getting off to a bad start. If it ever came out higher up that they had mislaid the coroner's report, his head would be on the block and no mistake.

"We need someone to go over the scene of the crime with a toothcomb," he explained. "Better late than never. Not that there'll be any clues after five days. And we have to interview the relatives. It might have been a family matter."

Never underestimate the passions that lie beneath a calm surface. That's what they'd taught him at police college and that's what he believed. The victim almost always knew his murderer.

Having received a grudging promise of two extra men, Sergeant Evans breathed a sigh of relief. Snatching a pen from the inkstand, he seized the original report and studied it carefully. Then with thudding heart he closed his door, warned that he was not to be disturbed and settled down to fill in a second report, dated retrospectively.

Upstairs in George's office, Moyna listened to the reading of the will. It was brief and to the point. George had left the house to her, a hundred pounds to Frank—

She nodded, waiting for the solicitor to continue. "And . . . ?" she prompted.

He drew a long breath. "Mrs Ellyard, I want you to understand that I knew nothing of the contents of this will. Your husband made this will years ago and hasn't altered it since. You mustn't feel . . . I'm sure there's a rational explanation . . ." He avoided her eyes and read on. "The business known as The Linen Store is to be sold and the proceeds shared between my wife . . . and an unnamed 'other'."

She stared at him without understanding.

He went on. "This aforesaid person to remain anonymous throughout."

Moyna's hands tightened in her lap. "Wait. *Wait!*" she cried. "An unnamed other? What on earth does that mean? Who is this . . . I mean . . . half the business? That's crazy. Impossible. George would never do a thing like that." As she uttered the words she thought of Miss Wheatley and felt a sudden coldness. But no, it couldn't be.

The solicitor was shaking his head. "I'm sorry, Mrs Ellyard, but 'unnamed' means exactly that. You aren't allowed to know the name of this person. That is quite explicit, I'm afraid."

"But you know it?"

He made no answer.

Moyna stammered, "Half the business? But how does he expect us to live?" Her mind whirled again. "Is it Mr Dunn?"

His lips tightened.

"Can't you nod or shake your head?" she asked.

"I'm not at liberty to reveal the name." He looked embarrassed. "I'm not trying to be difficult, Mrs Ellyard, but I must abide by the rules. Unnamed means just that. If we begin a process of elimination . . ." He shrugged, falling silent.

Moyna could see his point but still she persisted. She said, "It's Frank then!" Yes, she thought. She could bear that. George had probably decided to leave half to Frank in case he was ever forced to give up his musical career. She relaxed slightly. If that was George's thinking she could understand, but why "an unnamed other"? Why the secrecy? She glanced up.

The solicitor's lips tightened again, but she sensed that she had guessed wrongly.

"Not Frank."

He maintained his silence.

Stunned, Moyna closed her eyes, trying to make sense of the revelation.

"You'd better read the rest of it," she said. "There must be more. Some explanation. An apology even." Her voice trembled slightly as the shock was slowly replaced by anger.

Mr Levy shook his head. "That's all there is – except this letter for you. It might throw some light . . ." He handed her a slim brown envelope and, after a moment's hesitation, she tore it open with hands that trembled.

My dear Moyna, Please forgive me. This will come as a shock but there is no other way. To explain my reasons would be to cause you more pain and I want to avoid that at all costs. Do not blame yourself. God bless you. George

Moyna read it again and then a third time, more slowly, looking for a clue to her husband's motive. Finally she whispered. "It tells me nothing! Nothing at all," and handed it to the solicitor.

He read it in silence. "I'm so sorry," he said.

"And it's legal – this travesty of a will? Properly signed and witnessed?"

He nodded, handed the letter back and began to refold the document. Impulsively Moyna held out her hand. "Let me see it."

"I can't allow that."

"I need to know when it was written. That might tell me something. Surely there's no harm in that. Who's to know? I shan't tell anyone."

As though keen to offer something he said, "It was written in 1914."

"But that's years ago!" She did a quick subtraction mentally. It was now 1932, so he had made the will soon after they were married. "It makes no sense," she muttered. "At least, not to me . . . And it can't be Mr Dunn because he wasn't working for George then. He came much later."

Who else could it be? George's brother Dennis, perhaps – but hardly likely. Dennis had borrowed money from them

37

which he had never repaid. They owed Dennis nothing. And Dennis had died two years ago. She wondered whether it might be his mother, but she had been left a very wealthy widow. George had no other family.

Catching the solicitor's eye she saw his compassion and her anger deepened. Why had George done this terrible thing?

"So when do we have to sell the shop? How much time do I have?" She struggled to keep her voice free from hostility. It wasn't the solicitor's fault, she reminded herself. It was George's. Before he could answer she asked, "Who drew up this will for George?"

"My senior partner did it."

"Does he know why it was done this way? Would he talk to me?"

"Mr Brough has long since retired from the firm, but he would be bound by the same set of ethics." His expression had relaxed slightly. "But it isn't necessary for someone to explain the will he wants to make, no matter how bizarre. All the solicitor can do is give advice and draw it up in the proper legal terms. Even if you were to contact Mr Brough he couldn't help you. He couldn't tell you any more than I have done."

Moyna's mind whirled. Mr Brough might be a little more flexible, she thought. He was retired and might be persuaded to help.

"I'd like his address. I shall probably write to him." Moyna managed a challenging look. A small spark of anger flared within her. She was facing a wall of silence. It was beginning to feel like a conspiracy to defraud her and her son of their rightful inheritance. That was bad enough, but she was also faced with the knowledge that very early in the marriage George had done this thing and had kept it a secret ever since.

"Of course, Mrs Ellyard. I shall be pleased to do anything

to help you through this difficult time. Anything . . ." He hesitated.

"Anything legal. Yes, I understand that."

She was desperately trying to imagine what had made George do such a thing. An unpleasant thought occurred. Did he owe somebody a large amount of money? Was this his way to repay a longstanding debt? If so, was *that* legal? Perhaps it could be undone.

"Couldn't I challenge the validity of the will on grounds of . . ."

"Temporary insanity?" He shrugged. "You could try but – you see, there's this other person who will have to be informed and who would undoubtedly fight to keep the inheritance. Believe me, I do sympathise, Mrs Ellyard. It's a most unfortunate business." He took out his watch and looked at it with obvious relief. "Oh dear, I have to go, but do keep in touch. Call in at the office one day and we can talk further."

In his sister-in-law's kitchen, Michael Wheatley was toying with his food while she watched him, hawk-eyed. He pushed his plate to one side and said, "Very good. Thanks."

"You've left some!"

"You gave me too much."

"No more than usual."

He wiped his mouth with his napkin and turned his chair to face the range which gave off a comforting warmth. "You always make a good stew."

"Business not so good?"

Michael shrugged. His work at the theatre was hardly demanding, but then it didn't pay very well. But then nothing he did ever paid more than a pittance and that was the story of his life. He had driven a delivery cart for a baker until the horse collapsed of old age and what remained of the business was sold to a competitor. For a year he had endured life as a presser in a laundry until a clash of personalities had ended that job. He'd been a porter in a hospital, which he hated, and had spent one desperate summer as a deck-chair attendant. He knew he had potential if only he could find the right job, but he seemed to be dogged by bad luck. Iris could never understand that. He suspected that she saw him as a bit of a loser which irked him more than a little. At least he was still alive while his brother was rotting somewhere in a field on the banks of the Somme. For a few moments he gave himself up to memories of happier times when he and Stan were a couple of young tearabouts. At seven they were banging on doors and running away; at nine they were drinking from milk bottles on doorsteps and tying tin cans to dogs' tails. Even at sixteen . . . He shook his head. Better to leave it there. Stan had rushed to enlist or he, too, might have wavered a bit and ended up on the wrong side of the law.

"Business is lousy." He frowned. "Last night we were half empty. Poor old Bainbridge's doing his nut. He'll never make a go of it and it's a shame after all the money Wenter spent on doing the place up. I prefer a decent play but variety's better than nothing – or wrestling!" He stretched out long legs and surveyed his feet gloomily. "Mind you, some women love wrestling. Show them a couple of large, sweaty men pretending to make mincemeat of each other and they scream themselves hoarse."

Iris said, "Well, at least it's the Theatre Royal and not a cinema. That really would be the dregs."

He sighed. "But it's what they want. Blasted films. They should never have been invented."

"Time for a cup of tea before you go? The kettle's on."

"Might as well." He thought about his brother's wife, as he often did. After Stan's death he had hoped he might be in with a chance but she had never given him the slightest encouragement. Their relationship remained one of simple friendship.

He said, "I'm surprised Ginnie wanted to go to Ellyard's funeral. They're such dismal occasions and she's only been working there for a few months."

Iris shrugged. "It was her decision. She always said he was a decent stick and he'd just given her a rise."

"No accounting for taste."

"What's it to you? You hardly know him."

He shrugged. "I've seen him around."

Iris gave him a sideways glance. "No harm in her going, was there?"

"Except that she's missed the dentist."

Iris spooned tea into the china pot and added boiling water. "I've made her another appointment."

"I could never see what she saw in him. He was years older than her and hardly a charmer. Quite offhand with his staff, they say."

Iris poured milk in to the cups and stirred the tea in the pot. Was she avoiding his eyes?

She said, "Some women like older men and he was very kind to her. He lent her the money to buy her bicycle, remember."

"I would have helped her with it," he said sharply. "She only had to ask." At least he would have helped her if he'd been in funds. If he'd had a bit of luck on the horses, which he hadn't. For the past few months he'd been unluckier than usual.

"Michael! It didn't even enter her head to have a bike until he mentioned it."

"And he's a married man. Or was." Blast the man. Oiling his way into her affections. Not that it would do him any good now. He'd got his come-uppance.

Iris shook her head. "For heavens sake! Mr Ellyard was just a – a father figure. Maybe she needed one."

He stabbed a forefinger into his chest. "I'm her father figure. She didn't need one!" Why on earth did she have to defend the wretch?

She smiled at him suddenly. "Michael Wheatley! I do believe you're jealous!" She passed him a cup of tea and the sugar bowl. "Honestly, you needn't be. There'll never be anyone like Uncle Mike for Ginnie. You know that."

He forced a smile. "As long as we all know where we stand."

Iris regarded him with narrowed eyes. "Is anything wrong, Mike? I mean, you seem a bit mopey. You're not sickening for something? You would say, wouldn't you? You would see a doctor."

"I'm fine – and don't start that again. For the last time, I am not going the way of my father. Do stop fussing, Iris."

"I'm not fussing. I just hate to see you like this. It's not like you to be moody. Skint, yes. Drunk, yes. Bad-tempered, even. But not miserable."

"Thanks for the glowing reference!" Hurriedly he bent down, fished under the table for his shoes and fussed with the laces. Women! They were a sight too shrewd in his opinion, especially this one. He'd have to keep her at arm's length or she'd be giving him the third degree.

"Couldn't lend me a bob or two, could you?" he asked, blowing on his tea to cool it. He didn't like the way the conversation was heading and was keen to get back to the theatre.

She reached for her purse and handed him a shilling.

"Thanks. Be seeing you."

"Not if I see you first!" she laughed.

It was their usual parting but this time, as Michael left the house, he wasn't even smiling.

Three

G innie pushed her bicycle round to the back of the house, ringing the bell repeatedly to alert her mother to her return. She had never been to a funeral before and was excited – and guilty for having enjoyed all the emotions. Throwing open the back door she erupted into the kitchen where her mother, struggling with the daily crossword, looked up in relief.

"Ginnie, it's nearly five o'clock! I was beginning to worry about you." Iris stared at her. "I must say you don't look too depressed. How did it go?"

"Not as gloomy as I thought." Ginnie snatched off her jacket and tossed it on to a chair. "I did shed a few tears but I thought it would be worse. The vicar droned on a bit the hymns were a bit sad, but poor Mr Ellyard *had* died so I suppose they had to be sort of soulful." She threw herself on to a kitchen chair and saw her mother's expression. "What's up?"

Iris pointed to the jacket. "If you don't hang it up you won't borrow it again!"

"Let's hope I don't have to." With an exaggerated sigh, Ginnie rushed the jacket upstairs and replaced it on a hanger in her mother's wardrobe. She went downstairs two at a time to find a plate of stew waiting for her on the table.

"I can't eat that, Mum. I went—"

"Mummy not Mum! How many times—"

Ginnie pushed the plate away. "I'm not hungry. I went to the do afterwards. Ham and stuff. It's a nice house. Quite big really." She looked at her mother. "What's the matter now?"

"You went back to the house?" Iris was staring at her. "Were you invited?"

"Not exactly, but I heard someone else say they were going so I followed on my bike. It was all right. Nobody said anything. I was going to speak to his wife – I'd thought of a nice little condolence – but before I got my courage up she disappeared upstairs with one of the men."

"Ginnie!"

"Not like that!" She laughed. "She didn't look that type. Rather sober. Serious."

"Her husband has just died. She ought to be serious." Flustered, Iris consulted her crossword. "What's the name of the the other couple in *Macbeth*?"

"Which other couple? You mean Macduff?"

"Ah! Thanks." She pencilled in the letters. "That gives me an F for thirteen down . . . so that one can't be 'scree'. Blast!" She made a great show of rubbing it out.

"Why are you always doing crosswords?" Ginnie demanded. "They're a waste of time and brainpower." She eased her feet out of her best shoes – black suede with a buttoned strap – and briefly admired her slim ankles. "I dropped a flower on to the coffin. I hope he was looking down."

Iris looked up, startled. "Dropped a . . . ? Ginnie! You shouldn't have done that." She swallowed, her lips pressed together. "Look, dear, you weren't – You are just an employee. It wasn't your place."

"I don't care if it wasn't. I liked him. Deep down he was a kind man."

"Not much of an epitaph."

"And he liked me. I told you."

Mother and daughter stared at each other, but it was Iris

44

who dropped her gaze first. She drew a long breath, then said, "What am I supposed to do with this stew? Poor Sukey would have loved it."

"I expect there's stew in the cat heaven."

"I'm thinking of getting another kitten."

"For heaven's sake! This place is a deathtrap for cats. They won't stay in the garden. Look, give it to next door's tom. He'll love it."

"I'll have to but he doesn't deserve it. Always fighting, wretched animal!"

"We had duchesse potatoes with the cold meat," Ginnie pronounced it "dooshesse" with a humorous roll of her eyes. "And after that a luscious cherry tart with lashings of cream. The son arrived home from France – hopelessly late and missed the service. Missed seeing the coffin and everything, poor lamb."

Iris had fixed her eyes on the crossword. "The son?"

"His name's Frank. I heard someone say he was on holiday. Gone on a walking holiday with a friend in Brittany, wherever that is. He came back as soon as he heard. He's got beautiful hair. Naturally curly but you can see he tries to flatten it. Anyway I told him all about the service so he hasn't really missed anything. He's nice. Actually I could fancy a slice of bread with some of your lemon curd." Iris pointed to the bread bin and Ginnie helped herself. "You should have come." She smothered the bread liberally with lemon curd.

"What was she like? Mrs Ellyard. Fat? Thin? Ugly?"

"Why should she be ugly? You should have come into the shop more if you were interested. Not that she showed her face very often."

"Who says I'm interested in her?"

"She was slim. Well dressed. She had an older woman with her. A bit frail. Could have been Mr Ellyard's mother

45

– or her's. I sat at the back but they spotted me. The older
woman said, 'Who's she?' Mr Dunn was there but the others
didn't come. They were minding the shop. I thought they'd
close as a mark of a respect but they didn't. Mind you, we
did send flowers and I wrote the card. I was going to add a
line of kisses but Miss Crane wouldn't let me."

Her mother's head was once more bent over the crossword. "Colour from India perhaps. Six letters. I hate it when
they say 'perhaps'. You don't know where you are."

"Colour from India . . . ? Indigo. It will be interesting to
see what happens to the shop. Mrs Ellyard might have to
take over, but Miss Crane says that what she knows about
the business would go on the back of a penny stamp!"

"Indigo? How on earth—"

"India, cross off the last letter and add 'go'. I bet Mr
Dunn would like to take it over but Mrs Cook thinks he
probably hasn't got the money. He said a few words – what
a good employer he was and all that." She bit into the bread.
"I expect he was currying favour with Mrs Ellyard. Hoping
to stay on. Mr Dunn says the son should take over but Frank
says he's supposed to be going to study the piano somewhere
in London."

Her mother regarded her anxiously. "Did you get anything
about your rise in writing?"

It was Ginnie's turn to stare. "No . . . You don't mean . . ."

Her mother shrugged. "It would only be your word unless
Mr Ellyard told his wife or Mr Dunn. And why should he?
He didn't know he was going to die on the way back to work.
Mrs Ellyard might sell the business. Maybe you should keep
your eyes open. You might be looking for a new job before
the month's out."

The following day Moyna sat in the policeman's office
trying not to show how nervous she was. Sergeant Evans
was not at all what she had expected. He smiled a lot but his

eyes were hard. He shuffled the papers he held then leaned back, tilting his chair precariously.

"Now what can I say to reassure you, Mrs Ellyard?" Without waiting for an answer he went on. "I won't beat about the bush. We're not much further forward and have no leads at present but my lads have been hard at it ever since the – the incident. We'll catch whoever it was. Don't you worry on that score."

Moyna leaned forward. "So you are convinced it was an attack? I was hoping it might have been what you first thought – a seizure of some kind. I can't bear the idea that George was afraid at the moment of his death. A heart attack seems a much kinder way to go."

"Not really, Mrs Ellyard. Imagine the fear of being taken ill in the street, not to mention the pain. We'd all like to slip away in our sleep but . . ." He shook his head. "We can only go on the coroner's finding and he can only go on the evidence. The original report was incomplete and the bruising to the side of the face was only discovered later – bruises sometimes take a time to develop, you see. I'm afraid there was definitely an assailant." With a sigh, Sergeant Evans slipped the papers back into the blue folder. "We are still hoping a witness might come forward. My lads are still making enquiries. It's quite likely that someone who saw something may be reluctant to come forward. People don't want to be involved. They're scared of going into the witness box. It sometimes takes a second visit." He straightened his chair and smiled again.

Moyna took a deep breath. "I've told my son it was a heart attack. I don't want him to think that his father had enemies. George was a thoroughly decent man."

"Mrs Ellyard, it's easier to make an enemy than a friend. You have to work at friendship. You can make an enemy by a slip of the tongue. Are you sure your husband hadn't upset anyone? No unhappy business deals? No unpaid debts? No skeletons in the cupboard?"

"He would have told me," Moyna said stubbornly. This wretched sergeant was determined to think the worst, but the idea that her husband had been challenged by a violent stranger was too awful to contemplate. She said, "You're sure there was nothing stolen?"

"Nothing. So we've ruled out a robbery that went too far. Which makes it look even more like revenge by someone bearing a grudge."

Moyna's fingers tightened on her bag. She had come hoping to set her mind at ease. Instead she felt worse than ever. Unhappily she rose to her feet and held out her hand. "Then I mustn't waste any more of your time, Sergeant Evans. I know you're doing your best."

As she retraced her steps towards home she was aware of a growing panic. She was a widow, her financial future looked very insecure, and the manner of her husband's passing was an unpleasant mystery.

Thursday evening found Frank sitting beside Douggie's empty seat in the fifth row of the stalls below the newly decorated cream and gold ceiling of the Theatre Royal. His friend had returned from France a few days after Frank and had decided to cheer him up. He had bought two tickets for the theatre and Frank had been too kind to tell him he didn't want to be cheered up. What he wanted was to be left alone to come to terms with his father's death and what had followed.

It was bad enough to be told your father had died and to arrive home in England too late for the funeral. To then learn that his father had been killed added a further dimension to the grief which was already intense. His mother had also confided the contents of the will and that added to his confusion. The first half of the performance had passed in a blur but the interval had arrived and Douggie had darted away without explanation. All around him people scurried up and down the aisle heading for the bar, the Ladies or the Gents, while usherettes carried trays of tea and slices of fruit cake which had been ordered earlier. There was a buzz of sound as a hundred people aired their opinions or riffled idly through their programmes. Frank tried to remember the last time he and his mother and father had been at the theatre together. It was the gala re-opening of the Theatre Royal with Vosper's *Murder on the Second Floor*. "We must come more often," his father had insisted, but it hadn't happened. Now it was too late.

He glanced up to see Douggie squeezing his way back along the row, proudly bearing two ice cream tubs. In spite of his mood, Frank smiled at the sight. Douggie was instantly recognisable by his lanky frame and untidy fair hair. Ever since he was a child he had had a pathological dislike of having his hair cut and now, among the sleek heads of the rest of the men, he was instantly recognisable.

"There was a queue a mile long," Douggie told him. "But I was determined to get them. I got chocolate. I know it's your favourite." He handed one to Frank and gave him a small wooden spoon and sat down. "So – are you enjoying it?" He smiled hopefully.

Frank nodded. "It's awfully good."

"Shame it's half empty."

"It takes my mind off things."

Douggie smiled broadly. "That was the idea."

Douggie and Frank had been schoolfriends, a close friendship that was only interrupted by their different choice of career. Frank had chosen to carry on with his music while Douggie followed his father into their small printing firm.

While Douggie chattered away beside him, Frank ate his ice cream without really tasting it. It seemed incredible that his prospects had changed so quickly. Was it possible that he would not be able to pursue his musical career? A spoonful of chocolate ice cream paused halfway to his mouth. Suddenly giving up his music didn't seem such a disaster. His future, once slotted so neatly into its pigeonhole, was now opening up and Frank found the situation exciting. Security had been replaced by a dangerous uncertainty which meant that anything was possible and Frank was surprised to discover that he welcomed his new-found freedom.

What did not thrill him, however, was the mystery of his father's behaviour. Had he borrowed money to open the shop, as his mother suggested, or was there something more sinister emerging? Frank had rashly wondered aloud about blackmail but his mother had furiously rejected the idea. On reflection it did seem improbable and Frank was prepared to let it go.

"Frank! Wake up! Someone's calling you!"

A good-natured elbow in his ribs brought him out of his reverie. Three rows in front of them a young woman was waving at him.

"It's Frank, isn't it? I came to your father's funeral, remember?"

With a start he recognised her. It was Ginnie, who worked in his father's shop. She was sitting with a cheerful-looking girl with a freckled face.

"Ginnie!" His worries were immediately forgotten as they smiled at one another.

Douggie whispered, "She's wonderful! Where did she spring from?"

"She works in The Linen Store." He raised a hand. "Nice to see you again, Ginnie." He pointed to the empty seats in front of them. "Want to join us?"

The two girls exchanged glances and giggled. Then they left their seats and came up the aisle.

Douggie said, "Your Ginnie's a sweetie!"

Frank grinned. "I saw her first, remember."

As the girls settled into their seats Frank introduced Douggie and Ginnie put an arm around her friend. "This is Laura. She's awful. A terrible clever clogs. She was always beating me at arithmetic and history."

Laura said, "And cookery and geography!"

The girls went into fits of laughter.

Douggie said, "You can go off people like that!"

Frank smiled at Laura. "They're only jealous."

Douggie felt obliged to explain that he had persuaded Frank to get out and not mope about the house. "His dad wouldn't want him to be miserable," he insisted. "I wouldn't, if I had a son and I died. I'd want him to be sorry but I wouldn't want to spoil his life. When my Grandad died he left my Dad some money to take me and my brother to the funfair and buy us some toffee apples! It was a magical night and I'll never forget him."

Ginnie told them about her uncle who worked in the theatre. "He helps the stage manager and he's always getting complimentary seats so me and Mum get to see lots of shows."

The fire curtain was lowered and raised and they settled in their seats. Even if Frank had wanted to concentrate on the performance he couldn't have done so. Suddenly he was more interested in the girl in front of him. He watched the back of her neck and the way her hair moved when she laughed. Her laughter warmed his grief-stricken soul. Leaning forward surreptitiously he caught a whiff of "Evening in Paris". Ginnie Wheatley had entered his life and suddenly he didn't want to let her go.

George had gone from her but Moyna felt his presence with every passing hour. It was not the comforting presence she might have hoped for but an uncomfortable shadow from the past. Aware of the tone of the letter, she had lost the power to remember the good times. All she could imagine was the years she had lived with a stranger – a man who had signed himself "George" all those years ago. While Frank was at the theatre she had searched her mind for a possible reason for his unexpected cruelty. She had also searched the drawers of his desk in the study, reading every scrap of paper she could find, but without result. As time passed her fear crystallised into anger. She would not allow him to destroy what was left of her life, she told herself. Ferreting out the truth about the will had become a priority.

With that aim in mind, she set off next morning to visit Mr Brough. The retired solicitor lived in a semi-detached bungalow in Cliftonville but hardly in the style Moyna had expected. The front garden was overgrown with weeds and the paintwork on the door and windows was flaking off in patches. The air of neglect was quickly compounded when the door opened. She had telephoned to say she was coming and it was nearly eleven o'clock but the elderly man who answered her knock was still wearing pyjamas and a dressing gown and his feet were bare.

"Oh I'm sorry," she said, embarrassed. "I thought we'd agreed—"

"That's right. That's right. Come on in, my dear. I can't seem to find my slippers."

With some trepidation Moyna followed him along a passage to a small but sunny kitchen. Crockery was piled in the sink and the gingham tablecloth was stained and covered with crumbs.

"Make yourself comfortable, my dear."

Moyna cleared a pile of newspapers from one of the chairs and sat down.

Mr Brough stared vaguely round the room.

"I can see some slippers under the dresser," Moyna told him. She handed them to him and watched as he sat down and carefully put them on the wrong feet.

"I have a little lady that comes in every morning," he told her. "She'll make us some tea, I dare say. Every morning at half past nine." He glanced up at a clock on the wall which had stopped at five minutes to five. "A pleasant little soul. Mrs Simons, I think it is. Or is it Solomons?"

Moyna hesitated. "Mr Brough, it's eleven o'clock. She may have forgotten."

"I forget her name. Now what can I do for you, Mrs . . ." He cocked his head enquiringly.

Moyna told him her name and the reason she had come. Since her arrival she had resigned herself to the fact that this gentle but forgetful old man would be of no use to her. To her surprise, however, his face clouded at her words.

"Ellyard? Good Lord! I'd forgotten that Ellyard business. Very rum do. Very rum indeed. Tried to talk him out of it. Because I thought him a bit of a cad, actually. Not cricket."

Moyna felt the hair on the back of her neck rise at his words. He *knew*. "So you remember the will?"

"Oh yes! Funny business altogether. Not cricket, old chap, I told him, but he went ahead with it."

She waited, but he was suddenly lost in thought. Was it fair to take advantage of him and push for a name, she wondered guiltily. It wasn't ethical for him to reveal it, according to Mr Levy, but did she care? Who would know what the old man had told her? He himself would almost certainly forget as soon as she had left the house.

She took a deep breath. "This Mr Whatever-his-name-was – was it a very large debt?"

Staring round the kitchen, he appeared lost in thought. "Solomons. That's it . . . I think. Every morning, regular as clockwork. She always makes me a pot of tea, bless her. Because I get so very dry. Afraid to use the gas, you see. Caught the curtains alight once." He chuckled. "Caused quite a rumpus, so they tell me."

So he could remember some things. Hope flared. "Shall I make you some tea, Mr Brough? It wouldn't take a moment."

"No, no, no, my dear. Mrs Simons will do it. Now, why have you come? Remind me if you will."

Moyna said, "My husband, Mr Ellyard – he left me a letter with his will. He's just died, you see . . . He said he owed money to someone."

"Did he now?" He frowned. "Because I don't recall anything about a debt . . . unless it was a . . . Now what did he call it? A debt of honour. That was it precisely. Ah yes, it was Simmons. Miss Simmons. I didn't think I'd forget that because at the time I—"

"No!" Moyna corrected him gently. "Miss Simmons is the woman who comes each morning to clean up for you – although I suspect she's forgotten you today. I'm talking about years ago. Mr George Ellyard's will."

"Yes, yes, I know you are." His faded blue eyes met hers without a trace of vagueness. "I may be a mite forgetful these days but that day is quite clear in my mind. Because, you see, I was very worried by what he was doing. I took the will to my partner as soon as Mr Ellyard had left the office. 'Forget it, Bernard,' he told me. 'Ellyard will probably write half a dozen wills before he dies.' Because, you see, Ellyard was still a young man – in his twenties as I recall. Plenty of time to change his mind. That was the thinking and I was reassured."

Moyna marvelled at the clarity of his mind for the far distant past. "D'you think someone had some kind of hold over him? Blackmail, perhaps? Or could it have been a sleeping partner? If a man – a friend – had secretly put up the money for The Linen Store they might have agreed that the loan should be repaid on his death if not before . . ." She stopped. Mr Brough wasn't listening.

54

"There were two letters, I recall. One for his wife and another one for the beneficiary."

"Another letter!" Mr Levy had kept very quiet about that, thought Moyna angrily.

They were interrupted by a knock at the front door and Moyna bit her lip as she waited for his return. He came back accompanied by a middle-aged woman who carried a covered plate. She looked at Moyna in surprise.

"A visitor? How nice. I'm Mrs Solomons, the daily. I come in three times a week around this time. Bring him a bit of dinner and tidy round." She uncovered the plate and began to assemble knives and forks and the cruet. "A nice bit of boiled bacon, some carrots and mash." To Moyna she said, "His favourite!"

Without further ado Mr Brough sat himself down and began to eat while Moyna cursed the interruption. Fate was proving entirely unco-operative. Could she continue her interrogation with the daily woman present? Mrs Solomons was tying an apron round her waist and Moyna hesitated.

She said, "Mr Brough, can you recall anything about this debt of honour? I'd be eternally grateful."

The old man retrieved a piece of carrot which had fallen from his fork. Then he glanced up. "Debt of honour . . . Let me think . . . Yes, of course, I did try to find out more. I wanted to advise him, you see. It seemed a very rash thing to do . . ." He began to mash potatoes and carrots together into an unappetising orange mass and Moyna stifled her disappointment.

Mrs Solomons whispered, "He gets very confused, I'm afraid."

Moyna nodded. She had received very little information but at least the daily woman wasn't a figment of his imagination. Rising, she made her goodbyes.

A wasted journey but at least she had tried. There must surely be other avenues to explore. She would not give up at the first hurdle.

"I'd best be going then."

As she moved toward the door an idea came to her. She would consult a private investigator.

Mr Brough glanced up from his meal, dropping a piece of bacon on to the cloth as he did so. "It was so nice meeting you, my dear."

"Thank you for your time. You've been very helpful." A lie, she thought, but at least he had been more forthcoming than Mr Levy. At least she now knew that there had been another letter. "I'll let myself out," she told them and Mrs Solomons gave her a brief wave with a soapy hand.

She was halfway up the passage when she heard the old man. "That second letter! It wasn't addressed to a man, my dear. It was addressed to a woman!"

Less than a mile away, Eddie Tanner was having a very difficult morning. He had ignored several bills, lost the top of his fountain pen and had spent seventeen and a half minutes typing a very short letter. Now, desperate for company, he was telephoning an acquaintance on the other side of the town.

"Answer it, can't you!" he muttered as the ringing continued. When someone tapped on the office door it was almost a relief. He saw a woman silhouetted against the glass panel of the door and shouted, "Come on in!"

Eddie loved his office door. He loved the gold lettering which formed the words EDWARD C. TANNER and beneath them the legend PRIVATE DETECTIVE. It had been worth leaving the security of his job as a policeman just to see those words and to know that here he was king.

The woman who entered looked about his own age. She was well dressed and would have been good-looking if the expression on her pale face hadn't sharpened her well-shaped features. Eddie considered himself an expert on pretty women and he gave this one nine out of ten. He indicated the telephone and pointed to a chair. A breathless voice on the line said, "Who is it?"

Eddie smiled. "Charlie, it's me, Eddie. What took you so long?"

"I was halfway out of the door and had to run back up two flights of stairs. I'll have a heart attack one of these days."

"Never! All that golf and tennis! Know what I mean! You're the fittest man I know! Charlie, what about meeting up for a bite to eat? I know this place—"

"When were you thinking of, Eddie?"

"When? Today, of course. My treat. We'll go to the—"

There was an exasperated snort at the other end of the line. "Today? Eddie, you're mad. You forget I've got a life of my own to lead. I'm having dinner at the golf club with my brother. Another time perhaps, Eddie. Now excuse me. I'm late already." The line went dead.

Hurt by the summary rejection, Eddie stared at the phone then slowly hung up.

"Moody devil!" he muttered. Puzzled, he caught the woman's eye and shrugged. "Funny chap, Charlie. Pal of mine from the coroner's office. Never can get him to have a bit of lunch."

She said, "You didn't give him much notice, did you?"

He stared at her. What was she on about? "Notice? He's a mate of mine!"

"Ask him to lunch one day next week."

"You reckon?" He thought about it. "I might just do that. Nothing to lose . . . I suppose you're not hungry, are you? I know this place near the front. They do—"

Startled, she shook her head.

Another "No", he thought disconsolately. Obviously doesn't go for my type. Or likes her men shorter or leaner. Not that he was overweight. His last girlfriend had called him "a big cuddly bear" and the one before that had liked his round face. She'd compared him to a friendly puppy. He cringed at the memory – but suppose she was right. What was wrong with being friendly? He liked people. And dogs. He studied the woman opposite. Probably scared of men. He'd met the type. Pity she wasn't hungry. He hated eating alone.

"Mr Tanner," she began, "I don't have an appointment but . . ."

Maybe he'd just nip round to the Three Horseshoes and · have a pint and a pickled egg. That settled, Eddie turned his attention to his visitor. "No appointment? Not to worry. It so happens I'm not busy so that's OK."

"I'm Mrs Ellyard."

He raised his eyebrows. "*The* Mrs Ellyard?"

She flushed. "So you know?"

"Have to know, don't I? Always have to have my ear to the ground. Goes with the territory. Know what I mean? I'm sorry. It must be tough." He wondered how she looked when she smiled.

"Mr Tanner, it's actually worse than you imagine."

What could be worse than having your husband attacked and killed? "Cup of tea?"

"No thank you."

"Something stronger? A cigarette?"

She shook her head.

"So you think I can help – is that it?"

"I hope you can."

He was studying her carefully because he was trained to do so and because he enjoyed looking at her. Her eyes were not red-rimmed. So not the grieving widow? She was sitting straight and still in the chair. Most women in her shoes would be fidgeting with a handkerchief or clutching a handbag.

He said, "Want to tell me about it? I'm the world's best listener." Leaning back he locked his hands behind his head and wished he had emptied the ashtray.

Mrs Ellyard took a deep breath. "Mr Tanner, firstly, the police have told me that my husband's death was not an accident. Somebody attacked him. Who, I have no idea but the police think it was someone with a grudge. But, of course, finding the attacker is their business. I have come to you on a second point." She swallowed, glancing down at her hands, but then lifted her head and gave him a straight look.

"When my husband's will was read there was a shock waiting for me. George has left half the business to someone else. He didn't name the other person but I found out this morning it was a woman. He made the will eighteen years ago and has never altered it. I asked who this person is but they say it isn't ethical to reveal the details. But if I'm to be left in financial difficulty I'd at least like to know who to blame."

A fluent little speech, he thought and was strangely moved by her cool delivery. A very restrained account. Probably practised it. No hysterics, no name-calling and no self-pity. Just a controlled anger. Of course, if she'd cried he could have offered a manly handkerchief and maybe put a comforting arm around her shoulders. Pity.

He opened his mouth to say, "Another woman! The age-old story," but changed his mind. No need to rub it in.

"So you want to know who she is and why he has left her the money." Shouldn't be too difficult with his contacts, but it didn't do to let her know that.

"Can you do that?" she asked.

Eddie pursed his lips. "I can, but these things take time. Isn't hiring me going to be a bit of a strain on the old purse strings?" Now he had her worried. So she wasn't that flush with money. "Assets frozen, are they?"

"Certainly not!" She hesitated, frowning. "Could they do that? The bank? Freeze the assets? Does that mean what I think it means?"

"They can but not always. Forget I said that."

He told her his terms and waited. Take it or leave it. That was his policy. It didn't look good to offer a reduction. Sounded as though you didn't have enough work. Made you sound desperate.

She hesitated again.

What the hell! He *didn't* have enough work. He said quickly, "Let's just make a start and see how it goes. Know what I mean? If it takes longer than a week or two you can always call a halt. No offence taken."

She was still looking anxious. "How do you account it – or whatever you call it? I mean how will I know . . ." She stopped, embarrassed.

"How will you know I'm not taking your cash and sitting in the office eating a jammy doughnut?" He grinned. "I'll make a note of the day-to-day expenses and the times and places where I make my enquiries. OK? I may not be the handsomest private detective in Margate but—"

"Oh but you're not – I mean . . ."

He had flustered her, he thought, surprised. "I may be the homely type but don't be fooled." He tapped his head. "Beneath this too solid exterior there's a genius trying to get out. Sherlock Holmes? Forget him! Seriously, Mrs Ellyard, as private detectives go, I'm one of the honest ones. I promise I won't cheat you."

She gave an unconvincing smile and opened her handbag. "I expect you need something on account."

"Not from a lady. I'll send an account at the end of the week. Now, if you can give me a few more details . . ."

He kept her as long as he dared, offered her tea, whisky and cigarettes, and when she refused all three for the second time he ushered her to the door and opened it.

"That's me," he said proudly, pointing to the lettering.

She asked, "What's the 'C' for?"

"I can't tell you that," he said with a grin. "It wouldn't be ethical!"

Four

When Frank could no longer put off the moment, he set off to visit his father's grave. Seeing it, he knew, would be the final proof that his father was dead, and although he knew that with his mind, his heart said otherwise. He half expected to see him at breakfast immersed in his newspaper or settled in front of the fire in the evening, listening to the wireless. He waited for the background sound of conversation between his mother and father and was surprised by the continuing silence. Once he played his father's favourite sonata, hoping illogically for the approving pat of his father's hand on his shoulder.

His mother had finally admitted that his father's death had been the result of an attack. As Frank approached the church, self-consciously carrying a bunch of carnations, he wondered who might have hated his father enough to kill him. He also found himself wondering what exactly Ginnie had heard or read about it and whether it affected her opinion of him.

As he approached the newly formed grave which he knew must be that of his father, he came to an abrupt halt. A middle-aged woman was kneeling beside it, her head bowed as if in prayer. Before he could speak she seemed to sense his presence and turned, startled. She struggled to her feet, hesitated, then turned her back on him and walked rapidly away.

"Who on earth . . . ?" he wondered, but at that moment the vicar came hurrying towards him, hands outstretched, his dark robe fluttering around him.

"Frank! I was meaning to call on you one day this week. This is such a sad and difficult time for you. I thought we might pray together some time."

Frank hastily laid the flowers on the grave and surrendered his hands to the other man's grasp. "I'm sure my mother would appreciate that, Reverend."

"So sad, Frank, that you missed the service, but I'm sure your father understood."

The guilt returned. "I came home as soon as I got the telegram."

"I'm sure you did. Is there any news from the police about the man who did this terrible thing?"

"Not yet. At least I don't think so . . . Vicar, who was that woman?" He gestured in the direction she had taken.

"Woman? I saw no one." He glanced down at the grave with its hastily arranged turfs. "If your mother needs any help with the wording on the headstone . . ."

"Thank you, but I don't think she's got that far yet. We're just getting through one day at a time."

"Of course." He glanced up at the church clock. "Well, I must leave you, Frank. You know where to reach me if I can ever be of help." Smiling sadly he resumed his flight towards the gate.

Frank crouched down beside the wilting wreaths and said, "I brought you some fresh flowers . . . Father, I'm so sorry . . . about everything. They'll find who did it. I know they will." He tried to imagine the polished wooden coffin with its silent contents, but the image remained out of reach. What was his father wearing? A white gown? His best suit? Was the coffin lined with satin and if so what colour was it? His mother would know but he couldn't ask her. He glanced round him to make sure that he was alone.

"I met Ginnie, Father," he went on. "She came to your funeral. Then we met again at the theatre." More guilt. "It was Douggie's idea. I hope you don't mind. I'm going to meet her later . . . Mother's doing as well as can be expected but she's terribly hurt about . . . about the will. I wish you could have told us earlier. We might have been able to help you." He thought of the secret which his father had borne all those years and then carried to his grave. "Whatever it was you did, Father, I forgive you." He felt tears spring to his eyes and blinked them away. "I'm sure you didn't mean it. We all make mistakes."

He stood up, sighing heavily. Why hadn't he and his father talked more? As a young boy he had worshipped his father but as he grew older he was aware of a gap opening between them. He was also aware of the distance between his parents but assumed that was normal. Now, with hindsight and in view of the will, he began to see it differently. Would they ever know the truth, he wondered, as he made his way home.

Later that afternoon, Ginnie walked with Frank along the pier. Ginnie longed for him to hold her hand but doubted he would. Much too soon, she reflected. Frank was not like her previous boyfriends whose cheeky hands had to be slapped away at least twice during an evening. Frank was a sight more respectful. Courteous. Gallant, even. It made a nice change.

Side by side they leaned against the railing and stared down into the green sea which rolled and frothed around the supports of the pier. A few swimmers had braved the water but many more paddled along the edge or searched for shells. A yard or two further along the pier an angler stared patiently down at his line.

"One day," Frank said, "I mean to go to the south of

63

France. It's the Mediterranean sea and it's supposed to be blue. Reflecting the sky, I suppose."

"But sea water's green."

"Not everywhere. Maybe we could go together – you and Laura and me and Douggie."

She was astonished. "Go abroad – just the four of us? Good heavens, Frank! Mum would never allow it." She glanced at him, smiling and said, "Pity, though!"

"Perhaps she'd come too."

"You're kidding. Mum would never leave Ocean View. It's her whole life."

"Tell me about your father, Ginnie. You know about mine."

She turned to lean back against the railing and opened the small silver locket she wore around her neck. "Here he is. My darling Dad. Private Stanley Albert Wheatley, aged twenty-one. Mum bought it for me when he died. I was too young to understand but she often talked to me about him."

Frank studied the small likeness – a nervous young man in a very new uniform. "You don't take after him," he said.

"No. I take after Mum's side of the family. I wish I did look like him. I'd feel a little closer. I remember a few things – like the way his moustache tickled my face and the way he laughed. Apparently when I was a baby he used to throw me up in the air, but I don't remember that. Mum says I loved it but it gave her heart failure – oh sorry!" She laid her hand briefly on his sleeve. "She's never told me but . . . I think they had to get married in a hurry because of me. You know? Because I asked her once about her wedding anniversary and she wouldn't tell me."

Frank said, "It doesn't matter a jot to me."

"He was killed a few months after he enlisted. He'd done a few weeks training and they sent him to France. He hadn't been there long when Mum got the telegram. She's still got it. Poor Mum. She must have been lonely all these years, but she's never met another man to love. I used to hope she'd marry Uncle Mike, Dad's brother. According to Mum they're quite alike in lots of ways – him and Dad I mean – but she always says, 'I can manage without a husband, thank you very much!'"

At that moment a small girl ran past and somehow tripped and fell. Before Ginnie could move, Frank had picked the child up and dusted her down. He returned her bawling loudly to her flustered mother. Watching the small drama, Ginnie wondered if Frank was the marrying kind and let her thoughts drift delightfully until he coughed and said, "You were saying . . . ?"

"Oh yes! Uncle Mike. He's been like a father to me. He used to take me to the fair and the park and often, if he was out of work, he'd collect me from school and buy me an ice cream. Once a strange man was waiting at the school gate and offered me a bag of toffees. Of course I grabbed them! I was only five and I didn't know any better. He was crouching down, talking to me. Saying I had pretty hair and things like that. Nothing nasty. He called me his dear little girl and nobody had ever called me that."

"Oh Ginnie! Not even your father?"

She considered. "I suppose Dad might have but he died before I was old enough to remember. I was completely charmed by the man."

"I expect the toffees helped!" he grinned. "I must remember to bring some next time we meet!"

Ginnie gave him a playful punch. "I can remember it to this day. But then Uncle Mike arrived and went haywire. I suppose he imagined me being kidnapped – or worse. He gave the poor man a tremendous shove that sent him sprawling and threw all the toffees after him. Of course I burst into tears and Uncle Mike dragged me away. I twisted round to look back at the toffees and he'd picked himself up and was staring after us. He saw me looking and gave a little wave. But that's my uncle for you. A bit hasty, Mum always says. And talking of toffees, d'you want a pear drop?"

She pulled a bag from the pocket of her jacket and Frank helped himself. She looked at the one he had chosen and said, "Oh good. I don't like the yellow ones," and popped a pink one into her mouth. A beach ball rolled towards them and Frank leaped forward and dribbled it back to its owner – a young boy who looked about eight or nine.

Frank returned, smiling. "One of my many talents!"

Ginnie squinted up into the afternoon sun. "Mum'll never marry again. Her world revolves around me and the business – but not always in that order."

Next to them the angler pulled a fish from the water amid admiring exclamations. He caught Ginnie's eye and said, "Supper coming up!"

It was the first one he had caught that day, by the looks of things, and Ginnie hoped he had a small family. She turned to gaze seaward again, hoping Frank might be tempted to put an arm round her waist. After a moment or two he did.

He leaned closer and whispered, "You don't mind, do you?"

Ginnie's smile was dazzling. "I rather like it!" she said, acknowledging the understatement. She added, "But Laura wouldn't approve. She's taken rather a shine to you." She waited breathlessly for Frank to offer an opinion on her best friend.

"She's very nice," he said, "but not as nice as you."

The silence lengthened as they both allowed the moment its proper significance. Then he said, "Douggie was wildly jealous. He asked me where I'd found you and why I'd kept you a secret."

"Maybe they'll get together." She turned towards him, giving him the full benefit of her green eyes. His own eyes

were sending her pulse rate sky high. She said, "Your turn
to tell me about your family."

They began to stroll back along the pier with his arm still
draped around her waist. It pulled them closer together and
Ginnie could feel the delightful warmth of his hip through
the thin fabric of her dress. She found herself wondering
why today seemed so special. She and Laura had strolled
on the pier before with a variety of young men in tow but
Frank was different. She hardly knew him and yet she felt
close to him in a way that was more than physical. And
being with him seemed to have sharpened her senses. She
could smell the salt air and the subtle tang of hot sand
and seaweed. She could hear the strangled sounds of a
Punch and Judy performance further along the beach and
the "oohs" and "aahs" of the young audience. Even the
colours appeared brighter – the sky was a deeper blue, the
sea a softer green.

"There's not much to tell," Frank was saying. "I only have
one grandparent left and that's my mother's mother. There
was an uncle but he was badly shellshocked during the war
and took his own life some years later. Father's always been
quiet and very serious. I mean, he always was . . ."

His voice faltered and Ginnie took the opportunity to slide
her arm round *his* waist.

He went on. "I think he loved us, but he wasn't the sort
of man to show his feelings. He wanted to be proud of me
– I knew that – and as soon as he knew I could play the
piano that was it! I had to become famous!" His laugh was
rueful. "Mother went along with it, of course. She rarely
went against him. In a way I suppose we were both always
trying to please him so there was seldom any argument.
Douggie's parents are really fiery. They fight like cat and
dog but it never lasts. If my parents ever rowed they must
have done it very quietly. I can only remember one noisy
row and that was my fault. I couldn't eat something – I seem

to remember it was gristly meat – and Father insisted that I did. Mother said I'd be sick but he stood over me and made me eat it."

"Poor you!" She felt a rush of dislike for George Ellyard.

"I *was* sick. Mother said, 'What did I tell you!' and Father picked up my plate and threw it across the room. It smashed against the wall and the food dripped down the wallpaper. They both started to shout and I ran out of the house and round to my grandmother's."

"When I get married and have children I'm going to be really sensible," Ginnie vowed.

As she hoped, this provoked a reaction from her companion. "So you're planning on getting married?"

She thought she detected a note of caution. "Aren't you?"

"I hadn't given it much thought, to be honest." He stopped walking and stared earnestly into her eyes for what seemed an eternity. "But . . . maybe this is the time to start!"

Meanwhile, in her neat flat in Ethelbert Road, Mrs Stuckey was starting what she called her whist night routine. Tonight they would play in Mrs Crampton's front room and Mrs Stuckey liked to be smart. Bandbox smart, as her mother used to put it. People take you at face value, she used to say. If you're well turned out they respect you. But at sixty-eight being well turned out was no mean feat and required a methodical preparation. First, around two o'clock, she would tie her hair up in curling rags and then wrap her head in an ancient red turban. Next she would take off all her rings and attend to her hands, rubbing in olive oil and encasing her hands in old cotton gloves. The rings would be rinsed in warm soapy water and carefully dried. Then she would lay her chosen outfit on the bed to remove the smell of camphor. Today's choice was the dress she had made last month, a pale green linen with a centre pleat in the skirt, a covered belt and ten glass buttons up the front of the bodice.

Occasionally she found herself wondering if she should give up the whist evenings. Old Miss Cray was such a bore about her prizewinning petunias and Mrs March would go on so about her missionary daughter in South Africa. Mrs Stuckey, with very little to talk about, felt that they monopolised the conversation, but with no garden and only one sister remaining she was hard put to find something newsworthy to offer. Still, it was an evening out. It gave her a chance to wear her nice clothes and she felt she owed it to herself to have a little social life even if she was well on the way to seventy.

On this particular day she had just dealt with her hands when the front door bell rang. She tutted irritably, partly at the interruption to her routine and partly because she hated to be seen in the red turban and the gloves. The turban must stay but before she made her way to the front door she pulled off the gloves, wiped her hands on her apron and tossed the apron on to a chair.

By the time she reached the front of the house the policeman was turning away. He looked very young, she thought, peering from behind the partly opened door, more like a school prefect than a policeman – but these days all officials seemed younger than she expected.

He gave her an unconvincing smile and gave his notebook a perfunctory glance. "Mrs Stuckey? I wonder if you could spare me a few minutes of your time?"

"It depends," she told him. "I don't have time to waste. What's it about?"

"It's about an incident that happened near here about a week ago. May I come in?"

"I know nothing about an incident, young man, and I'm getting ready to go out."

"It'll only take a minute or two. We really do need the public's co-operation on this matter."

It occurred to her suddenly that a visit from the police about "an incident" might impress the members of the whist club. Also that her late father's late cousin had worked at Scotland Yard for most of his working life. Her mother had brought her up never to shirk her duty.

"If you need my help then of course you shall have it," she told him and widened the gap to admit him.

She led him up the stairs to her flat and into the front room which doubled as a sewing room. It smelled as musty as ever despite the Ronuk polish she applied liberally from time to time to all the wooden surfaces. In one corner of the room her new Singer sewing machine held pride of place and the shelf behind it was piled high with paper patterns. On a table in the bay window the aspidistra looked healthy, thriving as it did on a weekly application of cold Earl Grey tea.

He sat down and took out a notebook. He seemed to be in no particular hurry, she thought. Almost weary. Probably up half the night gallivanting. The younger generation appeared to have no idea of a reasonable bed time.

The policeman cleared his throat. "On Saturday, the tenth of September at about a quarter to one, a gentleman was knocked down and killed a little further along this road—"

"Doesn't surprise me at all, young man. You see, they all drive too fast. I wrote to the council about a year ago but they didn't even answer my letter. Much too fast. I'm surprised there hasn't been an accident sooner."

"Actually it wasn't an accident. We believe another man was involved. Apparently the postman heard raised voices while he was delivering a package, then found the victim lying unconscious on the pavement. He also saw another man hurrying away in the opposite direction. He ran to the nearest telephone box and called for help." He smothered a yawn. "We are trying to trace anyone who saw the—"

Mrs Stuckey leaned forward suddenly. "I saw a quarrel. Oh yes, I saw two men quarrelling. That would have been the Saturday. I know because I was on my way to the station to visit my sister."

With her words, the policeman's expression changed. His weariness was gone, replaced by eager attention.

"You saw a quarrel? Well now, that is helpful. You're sure it was this specific day?"

"The day I went to London to see my sister. The tenth. She gets lonely so I always stay a few days but—"

"Could you describe the two men?" Pencil poised, he was now all efficiency.

"Well, one was between forty and fifty, the other a bit younger . . . They were outside Mr Braggs's house – that's the man with the two poodles – and they were causing quite a disturbance. The men, that is. The dogs are very well behaved. Anyway, one said, 'You think I don't know—' I think that was it. 'You think you've got away with it!' That sort of thing. One of them, the one doing all the shouting, shook his fist in the other man's face and then gave him a push." She stopped to let the policeman catch up as he started a fresh page of his notebook. "I'm surprised Mr Braggs didn't hear them – unless he was out, of course. He plays a lot of bowls."

Mrs Stuckey was anxious to get on with her routine and she certainly regretted the turban, but this little chat might lead to something interesting. If the man she had seen had been the attacker she might be interviewed by a newspaper reporter. If that happened, she decided, she would wear the dark blue skirt and maybe a new blouse. Or maybe the spotted dress she had made for her neighbour's wedding.

The policeman said, "This is splendid, Mrs Stuckey. Very helpful. Do go on."

She said, "I must tell you I don't care for that sort of thing. Men behaving badly in the street. You see, this is

71

a very good neighbourhood and I *was* surprised. I averted my eyes if you must know and hurried on."

He said, "One of the men was George Ellyard from—"

Her heart gave a little jump. "Mr Ellyard? From The Linen Store? Good heavens!" She put a hand to her chest. "I thought one of the men was familiar, but then I thought I don't know anyone who would raise his voice like that in the street. You see what I mean."

"Indeed I do . . . Mrs Stuckey, could you possibly give me—"

"That's 'e-y' at the end of Stuckey."

"Yes. Thank you. Could you give me a description of the other man? Mr Ellyard was killed and we have to find the man who did it."

Mrs Stuckey closed her eyes in an effort to recall the scene. "He was tallish, not well dressed. I don't mean he was a tramp, but not a businessman. More a workman. I did notice his jacket was a bit shabby. A brown tweedy sort of thing."

"Any hat?"

"Not that I recall. But not a cap. I'd have remembered a cap . . . Dark hair . . . Oh dear, it was some time ago – but I'd recognise him again if I saw him."

The policeman was staring at her. "You would?"

"Definitely. I was quite close to them before I crossed the road. To avoid them, you see."

He stood up, positively bristling with new-found energy. "I'd be grateful if you could call in at the police station some time tomorrow morning. Then we can take a more detailed statement and you can sign it. My sergeant's going to welcome you with open arms – in a manner of speaking. This might be just the lead we've been looking for. Would you do that for me?"

He had a rather attractive smile, she decided. He reminded her of Bertie, her sister's boy, when he was that age.

She said she would be there. About nine.

He paused at the door on the way out. "Your information may turn out to be crucial, Mrs Stuckey. I wish we had a few more citizens like you!"

She watched him cycle away and wondered if this would be his big break. He might be made a sergeant and it would be all thanks to her evidence. With a smile she retrieved her apron and put it on. She pulled the gloves from the pocket and prepared to carry on with her preparations.

"Just you wait!" she muttered and began to plan the way she would tell her story. There would be no time for the daughter in South Africa and certainly none for petunias.

That evening, Moyna and Frank sat down to high tea of egg on toast with a rasher of bacon on the side.

"And don't tell me you're not hungry," she told Frank. "The doctor says we're going through a difficult time—"

"You've been to the doc?" He regarded her anxiously.

"Only because I can't sleep, Frank. Nothing to worry about. If *you* can't sleep you must tell me and—"

"I sleep like a log!" He passed her the bread and butter, then helped himself.

"I'm pleased to hear it. And we must eat even if we're not hungry. He says we mustn't neglect our health."

"I haven't lost my appetite either. Father wouldn't want us to suffer in any way."

"How can you say that?" She stared at him. "What he's done . . . Well, how can we *not* suffer? You won't be able to pursue your music and he couldn't have wanted that. He had such high hopes. I don't begin to understand all this."

He tapped his knife on the edge of her plate. "Eat up before it gets cold!"

Moyna put a forkful of egg and toast into her mouth and chewed it distractedly.

He said, "That girl, Mother. The one who worked for

Father. I get the feeling you don't like her, but she's really awfully sweet. She's only got her mother. Her father was killed in the war."

Moyna felt herself stiffen but she tried to keep her tone neutral. "If you say so, dear. It's not that I dislike her. How could I when I don't even know her? I simply felt that your father was showing her too much attention. Favouring her because she was young . . ." And pretty. She bit back the words in time. "It's hardly fair on the other two women who have been there all those years . . ."

"He was being kind, that's all. Ginnie thought Father was very nice. Considerate. And he was kind. It was just like him to give her the money to buy a bicycle—"

"*Lend* her the money, Frank. She was going to pay a little off each week. You know he was going to give her another half a crown a week. And she wasn't to tell the others." She fussed belatedly with salt and pepper. Since the reading of the will she had realised that her suspicions about George and this young woman had been ill-founded. There was a woman but it wasn't this one. Ashamed of her suspicions, she hoped Frank would drop the subject.

He didn't. "Probably he started her at a low wage to see if she was going to be any good. A probationary period, if you like."

Moyna shrugged. She had all but lost interest in Ginnie Wheatley since her visit to Mr Tanner. She had decided to tell Frank what she had done. She didn't want him to find out from anyone else. Both parents keeping secrets would hardly inspire him.

"Frank, I have to tell you something." She had finished the egg and bacon and now put knife and fork together, lining them up precisely. "I have engaged a private detective to look into this business for me. His name—"

"A private eye?" He grinned delightedly. "Just like the movies! What a good idea. When do I get to meet him?"

74

He helped himself to more bread, folded it and wiped the plate clean.

Moyna opened her mouth to protest but changed her mind. There were more important things at stake than table manners and anyway George was no longer here to express his disapproval.

She said, "His name's Tanner. His charges seem reasonable. He has contacts in the police – he used to be a policeman . . ." She broke off.

Frank was grinning. Once George had had just such a grin, Moyna reflected sadly and wondered exactly when he had stopped enjoying life. "A real-life private eye. What's he like? Does he wear a fedora pulled down over his eyes? Fag hanging out of the corner of his mouth?"

Moyna smiled at his enthusiasm. It was the thing she most envied about young people. She took the plates to the sink and began to pour boiling water into the teapot.

"Quite pleasant, in an odd way. Hardly handsome, but that's not what matters. Can he find this wretched woman? That's what he's being paid for." She brought the pot to the table and fetched a shop-bought fruitcake from the larder. "I didn't have time to make any," she said by way of apology.

Frank said, "Tall, short, fat, thin?"

She sat down. "I suppose burly is the best word. A round face that makes him look younger than he is – or younger than I think he is. I mean, he has touches of grey in his hair which is not quite curly but not exactly frizzy. Very dark hair and bright blue eyes. He's . . ." She had been thinking a lot about him but now found it difficult to find the right words. "Easy-going . . . No. Relaxed? I suppose he's relaxed and – and funny at times. Not middle-class but . . . a hint of the cockney sparrow, you might say . . . Let's just say I liked him much more than the police. Mr Tanner seemed to care. I wasn't just another case to him. He reassured me, if you see what I mean. I came away feeling better than when I went in which is more than I can say for the police station."

"Quite a speech!"

"Well, you did ask." She took a slice of cake and offered him the same then busied herself pouring tea. "His first name's Edward but his second name's a secret. Starts with 'C'."

"Cecil? Claude? Cyril? Or even Cuthbert! Oh Lord! Not Cuthbert!"

"Poor man. Whatever it is, it obviously embarrasses him." She could see him standing in the doorway pointing to the lettering. "That's me." She wondered why he had no secretary. Had he ever had one? Perhaps she was ill or he had sacked her. Moyna hoped she was at least sixty years old and very plain. Not dazzlingly pretty like Ginnie Wheatley.

"Do I detect a certain warmth?" Frank regarded her curiously.

"Don't be silly, Frank. Now, about this Ginnie."

"Yes, Mother, Ginnie." He stirred sugar into his tea. "I'd like to bring her home one day. You'd like her." He pushed back his plate and his expression changed. "And Mother . . . I want to say something about Father. I've been thinking. Whatever comes to light – whatever he did – I can't believe he did it to hurt us. He loved us. It must have been something that went wrong, and you know how he was. He would feel the need to right it. When I think how for all these years he's had it on his conscience . . . It must have made him the way he was."

"The way he was?"

"You know what I mean. Withdrawn. Haunted, almost, by something too terrible to tell us." He drew a deep breath. "We know it was a woman. So . . . Suppose he had a great-aunt who was rich and who lent him the money to start the business. Or a wealthy godmother. Anybody. Maybe his

76

pride wouldn't let him tell you he had this huge debt. Or perhaps he thought you'd worry about a large debt."

"Rather a lot of 'Or maybes'!"

He said, "Here's another one! Maybe the great-aunt didn't want her own family to know she'd lent the money to him. And suppose Father agreed to repay the money when he died. He would have expected to live much longer. He probably thought he'd have paid off the mortgage on the house and put me through college. Then he gets killed before his time. All I'm trying to say is that if we do find out the truth we should try to understand and forgive him."

Moyna, studying the earnest young face of her son, found herself close to tears. This was George's son and he was trying to salvage something from the ruins of the family. She was full of admiration and felt ashamed of her own anger. Frank was right. They must try to understand no matter how terrible the revelations. They must try not to let the past destroy the present and future.

She clasped her cup with both hands. "You're right, darling. I've been letting this thing overwhelm me. But it's not just what it was. It's how we are going to manage. Selling The Linen Store after all these years. I shall have to find a job and that's a rather frightening prospect. I can type, of course—"

"Can you?" He looked at her in surprise. "I didn't know that."

"Why should you? It was years ago. I spent a year at a secretarial school with the dreaded Miss Wickham!"

"You may not need to work. I shall find a job before too long. I called in at the Labour Exchange this morning."

Moyna regarded him carefully before she spoke. "Your grandmother tried to tell me you have never wanted to be a pianist."

There was a long silence. Then Frank looked up. "Grandmother was right. She's very canny. It was really what Father wanted. I dreaded all those hours of practice – I'm a lazy beggar at heart. And the public appearances. But I couldn't say 'No' because I wanted to make him proud of me. We both wanted him to pat us on the head and say 'Good dog!'"

"Frank! What a thing to say!" But even as she protested, Moyna knew he was right. They had both craved George's approval. She swallowed. "I think I failed him."

"Of course you didn't." He swallowed the last of his tea and stood up. "I must dash. I'm meeting Douggie." He bent down to give her a quick hug and she caught the glint of tears in his eyes as he hurried from the room.

Impulsively she ran to the front window and watched her son cycle away. She had been so wrapped up in self-pity for her own predicament she had almost lost sight of her son's needs. Frank was already being changed by events. He was facing up to their altered circumstances without complaint and had seen, more clearly than she had, the dangers of bitter, ill-considered judgements. The son George had given her was growing up. A faint smile touched her face. Frank was turning into the kind of man she admired. It was a landmark of sorts.

Merriedale House, next door to Ocean View, had once been another guest house, but the fading fortunes of the town had brought about closure and it was now a private residence. As Mr Levy knocked on the door he was vaguely aware of the fall in value of the properties in the area. He sighed. Margate's glorious past, so often trumpeted by his grandfather, was no more.

"Yes?" A dumpy woman had opened the door.

"Good evening, madam. I represent the solicitors Brough, Levy and Patterson and I'm—"

"I hope you don't want to sell me something."

A dog appeared beside her and she bent down to grab its collar.

"No, no. Nothing like that." Silly woman. He forced a smile. "I'm trying to trace a woman whose maiden name was Simmons, but she may have married. I wonder if you can be of any help."

"Well, I'm Mrs Garbey and it's not me and next door's a Miss Merry so she can't be the one and next door that side's a widow called Mrs Wheatley and she went out half an hour ago and she's been living there as long as I have and that's more than twelve years. Ocean View, they call it. They also call it a guest house but there aren't many guests these days. Opposite, over there—" She pointed. "That's the Vines. Two sisters and an elderly mother. Could be her but they're away at the moment." She leaned past him to point to a house further down. "Green door's a Mr Broadwood but his wife died recently so it could have been her, but he's a bit funny in the head. Next to him's empty. Been empty for years now but was a Mrs Sloane – or might have been Stone." A child began to cry inside the house and she turned. "I'm coming, lovey!" She turned back to her visitor. "Sorry. No Simmons. Can't help you."

She closed the door abruptly in his face and Mr Levy muttered something uncomplimentary under his breath. He hesitated then took out his watch and studied it. "Blow Miss Simmons!" he muttered with an uncharacteristic lack of gallantry. And blow Mr Ellyard. Why hadn't he updated his will when Miss Simmons married? He shrugged. It happened. Probably pushed the whole business to the back of his mind.

He hesitated. Knocking on doors was not part of a senior partner's work and he disliked it intensely. He came to an abrupt decision. The advertisement would appear shortly and might bring results. If not, hopefully, their junior clerk would be back in the office tomorrow. He snapped the watch shut and set his feet towards home.

Five

W hen Moyna entered Eddie Tanner's office she found him sitting at a typewriter on a side table.

"Damn and blast!" he muttered, turning at the sound of the jangling bell. His frown vanished instantly and he leaped to his feet. "Mrs Ellyard! What a sight for sore eyes! Come on in and sit yourself down. Sorry about the language, but typing's not my forte."

She waited until he snatched some files from the chair and then sat down. "Don't you have a secretary, Mr Tanner?"

"Good question!" His face broke into a broad smile. He propped himself against the desk, crossed his arms and stared at her with undisguised delight. "From time to time secretaries do come my way but they never last. Don't ask me why. Course, they all have an excuse. He held up the fingers of his left hand and ticked them off. "Miss Whatsername left to get married . . . Miss Sourpuss went to a tearoom to be a waitress – for the tips, she said . . . The last one couldn't stand the muddle! Now I ask you . . ." He waved his hands helplessly. "Would you call this a muddle?"

Moyna was toying with the idea of a lie when he answered his own question.

"Certainly not. It's a working environment! Cup of tea? Biscuit?" He sprang away from the desk and hurried to a battered grey filing cabinet from which he extracted a large tin. He peered inside. "Two ginger nuts. One each. The secretaries are supposed to see to the supplies. Biscuits, tea and stamps and stuff."

Moyna held up a hand. "Wait, please. I had a visit from the police yesterday evening and they were not very happy. They were annoyed that I hadn't told them about the unnamed person in the will and . . . I'm afraid they insist that I cancel our contract."

"They do, do they? Blooming cheek!" He shook the tin. "I love ginger nuts."

He disappeared into a small room and she could hear him filling a kettle. She stood up and crossed to a row of photographs on one wall. One of a much younger Tanner in his police constable's uniform, one of Tanner in the third row of about thirty newly fledged constables, and a framed newspaper cutting which she read with interest. It seemed that he had received a commendation for being instrumental in arresting a man who had attacked three women. He came back into the room and saw what she was reading.

"That," he said. "Did myself proud with that nasty piece of work and I thought why not be a detective instead of a uniform man. You see I did a bit of detecting in my own time because I enjoyed the hide and seek."

"So why didn't you?"

"Become a detective? The blighters wouldn't have me. Not detective material, they said. In other words my face didn't fit. Know what I mean? So I thought I'd get out and go it alone. Good thing I did because here I am in a splendid office with an efficient secretary who adores me and a queue of would-be clients!" He shrugged. "That's what you get for believing in yourself."

"I believe in you, Mr Tanner. I'm really sorry about the contract."

He winked. "Don't be. You're still my client. How many sugars?"

"Two, please." She followed him and stood in the doorway. The small scullery was as untidy as the office. "Still your client? How d'you mean, exactly?"

"We let them think it's cancelled. I won't tell if you won't."

She retreated as he carried a tray with two mugs on it. There was nowhere to put it down so he said, "Dump a few of those files on the floor."

Moyna moved them instead to a nearby windowsill and sat down again. His words had given her fresh hope, and she realised for the first time just how disappointed she'd been at the prospect of losing him. He sat down on his chair and surveyed her over the rim of his mug.

She said, "I didn't want to terminate the contract but they insisted. Said it would muddy the waters."

"Forget it. Unless it's the money. If you can't afford me I could transfer you to another tariff."

"Oh no! It wasn't the money. They said—"

He snapped his fingers. "I've got it. We tear up the contract. Then if they ask you, you can say "Yes" with a clear conscience. No need to mention our new verbal contract. A slightly lower rate for an established client. And the new one will include some security work. Which means I shall keep an eye on you and your son. A bit of surveillance now and then on the house. Stuff like that."

Moyna stared at him. "Security? Why? Are we in some danger?"

"Who knows? Someone killed your husband."

"But . . . what have *we* done?"

"Nothing except that you're the wife and son and we don't yet know who killed him or why."

"Which reminds me – the police have a witness. The killer was a man."

He nodded. "Mrs Stuckey saw your husband and a man quarrelling just before he was found dead."

"You *know*?"

He tapped his nose. "I told you I have contacts. Eyes and ears everywhere. What we don't know is if there is any connection between the unknown assailant and the female beneficiary. We must never jump to conclusions. There may be no connection at all. Have a biscuit."

"Thank you." She nibbled the edge cautiously.

"Dunk it. It's safer." He demonstrated. "And you'll never guess who I'm having lunch with tomorrow. Charlie. Gave him a ring yesterday. That's one I owe you."

They smiled at each other like two conspirators. Moyna dunked her biscuit and wondered how many times George had reprimanded Frank for doing just that. She was making the bisuit last, reluctant to leave the office.

She said, "I always used to take cakes into The Linen Store on a Saturday. Fairy cakes mostly. I – I could bring some in for you next time I bake if . . ."

"Fairy cakes? Well I'm blowed! They're my favourites. Couldn't stick a cherry on the top, I suppose?"

"Of course! They'll keep in your bisuit tin."

He grinned. "They won't get the chance to keep! I'm a great believer in eating fairy cakes while they're fresh." He put down his cup and leaned forward. "I don't suppose you can type, can you? I mean with more than one finger."

Startled she said, "I could once but I haven't touched a machine for years."

He pointed to his typewriter. "How about you finish that report for me and I'll owe you then so I'll be able to take you out to lunch by way of a 'thank you'. Today."

Moyna, hesitating, was suddenly breathless. She desperately wanted to go along with the idea but was it right and proper?

He said, "A business lunch, naturally."

"I'd like to—" She wondered if anyone would see them and if it would matter if they did. She hadn't been out to lunch with any man except George for more than eighteen years and she hardly knew Mr Tanner, but the idea of a table for two in a discreet corner of a restaurant appealed to her enormously. It seemed at once slightly dangerous yet infinitely desirable. She felt that there was something significant about her answer and the silence lengthened as she struggled with her doubts.

He said, "Perhaps it wasn't such a good idea."

"Oh no!" she cried, making an instant decision. "Let's do it!"

She used a scrap sheet of paper while she acclimatised herself to the typewriter, then reinserted the original sheet. It was report which dealt with a surveillance on an erring husband. She worked from a handwritten sheet and initially found it difficult to read Tanner's scrawl. She was halfway down the second of three sheets when he decided to pop out and "see a man about a dog". Intrigued, Moyna watched him go. Did he have informants scattered throughout the town, she wondered. Was he good at his job? Why did he have so few clients?

She was surprised to discover that her typing skills had not entirely deserted her, although she was much slower now from lack of practice. She had once been able to use shorthand but that, too, was probably very rusty. The report was fascinating in a sad way. She came to the end of it.

To summarise, your husband has spent time with Miss Amanda Braithwaite on three occasions since I took on this surveillance. On two occasions they had a meal together at the Belvedere Hotel but did not rent a bedroom. The third occasion took the form of a long walk along the beach during which time I observed no impropriety. I would assume from this that you have no grounds for divorce but you might wish to confront him with this report. It may be enough to cause him to terminate the affair, if that is what it is.

An account of my time with an accompanying invoice is attached.

Moyna was re-reading it for errors when the phone rang. She stared at it, shocked, hoping that Tanner would reappear to answer it. It might be important, she told herself. Reaching for it she said, "Edward Tanner's office. How can I help you?"

A pause, then a man said, "You the new secretary?"

"Not exactly. Helping out today." She reached across the table in search of a notepad and found it under a pot which held a drooping primula. "Can I take a message?" There must be a pencil somewhere.

Another pause. "Tell him Matthews called. No luck with the Austin crash. The only witness is as blind as a bat. OK, sweetheart?"

Sweetheart! She said, "Fine, thank you, Mr Matthews," and heard the caller hang up. She watered the primula and looked in vain for some polish and a cloth. Tanner came in then carrying a newspaper which he tossed on to his chair.

Then he said, "Dinner awaits, my lady!" with mock ceremony and they left the office, locking the door securely behind them.

Ten minutes later they were sitting opposite one another at a corner table in Bert's Pie and Mash Shop on the seafront. Condensation ran down white walls and a few flies buzzed overhead but the oil cloth that covered the table was spotlessly clean. On the table there was a large cruet set which had seen years of service and this contained salt but no pepper or vinegar. As soon as they sat down a small mongrel dog slid from behind the door and hurried over to greet them.

Tentatively Moyna stretched out a hand to pat it.

"He's got fleas!" the proprietor told her from behind the counter.

Tanner said, "Bert's having you on!" and tickled the dog behind the ears.

Bert was a huge man who obviously snacked regularly on his own pies and mash. He wore a vast apron which had once been white and was tied round his waist with string and he strode up and down behind his counter with a scowl for everyone. The tiny cafe was packed and three men hovered impatiently for a vacant table.

"There's pie and mash or bangers and mash," Tanner told her. "I recommend the bangers. I've never trusted pies after Sweeney Todd. Know what I mean?"

Moyna chose the sausages and Tanner passed the order to a small boy who looked about eleven.

"This is his kid, Sid," Tanner explained, by way of introduction. "Or rather, one of them."

The boy said, "My Mum and Dad breed like rabbits!" then ducked, grinning, as Tanner threw a playful swipe in his direction.

"Kids!" he muttered. "No respect!"

"Do you have any?" Moyna asked. In her experience those who professed to know most about children had never had any of their own.

"Hope not. I've never even had a wife. I suppose I'm not the marrying kind."

"Really?"

"Who'd have me?" He shrugged. "Not exactly a deb's delight, am I!"

"Oh, I don't know . . ." Moyna didn't know how to answer. She had imagined him with a cheerful buxom wife with three or four children. So she was wrong. What did he do, then, when he wasn't being a private detective? Where did he live? How did he live? He intrigued her more than she cared to admit even to herself, and she was pleased that he was single!

She said, "Don't tell me you don't have a – a ladyfriend."

"Not just now. But I've had my moments. There was Molly and Polly and Jenny and Penny and—"

She almost said, "And now there's Moyna" but instead she said, "Serves me right for asking!"

"And you?" he asked, his expression changing. "Are you happy? I mean, *were* you?"

She could only stare at him. How did he know, she wondered. Was it so obvious? Written in large red letters across her forehead? "I don't —" she stammered. "I can't . . ."

"I'm sorry. I shouldn't have asked. None of my business." He looked contrite. "It gets to be a habit, this private detective stuff. If you're the nosey type, like me."

"I'm sure you're not nosey," Moyna protested. "It's people, isn't it. They *are* fascinating. Even the awful ones you can't like."

He nodded. "'Specially them! But let me ask you something else. What family have you got?"

Moyna let out her breath. "Just Frank. He's eighteen. He had a sister but she died when she was six weeks old."

She heard her words with a sense of shock. What on earth had inspired that confidence? She never spoke about Louisa or the grief they had endured then and since. A sniffly cold had turned into congestion of the lungs and that had led to pneumonia. Their beloved little girl was snatched away before they knew what was happening.

He said, "That must have been terrible. I'm really sorry." He reached across the table and for a moment his hand covered hers in a gesture of sympathy. It was firm and warm and comforting, but almost immediately he withdrew it. Moyna wanted to cry, "Leave it there!" but it was out of the question and she simply muttered, "Thank you," and swallowed hard to force back unexpected tears.

The dog sank down on to Moyna's feet. Mindful of Bert's comment about the fleas she tried to dislodge him, but without success, and eventually resigned herself to overwarm feet.

"Prince doesn't usually take to women," Tanner told her and she felt absurdly pleased.

"His name's Prince?" Moyna hurriedly stifled her laughter but Tanner grinned with her.

"Poor old Bert was sold a pup, literally! He wanted an Alsatian to guard the premises. They swore blind it would grow into an Alsatian. By the time he realised he'd been diddled it was part of the family. Prince wouldn't hurt a fly, poor little mutt. As for intruders, he'd lead them straight to the till and say 'Help yourself!'" Two men took the spare seats at their table and from the smell and their clothes Moyna guessed they were fishermen. She moved her chair to accommodate the one who sat on her side. While Tanner talked easily to the man beside him – an obvious acquaintance – Moyna struggled for something to say to her companion. She could think of nothing which he might find remotely interesting and in desperation said, "They're busy here today."

"Like always." He gave her a quick glance and, seizing the cruet, shook some salt on to the table, snatched up a pinch and tossed it over his shoulder. Wondering if she had put some kind of jinx on him, Moyna lapsed into a nervous silence.

She looked around her. The little cafe was hot, cramped and noisy. Everybody was either eating or talking or both. Steaming plates of food were passed across the counter with dizzying regularity until finally their own meals were dumped in front of them.

Moyna gasped, "I'll never manage all this!" Her plate contained four large sausages, and a mountain of potato, all covered by a dark glutinous gravy. Tanner drew a ten shilling

note from his pocket and handed it to Sid. Within moments
the boy was back with a handful of change. Beneath the
table Tanner held out the handful of coins to show Moyna
and laughed.

"He doesn't always let me pay," he told her. Four
half-crowns gleamed in his palm.

Moyna looked at him. "But that's what you gave him.
Ten shillings . . . You mean he doesn't charge you?" she
whispered.

He slipped the money into his pocket and shook his head.
Passing her the salt he said, "It's his way of repaying a favour
I did him once when I was still in the force. Sorted one of his
kids out before he went to the bad. Sid's big brother was a
proper little oik. Cheeky, stroppy and his language! Always
bunking off school and then he got in with some nasty little
thugs. Real bad lot. His Mum and Dad were in despair."

He stopped talking to wave to an elderly lady who hobbled
in on the arm of a brawny man who called out, "Hey up there,
Eddie! See you've brought the wife along!" and roared with
laughter.

Tanner glanced at Moyna. "That's Harry and his old
Mum. Take no notice. They always pull my leg. He didn't
mean any offence." He cut a sausage into quarters and
stabbed at a piece with his fork. He said, "These bangers
are the best in Margate," and for the next few minutes was
busy eating.

Moyna, lost for words, ate also. In this friendly, bustling
place she felt totally out of place, like a creature from
another planet. It was far from the discreet restaurant she
had imagined earlier, but here everyone was alive and open
– or so it seemed. In her newly awakened state, she wanted
to believe that everyone had a heart of gold. Different
rules applied here to any she had known before and she
longed to be part of the scene, accepted in the way that
Tanner was.

He said, "I kept the lad out of prison. It was touch and go but I did it. This is Bert's way of thanking me."

Moyna began on the sausages and found them delicious. The mashed potatoes were lumpy but the savoury gravy, thick with chopped onions, easily made up for any deficiencies. For the first time since George's death she found she was hungry and was soon eating heartily. Tanner was also enjoying his meal. He asked the lad for mustard and, giving the pot a quick stir, helped himself generously.

After he had taken the edge off what appeared to be a ravenous appetite he said, "Good, isn't it?"

"Absolutely delicious."

Finally defeated, she left one sausage, but Tanner, with a glance at Bert, gave it to Prince.

"Eat it quietly!" he advised and then winced as the dog demolished it in three determinedly noisy mouthfuls.

Tanner said, "What about a pud? No expense spared when Edward Tanner takes a lady out to dine. It's spotted dick or spotted dick. With custard, naturally. Tomorrow will be apple pie and custard, the next day treacle tart—"

"And custard!"

"Good guess! So what d'you say? Go the whole hog? Bust your braces?"

The two fishermen sniggered.

"I'm full up," she said.

Before they left, she remembered to pass on the message from Matthews. Tanner nodded. "You're lucky to have that Mrs Stuckey with her twenty-twenty vision. No way the defence can talk their way round that kind of evidence. Know what I mean?"

Outside, Moyna drew in a trembling breath. In one way it was a relief to be out of the noise and bustle, but it was also time to go home. Frank might be out and she dreaded the empty house.

She said, "Thank you for lunch, Mr Tanner. I really enjoyed it."

"Thank *you*, Mrs Ellyard. And thanks for doing that bit of typing. I'm off to the church in Thanet Road to have a look through their records. Might get lucky."

"How exactly?"

"Might find your beneficiary. Soon as I do I'll let you know. Oh, by the way, her name's Simmons." Grinning, he tapped the side of her nose. "Don't ask! But does the name ring a bell?"

She thought hard and was about to shake her head when her thoughts reverted to Mr Brough. Simmons, he had said. She cursed her stupidity. "Yes it does."

"Well there you go! Take care."

And he was gone.

Ten minutes later Moyna was standing outside the office in The Linen Store. She straightened her back and drew in a deep breath. Be businesslike, she reminded herself. But how? She thought feverishly . . . Do not give Mr Dunn the impression that you are just a housewife – even if you are. You are now the owner – the *part* owner – of a thriving business and you must at least appear confident and capable. Speak clearly. Do not allow him to ruffle your composure. She reached for the door handle, but was immediately consumed with further doubts and withdrew her hand. Should she walk straight in, she wondered. He was in charge but he was, after all, only the manager. Perhaps she should knock and wait. Deciding on a compromise, she knocked on the door of the office and went in. Stanley Dunn was waiting, an expression on his face which she did not recognise. Certainly not the dismay she had anticipated.

"Do please sit down, Mrs Ellyard," he urged. "I've put the kettle on . . ."

"No tea, thank you," she told him, with what she hoped

was a businesslike smile. "I've just had an enormous lunch." She was tempted to ruffle him just a little. "Do you know Bert's Pie and Mash Shop by any chance?"

He blinked. "You mean, on the front? I know *of* it."

"Next to the rock shop." Moyna smiled. "I can recommend the bangers and mash. Very tasty and a reasonable price. But let's get down to business, Mr Dunn. You wanted to see me about a proposition." She was beginning to relax.

He sat down opposite her and leaned across the table. Was it her imagination or did she see suppressed excitement?

"Mrs Ellyard, you were kind enough to confide in me about the contents of your husband's will," he began. "I have to admit that I cannot bear the idea of The Linen Store being sold off to accommodate your husband's wishes. Nor, I may add, am I happy at the way this situation has come about. But that's not your fault." He cleared his throat. "I took the liberty – and I hope you'll forgive the presumption – of consulting my bank manager. I explained the position and asked whether or not he would consider lending me an amount sufficient to buy this 'unnamed person' out." He paused dramatically. "After deep discussion he replied in the affirmative."

He drew a long breath and Moyna thought she could see what was coming.

"So . . . Mrs Ellyard, I am now in a position to ask whether you would consider us becoming partners in ownership of The Linen Store – *if* this person is willing to sell at a reasonable price. I'm sure we could work amicably together."

She could almost feel the tension as he waited for her answer.

She said, "It's a rather large 'if', I'm afraid. But I'm impressed, I admit. The idea of such a partnership had never occurred to me. I'd have to think it over, Mr Dunn – and talk

to Frank, of course. I have to consider his future now that –
that our circumstances have changed."

"Oh, but of course you must. Take all the time you need. I
know it would halve your income, but at least I would share
the responsibilities with you and the store needn't fall into
careless hands." He leaned forward. "And I do have years
of experience. We could consult a solicitor together – or
separately if you wished . . ."

Moyna had been watching him closely. She had gained
the impression that he had more to say and waited to see
if she was right.

After a pause he said, "Of course, if you decided against
the idea I would – *might* then approach the unnamed
person—"

"Her name is Simmons. A Miss Simmons."

He blinked. "A woman!"

"Yes."

The silence lengthened.

Deciding against comment he said, "I would then approach
the unnamed person and discover whether he – whether *she*
– would agree to a partnership if you would sell me *your*
half of the business."

His face had coloured and he dropped his gaze to study
his hands.

Moyna regarded him steadily. "My half? You mean that
whatever happens you would want to become a partner?"

"Exactly so, Mrs Ellyard." He ran thin fingers through
his hair and sighed heavily. "I have talked to my wife and
we have agreed this might be our only chance to go into
business on our own account. There might never again be
such a chance. It would be a struggle for us, I don't pretend
otherwise, but I know the business like the back of my hand
and we can do it! I know we can." He drew a couple of sharp
breaths and was obviously trying to relax. He leaned back
in his chair. "It rather depends on your own plans. If you

were no longer connected with The Linen Store what would you do? We have no intention of causing you any further difficulties. You will need a little time, I know, to think it over and take advice."

"And to discover what the wretched Miss Simmons wants to do with her half. She might be dead, of course."

He looked shaken. "Dead? Oh do you think so?"

"I only said *might*. It would create further problems for both of us. They would have to trace her descendants – if she has any. Or her relatives if she remained single." She decided to be honest with him, as far as she was able. "Mr Dunn, I have barely come to terms with George's death and I haven't come to any decisions about the future. I am taking one step at a time, as you can imagine, and as soon as I have definite news on Miss Simmons I will be in touch with you. I approve your candour and – and I appreciate your suggestions. I think we may well come to an amicable arrangement one way or the other and I would certainly be happy to work with you, but we must just be patient for a little longer."

She didn't tell him that the police had not inspired her but that she had engaged a private detective. Better to leave Tanner out of it, she thought. Stanley Dunn would never understand.

Eddie Tanner met the vicar halfway along the path to the Rectory. The Reverend Parker was a tall thin man with thick grey hair and a harrassed expression. He was carrying a box full of papers and blue folders and gave the impression that he ought to be somewhere else and soon.

Eddie produced his card and held it up and watched the vicar's expression change.

"A private detective? What on earth . . . ?"

Eddie smiled as he slipped his card back into his pocket. "The police are trying to trace someone and I am helping with the enquiries." It wasn't far from the truth, he argued silently. He *was* helping, although he was actually helping Mrs Ellyard. "I need to have a dekko at the record of marriages. We think that a Miss Simmons married someone in Margate. Eighteen years ago or thereabouts – and it may have been in your church."

The vicar pursed his lips. "People do look through the register from time to time but usually they are seeking an ancestor. Compiling a family tree. That sort of thing. Quite a few people come from America." He smiled. "They are very appreciative – and generous. You say you're working for the police . . . Has this Simmons woman done something wrong?"

Eddie laughed. "Bless you, no! Quite the opposite. It's a matter of a will. Something to her advantage, in fact." He raised his eyebrows. Seeing that the vicar still hesitated he said, "Of course, you must make a fee for a search. Or could I make a small donation to church funds? Taking up your time like this when you're a busy man . . ."

"I'm due at a meeting, as it happens." The vicar glanced up at the church clock. "If it's an official fee I'd need a receipt but a donation . . ."

They settled on a donation of three shillings and Eddie was led into a small room behind the altar. A large ledger was produced and laid on the table with due ceremony before he was left in peace to study the various entries. For a while he leafed through the pages out of curiosity, seeing the handwriting change here and there – a visiting vicar, maybe. The first entry was dated 1905 and eventually he turned the pages to the required year. It occurred to him that he might find the Ellyards' marriage. Then he would know her maiden name. There was such a lot he would like to know about her – about her life before they met. What sort of child had she been? Probably dutiful. No doubt went to a private school –

maybe a convent. He tried to imagine her in a crocodile led by nuns.

"I bet you had pigtails!" he muttered smiling.

Had she been happy, married to Ellyard? There was no way he could ask. How did she grow up and how did they meet and was it love at first sight? For some reason he hoped it wasn't. He would like to meet Frank but could think of no excuse to do so.

The meal at Bert's place had been a bonus. And she had enjoyed herself. At least he hoped so. No doubt she was too polite to say otherwise. Shame about the wisecrack about "the wife" but she had taken it in her stride. He grinned. His friends had been hinting for years that he should marry but he had never given it much thought. His own parents' marriage had not been a success and hadn't inspired him to find a wife of his own.

With a small shake of the head, he forced his mind back to the business at hand. He didn't expect to find the Simmons woman but he had to start somewhere. He knew she could have married in one of the other churches or even in another town, although he hoped that was not the case. Slowly, methodically, his finger slid down the pages until – at last! He had found a Simmons.

Alec Reginald Simmons . . . Elsie Agatha Brownlow . . .

False alarm. He sighed and muttered "Are you in here, Miss Simmons?" and carried on, page after laborious page, for another quarter of an hour. Five minutes later he had it! His finger traced the names with a feeling of triumph.

Iris Brenda Simmons and Stanley Bernard Wheatley . . .

"Bullseye!" he muttered. He'd found her at the first attempt. Lady Luck was with him this week. He copied the details into his notebook and sat back with a satisfied smile on his face. So now he was looking for a Mrs Iris Wheatley. And so were the solicitors, presumably. He closed the ledger and stood up. Then he sat down again. He reopened the ledger and found the relevant page.

Staring at the entry he thought about it. "Was anything going on, Iris?" he muttered. Many women who married were already pregnant. Was it worth pursuing? Mrs Ellyard would be satisfied with the progress he had made but instinct made him want to dig deeper. Closing the ledger he returned it to the cupboard and as he replaced it he looked for another ledger. *Births and Deaths.* "Aha! This could be *very* interesting!"

With a quick look round to reassure himself that the vicar had not returned unexpectedly, Eddie carried the book back to the table and resumed his labour. This time he was looking for a child, born to Iris and Stanley Wheatley. Most people had their children christened by the vicar who married them.

So where were the children? "If you exist."

Again his patience was rewarded.

"*Virginia Rose* . . ." And Stan Wheatley had signed the register.

Eddie looked at the date of birth and screwed up his face in dismay.

"Oh Lord!" he whispered.

George Ellyard had left half his worldly goods to a woman who had had a child only six months after her wedding to another man. Had Iris Simmons been two-timing Wheatley? Had he found out and left her? Maybe she had been forced to choose between the two men. The possibilities were endless, the coincidences coming too fast for comfort. Suddenly another thought entered his head – an even worse scenario. He groaned. If his suspicions were correct George Ellyard might well be the father of Iris's child.

He frowned. "Do I really want to know this?" he muttered.

He was beginning to wish he had not been quite so

thorough. There was no way he would pass on all his suspicions to Moyna Ellyard. Nobody likes to hear bad news. Nor do they like the bearer of that news. He stood slowly, staring through the open doorway into the nave of the church.

"I can't tell her," he told himself, imagining the hurt and shock in her eyes. Yet part of him – the professional man – longed to show her how clever he had been. He had solved the puzzle; he had done exactly what she had paid him to do and in double quick time. So why not declare his success? Because it would cause her too much hurt. All he needed to tell her was that he had traced the mystery woman who was Iris Wheatley née Simmons.

"Although it's going to come out sooner or later," he argued. And when it did he would get no credit for his expertise.

Deep in thought he restored the book to its rightful place and went back into the church. He was not a churchgoer now but as he looked around him distant memories surfaced. Every Sunday morning he had attended church with his parents, dressed in his Sunday clothes. Every afternoon he had attended Sunday school, listening earnestly to pretty Miss Moss and collecting the weekly stickers in a little book which, when full, would entitle him to a seat on the bus which would take them for their annual picnic. He stood in the aisle, breathing in the familiar smell of polish, old wood and decaying flowers. Did Moyna Ellyard go to church, he wondered. On impulse he edged into the first pew and knelt, hiding his face with his hands.

"Dear God . . ." he began, then stopped. What should he pray for? He had his health and enough money to get by on. He wasn't a greedy man but there must be something he wanted. He tried again. "Dear Father in heaven . . ."

It was no good. He dare not ask for the one thing he wanted because he had done nothing to deserve it. He struggled to his feet and tiptoed along the aisle. Miss Moss had told them that He knew the inner workings of everyone's heart. So – He could work it out for Himself.

Eddie stepped out of the porch into what was left of the afternoon. He would go home and ponder the dilemma. He was going to present his findings to his client but how much would he reveal? He wanted to rush over there immediately but that would be a mistake. He had already seen her today. If he waited he would have an excuse to see her tomorrow. Maybe he would turn up on her doorstep unexpectedly and maybe she would ask him in for a cup of tea. Better and better.

He smothered a deep sigh, squared his shoulders and forced himself to walk back to the office.

Six

That evening, the bar of the Three Horseshoes was as noisy as ever. The room was full of smoke from countless cigarettes, a couple of dogs bickered half-heartedly among the chairs and a few red coals smouldered forgotten in the grate.

Michael sat back in his corner and watched the rest of the customers through half-closed eyes. He was at once depressed and angry. The news about the theatre wasn't good. Rumours were flying once more. If the present manager pulled out he, Michael, would be out of a job. So would the rest of the staff – the usherettes, the box office managers, the scenery shifters and cleaners. Everyone. Perhaps he ought to start looking for another job now, before the rush began. Why on earth had he ever got into the theatre business, he wondered. It was notoriously insecure.

He lifted his mug and drank deeply. If ever there was a night for getting drunk, this was it. He wiped froth from his upper lip.

"Mike! By all that's holy! It *is* you!"

He turned to see an old friend bearing down on him and at once his mood grew darker. Alfie Lowe! As if he didn't have enough to worry about! Of all the people he knew, Alfie was the one he would least like to see heading across the room. And with a tarty-looking woman in tow.

"Alfie!" He forced a smile and stood up.

The man was built like a barge and his face was broad and untouched by anything more immediate than present pleasures. He had never bothered with the future and now, Mike hoped, he had forgotten the past. The two men had gone to school together in Dorset and had later got into mischief together.

Michael slapped him on the shoulder and said, "Well this *is* a turn up for the books!" and tried to look more enthusiastic than he felt.

Alfie grabbed his companion round the waist and said, "This is Jen. What d'you think? Who's a lucky man, then?"

Jen was about thirty, overblown, with peroxided hair. The sort of woman he despised.

"Nice to meet you, Jen."

She said, "Likewise!"

She appeared to have been poured into her skirt and her satin blouse strained over a generous bust.

"What are you both having?" Michael asked.

"Rum and blackcurrant, thank you kindly, sir!"

He collected the drinks and refilled his own glass but his heart was heavy. What was this man doing here? He had hoped he would never have to set eyes on him again.

They chatted for a few moments, but it was mostly Alfie who did all the talking while Jen fluttered her eyelashes at every passing man.

Alfie bought a round and then Michael bought another. Around them the noise grew, the dogs fought in earnest and were thrown into the yard – and the fire went out. Jen looked bored.

Alfie said, "So how's life with you, mate?"

"I'm doing OK. Working in the theatre. Assistant stage manager. Nice cushy number."

"In the theatre?" Alfie glanced at Jen. "Couldn't wangle

101

an audition for this one, could you? She's got a lovely singing voice. I keep telling her—"

"Alf*ie!*" She gave a shrill little laugh. "You mustn't go on about me!" But she had perked up a little and now fussed with the frilled neckline of her blouse, managing to expose a little more of her cleavage.

"Why not? You've got a lovely voice. If Mike here can get you an audition—"

"Sorry, but I can't." Michael tried to sound regretful. "You'd have to approach the manager. The house manager. Different department altogether."

"You could at least try." Alfie blinked balefully.

"Sorry. No go." He was wondering how he could get rid of them.

Alfie leaned over to Jen and gave her a hug. "You OK, sweetie?"

She shrugged, obviously bored again.

Michael said, "She doesn't say much."

Jen bridled. "Can't get a word in edgeways with you two rabbiting away!" She tossed her head and reached for her glass.

Alfie leaned back in his seat. "We've got a lot to catch up on," he told her. "We go back a long way. Lot of water under the bridge, eh, Mike?" He winked.

Michael wanted to throttle him. Here we go, he thought. It's all going to come out. Damn and blast the man!

Alfie leaned towards Jen. "We shared a bit of bother once. Know what I mean?" He tapped his nose. Lowering his voice he said, "Few weeks' holiday by kind permission of His Majesty!"

Her eyes widened. "You don't mean . . . ? What you and him in the nick? Alfie Lowe! You kept that quiet!" Her voice rose.

Michael said, "Keep your voice down, can't you!" Silly cow.

"What did you do then? Rob a bank!" She giggled.

Mike gave her a filthy look and said nothing. It was all in the past and the way things were now, he didn't even want to think about it.

Alfie said, "Bit of a rough and tumble, that's all. A dust-up in a pub!"

"Ooh! You naughty boys!" She rolled her eyes humorously and Michael longed to slap her. "Fighting over a woman, were you? I bet you were!" She fluttered her eyelashes at Michael. "Now don't you two start a rumpus over me, will you."

"No chance!" he muttered into his beer.

"What was that?" Alfie regarded him blearily. "What did you say?"

"Nothing." His pulse raced. He'd got to get out of here before he blew his top.

"You said 'No chance' – I heard you!"

Jen said, "Now, now, boys!"

Michael stood up. "I meant no chance. She's your girl."

"I should hope not! You getting another round?"

"No. Got to see a man about a dog." He swallowed the last mouthful and forced another smile. This time it was harder than before. "Back in two ticks." He stumbled towards the Gents, praying that Alfie wouldn't decide to join him. He didn't want any reminders about the past. He didn't ever want to do another stretch in prison.

"Oi! Mike! Hang on a minute!"

He heard Alfie push back his chair but he was desperate to escape. He practically ran through the passage to the outside toilet. There were footsteps behind him. Damn the man! Mike dodged behind a stack of crates and watched Alfie go into the toilet. Then he ran for the gate and up the road. Alfie knew too much about him – but he'd said he was only down here for a few days' holiday.

"Thank God for that." He'd be gone soon. Two days.

Mike made up his mind to keep out of sight as far as that was possible. He stopped to relieve himself in a hedge then stumbled on. When he reached Ocean View he paused on the steps to draw breath and to collect himself. His heart was beating rapidly and he gave vent to his feelings with a few ripe curses. As he stumbled round to the back of the building he was trying to rid himself of the idea that Alfie turning up like that was bad news. A ghost from the past. A very bad omen.

Earlier that same evening Iris had found half an hour to herself – a rare luxury – and she was in the residents' lounge, running through her dance exercises. Once she had thought she might one day pick up her career but now she knew it was a vain hope. But that didn't mean she needn't keep herself supple and when occasionally she had time on her hands she would run through a short routine. Now she stretched forward each leg in turn, moving her foot from side to side. She was glad Ginnie had inherited her shapely legs. Iris had appeared at the Theatre Royal once as a child, one of seven fairies in a pantomime, and she could still remember the feel of the blue net skirt and the anxiety she felt over her wings which threatened to fall off.

The local paper lay on the coffee table. In it she had read and re-read the news item about George Ellyard's death. It now seemed certain that someone had killed him. It was not a robbery that had gone wrong – it was a beating of some kind and she found that impossible to believe.

"Poor old George!" she murmured as she raised and lowered her arms in an elegant curve. "He doesn't deserve to be dead." She tried to imagine him fending off an assailant and shuddered. "Who'd want to kill you?" She put her heels together and turned out her toes. "What did you do to him – whoever he is?"

She bent her knees, slowly and carefully because she

wasn't getting any younger and she had the business to run and couldn't afford to pull a muscle. George must have done something terrible to inspire such hatred, but that seemed so hopelessly out of character. He was a mild-mannered man. Wouldn't hurt a fly. She smiled faintly. "I was mad with you for a long time, but even I don't want you dead."

She made a few light springs, throwing out her hands by way of balance. Feeling that she had loosened up enough, she tried a few high kicks, but her heart wasn't in it. She could still kick with the best of them but what was the point. She said, "Oh blast it!" and gave up. She sat down but felt vaguely lonely. It was at times like this that she missed her cat. There had always been a Sukey to pet and cuddle and she missed the warm bundle of fur in her lap. Perhaps she would get another kitten. Ginnie might sneer but a cat was a homely thing to have about the place.

To cheer herself up she went into the dining room and wondered whether a change of lighting might be a good thing. She didn't want guests coming year after year to find the place exactly the same. There had to be alterations, no matter how trivial. They had to feel that she moved with the times. Perhaps the overhead lights could go. She would replace them with wall lights, or with tiny lamps with red silk shades. Pleated silk with gold braid.

The door bell rang and Iris made her way to the front door. It would be Mrs Loame, back from her after-supper stroll.

She opened the door, feigning polite surprise. "Mrs Loame!"

The old lady tottered inside, pulling her fox fur close around her neck. "I seem to have mislaid my keys," she said. "So sorry to trouble you."

"No trouble at all." Looking into the vague eyes, Iris was tempted to say that Mrs Loame had no idea what real trouble was, cushioned from the world as she was by the wealth her husband had left her. But she forbore. Troubles, as she well knew, were relative. Hers were money and her daughter's future. Mrs Loame's were loneliness and increasing disability.

"Is the local paper anywhere about?" she asked Iris. "I rather fancy a trip to the cinema – but don't tell your brother-in-law!" She gave Iris a conspiratorial wink. "I know he doesn't approve. Mrs Tenant went last week and says she quite enjoyed it. I know it's simply celluloid and not the real thing but I find them entertaining. Not like the old music halls, of course. Now they *were* the real thing. All those old stars – especially Marie Lloyd. She was a cheeky little thing. I remember her song about the umbrella. There was such a fuss about that song. I pretended not to understand it so as not to shock my husband." She rolled her eyes. "Poor Marie. Sad about her private life, but then famous people are so prone to unhappiness . . . And Hettie King. My mother loved Hettie King. Still those days are gone and we must move with the times."

Iris gave her the local paper and watched her slow progress up the stairs. She returned to the kitchen and reached behind the dresser to produce an ancient photograph album. Sitting down, she held it on her lap for a long time before opening it. When at last she turned the first page the sight of George's smiling face brought the familiar tears to her eyes.

"Silly sod!" she murmured with affection. "What on earth did you do to get yourself killed?"

Their affair had been passionate but short-lived. Iris stared at the photograph taken by a beach photographer. It showed a darkly handsome man with his arms round a young woman who was smiling radiantly into the camera. A travelling salesman, George had told her, and she believed him. She had believed everything he told her. Why should she have doubted him? She was in love with him from the first moment she set eyes on him.

George Ellis. That's what he called himself and she had wondered at the time why his friend had laughed. George had come to Ocean View to meet a friend who was staying in Margate for the weekend with his elderly mother. Iris searched her memory for the friend's name . . . Ah yes! Reggie Vine.

"So long ago!" It was almost like another life.

At the time the guest house had been run by her parents and she was helping out. General dogsbody, she called it. Making beds, clearing waste-paper baskets, emptying slop buckets and lugging huge jugs of hot and cold water to the bedrooms.

She was serving breakfast when George came in and her heart did a sort of somersault. She had read about that in books and suddenly she experienced it for herself. Her heart gave a definite skip inside her chest.

"You were a real smasher!" she told his photograph. "Too good to be true, in fact!"

She turned the page. A photograph of George taken by her with the Brownie camera her father had given her for her birthday. She couldn't pretend to be an expert photographer – George's head was squeezed into the top left-hand corner of the picture and his knees loomed large in the foreground. It was one of the few snaps she had managed to take while his attention was elsewhere. George had hated her taking his photograph. Later, when it was too late, she realised why that was.

"Evidence!" she told him now, caressing the photograph with her finger. "Mustn't be caught on camera in case Moyna sees it. Moyna, Moyna, Moyna!" Nineteen years later she still hated the name. "What sort of name is that?" she'd demanded. "She's not Irish, is she?"

She shook her head at the row that followed his revelation about his engagement to Moyna. His excuses had been so thin. "We just drifted into the engagement." He'd insisted that he knew he'd made a mistake and for months was always on the point of telling Moyna that the engagement was off.

"But you never did, did you? Too cowardly by half . . . No." She regarded him earnestly. "Too kind." He couldn't bring himself to break Moyna's heart so he'd broken hers instead. She sighed.

There was another snapshot on the next page – the two of them at Reggie's wedding in Hastings. Iris smiled at herself in the blue outfit with the matching satin shoes and head-hugging hat.

"You were a smasher, Iris!" she reminded herself smugly. Everyone had admired her and George had been so proud. She had imagined herself walking down the aisle with George. It had been such a happy day. The very next week he had broken the terrible news.

"She's expecting a baby. I've *got* to marry her. You must see that, Iris."

"A baby? But whose baby is it? Why do *you* have to . . ." The truth hit her like a blow, knocking the breath from her body. "You don't mean . . . ? Not her as well!"

That was the one and only moment she had hated him. Before that they had been desperately in love. After that she had forgiven him out of compassion for his dilemma and for the lie he would have to live for the rest of his life. She had transferred her hate to the woman who had somehow trapped him into a loveless marriage.

"I'll make it up to you," he told her. "Somehow. I *will*, Iris. I promise I will."

Her parents were bewildered when she broke the news. The young man they had so admired and had welcomed into their home had betrayed and deserted their beloved daughter.

"But we – we thought it was a love match!" Her mother regarded her, white-faced.

"I'll kill him!" Her father shouted, anger hiding his humiliation. "I'll sort the blighter out! No man does this to my daughter and gets away with it!"

They were devastated a month later when Iris discovered that she, too, was pregnant. Even now Iris's mood changed as she recalled the shame her parents had suffered. Not *their* daughter. Not *Iris*. They had brought her up to know right from wrong.

"And so on!" Iris sighed as she turned the page. "All very sad and messy."

Her face brightened. There was Ginnie at six weeks, smiling up from the cot Iris's father had bought. And there she was again on her first birthday in the arms of her devoted grandmother. The magic of a baby. If only they had lived to see the young lady Ginnie had become.

"George gave her to me," she whispered. "And now he's dead."

She closed the album, crossed to the cupboard where she kept the cooking sherry and poured a small glass. She downed it in a couple of mouthfuls but it didn't stop the tears. Alone, she gave in to the emotion but it was short-lived. She had wiped her eyes and blown her nose before Michael let himself in the back door. His eyes were dulled and his cheeks flushed. Obviously he had been drinking.

That makes two of us, Iris thought. Now what does he want at this time of night?

She said, "Cup of tea?"

He shook his head and sat down.

"You look all in," she said, her voice heavy with sympathy. "Had a tough day?"

He looked across the table and saw the album.

She said, "I was feeling a bit maudlin. You know how it is. Ginnie all but flown the nest and I'll be on my own." Afraid that he would want to look at the photographs she hastily closed it and pushed it into the dresser drawer.

Pamela Oldfield

He peered into her face. "You've been crying!"

"Just a bit – for the old days. When Stan was around."

He gave her a sharp look. "Poor old Stan! Poor, stupid old Stan!"

"Michael! Your own brother!" She had never seen him quite so low. "You OK?"

"None of your business."

"Then don't make it my business!" Her tone was sharper than she'd intended. "Go home and sleep it off."

He leaned back in the chair and gave her a long look. "He was too good for you, my brother. Too good by half."

Chilled by the look in his eyes she stammered, "Why . . . What d'you mean? You've never—"

"I'm not daft, you know. You under . . . estimate me, Iris. Underestimate me. Always have done."

"Have I?" What on earth was he talking about? Her eyes narrowed. "Has something happened? Somebody said something to upset you?"

He covered his face with his hands. "You could say that. Some stupid bastard." He looked up. "I ran into an old pal this evening. So-called."

She was beginning to recover. "What did he say, this man?"

"We went to jail together. That's what. And he had to bloody well remind me."

Iris bit her lip. Stan had never told her this . . . but had Stan known about it?

As though reading her thoughts he said, "Stan never found out. He'd have been off his head about it. He was a bit of a prig, our Stan. A stupid prig if you see what I mean."

She didn't see and regarded him warily. Where on earth was all this leading?

He said, "It was nothing. A mistake. A brawl in a pub and they had to pin it on someone. They picked on me and Alfie. Blamed us for starting it. That's the law for you. They

110

don't care who it is as long as they collar someone. Keep the books straight!" He clutched his stomach. "I feel bad."

"D'you want something to settle your stomach?"

He nodded and she hurried to the bathroom. A minute or two later she watched him drain the glass. He had drunk too much beer, she guessed. Probably eaten nothing. "Fancy a bit of toast, Michael? Bread and lemon curd?" Soak it up, she nearly said but didn't. He was in a strange mood and she didn't like it. She was glad Ginnie was already asleep.

He belched and said, "Pardon me!" with mock courtesy.

"Granted." She was worried. Why was he calling Stan stupid? He'd never done that before. She tried to think of a roundabout way she could ask him. Before she could think of a way he said, "Didn't he ever know the truth – about the kid?"

She felt cold all over, her stomach churned and her mouth grew dry. She had held that secret close for eighteen years. Or thought she had. But Michael knew. She felt dizzy with shock.

He was staring at her in triumph. "Didn't know I knew, did you?"

"How . . . Who told you?"

"That's my secret, Iris. But I know. You fobbed that kid off on my brother. No wonder you changed your mind so fast. First of all it was, 'Oh no, Stan' and 'I don't love you, Stan. It wouldn't be fair to you.' Then it was, 'I was wrong about us, Stan. Let's get married.' And the poor stupid sod fell for it. All the trimmings – white dress, veil, big bouquet. The works! And all the time you were laughing up your sleeve at him. Poor Stan!"

For a second or two Iris wondered if she could bluff it out, but immediately rejected the idea. "I wanted to tell him the truth," she told him. How could she convince him that she had longed to be honest? "I knew if I did tell him, he would stand by me. Because he loved me so much—"

"More fool him!"

"He would have stood by me," she insisted, "but the child would have been spoiled for him. A constant reminder. As it was, he adored her. She made him happy. I thought we'd have other children but we didn't. That would have disappointed him. The thing is, Michael, that Stan went to his grave happy about her. Wasn't that the best way?"

"Best for you, granted."

"And for him."

"And for Ginnie. Let's not forget Ellyard's daughter."

With these words, Iris felt as though a great weight had descended on her. Her one thought was that Ginnie must never know the truth. She had brought her daughter up to love the father who died for his country. She whispered, "Stan loved me. What was so wrong? He wanted to marry me. I made him as happy as I knew how."

"You tricked him into bringing up another man's kid! I've known it for years."

"But *how*?" She stared at him, perplexed.

"Read your letters. The ones in the top cupboard."

Iris clapped a hand to her mouth in dismay. Her letters! Three precious letters from George telling her again that it was only because of the child; insisting that she was the only woman he would ever love; telling her that in his eyes Moyna would never be his true wife. Underlining his signatures with rows of impetuous kisses.

"Oh God!" she whispered. She knew each letter off by heart and considered them a part of her very soul. She had thought them safe from prying eyes in their hiding place above the wardrobe, but Michael had found them.

"What were you doing in my bedroom?" she cried angrily. "You had no right to sneak around my house!"

"I was looking for something."

"On top of my wardrobe! Don't be ridiculous. You were searching for something. What was it?" The thought of him rifling through her clothes sickened her.

"You were out. Gone to fetch Ginnie from school. If you must know I was looking for your savings book. I wanted to borrow some money and I—"

"Savings?" She laughed harshly. "When did I ever have any savings?"

"I didn't know that. I hoped you did have some."

"Money for what?" Had she ever known this man, Iris thought wildly. She had always trusted him. Stan's beloved brother. Ginnie's adored uncle. Was anybody who they pretended to be? Was she?

"I owed a bit." He looked a little shamefaced. "A lot, really. A bet that went wrong. A so-called certainty." He pulled himself up sharply. "Not that it matters now. It was years ago and none of your business."

"I never saw you as a gambler," she told him.

"And I never saw you as a cheat and a liar!"

The barb struck home. Iris opened her mouth and shut it abruptly. He was right. Pot calling the kettle black. "So you read my private letters."

"Of course I did. Curiosity. But I expected them to be from Stan. From your husband. Not from Ellyard. Letters from the man you really loved – because you never truly loved my brother."

There were tears streaming down his face and Iris stared at him appalled. Now what was going to happen? She remembered suddenly that Michael had wanted to marry her after Stan had died. He had offered her security – of a kind – but she had turned him down. A few years later he had stopped asking. Now she knew why. She swallowed hard. This made her very vulnerable. If she didn't deal with this carefully Michael might tell Ginnie the truth about her father. But would he? He loved the girl. She was sure of that . . . But she had also been sure that no one knew the truth about George and she'd been proved wrong.

She said, "I tried to love him. I did love him in a way that you wouldn't understand. I loved—"

"And Ginnie, my little niece. She's no such thing, is she? She's nothing to do with Stan or with me. Nothing!"

"Michael, please!" Hands clasped in an agony of despair, Iris leaned towards him. "I beg you, don't tell Ginnie. You know what this would do to her. I don't care about myself but . . . Michael?"

His eyes were closed now and his breath came thickly. She leaned forward and shook his shoulder.

"Michael . . . Are you all right?"

At last he lifted his head. "I'm going home!" he muttered. "Going home."

She wanted to see the back of him – to have time to herself to think – but could he get home without assistance? Suppose he got himself run over? "You could sleep here, if you like," she offered reluctantly. There were always spare rooms at Ocean View.

He stood up, "Going home."

"Michael . . ."

He walked to the door steadily enough. Perhaps he would manage. His bed-sitter was less than a quarter of a mile away. Iris followed him out into the back garden and plucked at his sleeve. "Michael . . . Please listen to me. About Ginnie . . ." She could forgive him anything, would do anything for him, as long as he didn't tell Ginnie. But he went slowly down the garden to the narrow lane that ran along the back. He didn't look round and was quickly swallowed up by the darkness.

The next morning Frank closed the front door behind him, heading for the Labour Exchange in search of any suitable openings. Ginnie had promised to ask her uncle if there was a job going at the Theatre Royal but she wasn't holding out much hope. A well-dressed stranger approached him.

"Mr Frank Ellyard?"

"Yes." Aware of an unfriendly tone he was instantly on his guard.

"I'm Detective Sergeant Fox. I wonder if you'd accompany me to the station. We'd like to ask you a few questions."

Astonished, Frank stared at him. "A few questions? About what?"

"Your father's death."

"Hang on a minute!" Instinctively he moved back a step or two. "What is this? Are you arresting me?"

DS Fox raised his eyebrows. "Why should you think that, sir? We would like to ask you some questions, that's all. Someone killed your father and we have to explore every avenue." Frank turned and rang the bell.

The detective moved closer. "You do want us to find your father's killer, don't you sir?"

"Of course but—" The door opened and Mrs Locke stared at them nervously.

Frank said, "I'll come with you but I must first warn my mother. She will wonder where I am." He pushed past Mrs Locke and hurried into the lounge where his mother was arranging flowers in a glass vase.

He explained briefly, adding, "It's nothing to worry about, Mother. I shan't be there long."

She looked doubtful. "Are you sure you should go?"

"Why not? I don't know anything and haven't done anything."

She hesitated. "But, Frank, what about your friend Ginnie? She's coming to tea."

"That's hours away. I'll be back in plenty of time. It's only a few questions. I must go with them or it will look very suspicious. It's nothing to worry about, I promise. I can sort things out."

Ignoring him, she followed him to the door and glared at
the detective. "Is my son under suspicion?" she demanded,
white faced. "If he is then—"

"Certainly not, Mrs Ellyard." The detective touched the
brim of his hat respectfully. "You surely must realise
we have to question everybody we can. Your son may
know something that will prove valuable to us. People
often know something without being aware of its significance."

"I'll come with him," she replied.

Frank laid a restraining hand on her arm. "I'd really prefer
you didn't, Mother. If I do know anything useful I'll be glad
to pass it on."

Leaving her on the doorstep with Mrs Locke, Frank
climbed into the detective's car and gave his mother a brief
wave. In spite of his brave words, his heart was hammering
against his ribs.

The interrogation room was small and almost airless, and
reeked of tobacco smoke and sweat. There was a small
window high up in the wall, but when Frank suggested
they open it he was told that it had been stuck shut for at
least ten years.

He sat on a hard wooden chair facing the detective.

"Did you have any idea, Mr Ellyard, that your father
intended to leave a large portion of his estate to a woman
named Iris Simmons?"

"None at all." Better, he thought, to say as little as
possible.

"Can you hazard a guess as to why he did this?"

"I'm afraid not."

In the corner, a young constable was apparently scribbling
his answers in a notebook. Frank caught his eye but he
looked hurriedly away.

The detective coughed and Frank gave him his full
attention once more. "So you are not aware of the cause

116

of the rather odd bequest. Odd and unexpected to say the least of it!"

"Perhaps she lent him some money at some time. We wonder if perhaps—" He broke off. Stop rambling, Frank. Don't offer anything.

"You wonder what?" The grey eyes were shrewd.

Frank shrugged.

"You were going to say?"

"That perhaps she was a 'sleeping partner'. Investing money secretly, for some reason."

"But why would a sleeping partner want to kill your father?"

"I don't know. None of it makes any sense."

"Unless your father refused to repay the money."

"That's possible. Unless it was a random killing. Perhaps it *was* a robber but he was disturbed before he got Father's wallet."

"But the odd bequest does suggest a connection, doesn't it?"

Frank shrugged again.

"Mr Ellyard, I must ask you again – do you have any idea who this Simmons woman is? Do you know or can you guess?"

"I'm afraid not."

"Do you know anyone else who might have hated your father? Someone at work, perhaps?"

Frank was startled. "At *work*? There are two elderly ladies and a middle-aged man. They all rely on The Linen Store for their livelihoods. Why should they kill the golden goose?"

It was the detective's turn to shrug. "You can see, sir, how difficult this enquiry is proving. Did you and your father get along? A good relationship?"

"I miss him terribly." He hesitated, reviewing the relationship in his mind. "Lately we haven't seen too much of each other. I was at school – homework every night plus piano practice. Father was at the shop most of the time. Sometimes until seven or eight in the evening."

The grey eyes narrowed. "You *know* he was at the shop? Could he have been anywhere else? With someone else? Another woman, perhaps?" As Frank protested he held up a placatory hand. "We always have to explore the jealous husband angle, however unlikely. Or he might have been a secret gambler. He—"

"Father? Gambling? Never in a million years!"

"He might have been a secret drinker, offended someone who was out to get revenge . . ."

"That's a bit far-fetched, isn't it?"

"Someone had a grudge."

Frank said, "It might have been a mistake. Maybe someone killed the wrong man. Mistaken identity. It happens."

"Rarely in my experience."

Frank bit back an angry retort. There was no point in antagonising them. He said, "Look here, am I under suspicion or not? I'd like to know."

"Should you be?"

"What do you mean?"

"Should you be under suspicion, Mr Ellyard?"

"Of course not. It's hardly likely I'd kill my own father—"

"You might want to do just that if you had found out about the mystery beneficiary. You might well feel murderous." He stared at Frank through narrowed eyes.

"But I didn't know until after the funeral! And even if I had somehow found out, why should I kill him? It would simply bring about the disaster sooner than necessary. You surely aren't serious about this. About suspecting me. It wouldn't make sense." Were they convinced? They gave no sign one way or the other. Probably part of their training. Rule One. Give nothing away. He stopped for breath. The relentless scrutiny was difficult to bear. That was probably Rule Two.

"And anyway," he added, in sudden relief. "I was in France at the time it happened. You know I was."

Both men looked at him. The detective said, "We know you had a ticket to France and were supposedly on a walking holiday."

"There you are then."

"We don't know whether or not you came home early without telling anyone."

Frank stared from one to the other, his throat dry with shock. They really did suspect him.

The detective said, "Wouldn't be difficult, would it. *Did* you pop home, Mr Ellyard?"

"Pop home? From France? Of course not! That's a ridiculous thing to say! Ask my companion. Ask Douggie. We were together."

"He could provide you with an alibi, I agree. You might have persuaded him to back your story. Stranger things have happened, Mr Ellyard."

The small room was beginning to feel claustrophobic. The clock on the wall ticked loudly and as the minutes passed Frank felt as though he was being drawn into a nightmare. Whatever he said they had an answer. Presumably they had no other leads and were now determined to pin the murder on him. He felt the beginnings of fear. Agreeing to answer questions had been a mistake. He must bring the interview to an end and get out of the place. With an effort he clutched the edge of the table and stood up on legs that trembled. "I – I won't listen to this! You're accusing me of – of—"

The detective feigned surprise. "We're not *accusing* you of anything, Mr Ellyard. We're merely asking a few questions. You said you were willing to answer them. Have you changed your mind?"

Frank drew on all his resources. "You're damned right I have!" He pushed back the chair and it fell with a crash.

"Either charge me or let me go!" His voice had risen, tight with fear.

"You're free to go, Mr Ellyard." DS Fox stood up and the constable closed his notebook. The detective began to thank him for his time but Frank pushed past him blindly and left the room. Outside in the fresh air, a little of his confidence returned but he had no wish to go home until he was sure he could deal with his mother. He didn't want to alarm her by appearing in this overwrought state so he walked rapidly along the street and dived into the first pub he came to.

"Half a pint of mild!" As the barman reached for a glass he said, "On second thoughts, make it a pint!"

Seven

Moyna placed a lace doily on one of her best plates and arranged a dozen iced cakes on it for maximum effect. She was going to a lot of trouble to prepare the tea, partly out of a desire to please Frank and partly from a need to assuage the guilt she felt. She was sure now that she had been wrong about the girl. If Frank liked her, Moyna would like her. Frank was hardly likely to start a relationship with a woman who would have an affair with a married man. And if Miss Wheatley had been a gold-digger, she would certainly not be wasting her time with an impoverished student.

She glanced at the clock and fretted that he was still not back from the police station. What could he possibly tell them that would help their enquiries? He wasn't even in the country when George had been killed. On impulse she went to the window for another glance up the road. He had gone to the station in a police car but they might not bring him back. He might have to walk home. Unless they were keeping him in for some reason. She went cold at the thought.

Suddenly alert, she muttered, "Now what are *you* doing?"

The car parked on the opposite side of the road was still there. It had been parked in the same spot for more than an hour. The driver was still in it and had made no move to get out. Curious. She stepped back but continued to watch from behind the curtains. What was he doing? And why

121

here, of all places? She felt a prickle of unease. He was reading a newspaper – or pretending to read it. Suddenly she remembered something Tanner had said – that whoever killed George might intend harm to herself and Frank.

"Oh no!" she whispered and an anxious hand crept to her heart. "Surely not!"

As she watched her anxiety grew into fear and her imagination took hold. She saw Frank returning home to find her lifeless body on the floor of the sitting room. Then whoever had killed her would step from behind the door and attack him.

She rushed to the telephone and dialled Tanner's number. He had promised help. Night or day. He would come round . . . The telephone trilled on but no one answered it. He was out, no doubt still trawling through dusty records in one of the churches – or even busy on another case entirely. He really should get himself another secretary. How much business was he losing without someone to answer the telephone? She replaced the receiver and sat down in the kitchen. Then, unable to settle, she jumped to her feet and stared out into the back garden. She was tempted to go back to the front of the house, but suppose the driver was missing now . . . He would hardly try to gain entry through the front of the house where he could be seen by any passer-by. Suppose he was on his way to the back?

She was going to have to call the police but the idea had no appeal. They had bundled her son away and hadn't sent him back.

"Think, Moyna!"

She was trying desperately to calm herself. Perhaps she was panicking for no good reason. The driver of the car might be perfectly innocent. Waiting for a neighbour. He might be a debt collector. Or an insurance man waiting to collect a weekly contribution. He could be anybody.

"Give it five more minutes, then Frank might be back. Finish laying the table," she told herself. Play for time.

She brought in a Dundee cake which she had made earlier in the week and a plateful of cucumber sandwiches which she covered with a clean tea towel. Still no sign of Frank, and a quick check showed her that the man was still outside. She was buttering scones in the kitchen when an idea occurred to her which seemed little short of brilliant. If the man was still there then she would go out and challenge him. He could hardly stab or strangle her in the middle of a street in broad daylight. She would demand to know what he was doing there and threaten to call the police if he refused to say.

Before she could lose her resolve she hurried to the front door and down the steps. She crossed the road and rapped sharply on the car window.

The newspaper was lowered – and she gasped.

"Mr Tanner!"

Weak with relief, Moyna watched him climb out of the car. He was smiling, totally at ease.

"Mrs Ellyard!" he said. "What can I do for you?"

Somehow she refrained from hitting him – or from throwing her arms around his neck in a grateful hug. "What are you doing here?" she demanded shakily. "You frightened the life out of me!"

He was genuinely astonished. "Frightened? Oh Lord! Don't say that. I told you I'd throw in a bit of surveillance. Just sitting, waiting to see if anyone suspicious would show up. What we call an 'obbo'. Observation, get it?"

"Why didn't you let me know? You – you could have warned me."

"I'm really sorry."

They stared at one another. "I rang you," she said. "To tell you there was a strange man spying on me. Or so I thought. I almost rang the police." She caught hold of his arm. "But never mind that now. Ginnie's coming to tea but they've taken Frank down to the police station. He's been there for hours and . . . and I don't know what to do . . ." By the time they were inside the hall Moyna was on the verge of tears.

"There, there!"

Tanner put his arms round her and they stood together in the hallway, saying nothing as the tears flowed. But as Moyna's fear faded she became aware of other things – the strength in Tanner's arms, his comforting closeness, the faint musky smell of shaving lotion plus a hint of camphor which she guessed came from his wardrobe.

"I'm sorry," he said at last. He drew away a trifle self-consciously and she resisted the urge to cling on to him. "Here, have a good blow!" He produced a large blue-edged handkerchief from the pocket of his suit and she took it gratefully. She blew her nose as she led him past the dining room.

"Mm!" he said appreciatively. "Lucky old Ginnie!"

Moyna offered him the handkerchief and he stuffed it back into his pocket.

She said, "Would you like to stay to tea? There's plenty of food. I made some fruit scones."

"Tea with scones! How could I refuse. Yes, I will, thank you kindly."

They continued into the kitchen where Moyna began to relate the events of the past few hours, but they were interrupted almost immediately by Frank's return.

After the introductions they sat round the kitchen table sipping tea and Moyna began to feel a little less stressed. Her son was back safe and sound and there was no menacing stranger spying on her. At that moment she couldn't ask for more.

Tanner listened intently to Frank's account of his inter-rogation, tutting from time to time and shaking his head.

"They've got nothing," he concluded. "They're getting

desperate. I know. I've been part of it, remember. It's an old trick. Rake in anyone remotely connected with the crime and try to rattle them. They usually go for all the males. In a way you can't blame them. They're doing their job. They know that if you're innocent you've got nothing to worry about. They're just hoping to get lucky. You see it's often the one you least expect who's the killer. Nine times out of ten it's a family member."

Frank rubbed his eyes tiredly. "I – I feel as though I've been through the mangle!" he muttered. "The thing is – have I convinced them?"

"Of course you have. They've got a witness, you see. And since you probably don't match the description, they know it can't be you. But they have to be seen to be doing something! If it will make you feel better, I'll pop into the station tomorrow and have a word."

Moyna smiled at her son. "So you needn't worry any more."

He stood up and held out his hand to Tanner. "Thanks for everything, Mr Tanner." He gave his mother a pat on the shoulder. "I'll get upstairs and change my shirt before Ginnie gets here."

When he had gone Tanner said, "He's a nice lad. You must be proud of him."

"We are – I mean, *I* am. Oh dear! It's all so awful! I can't believe our lives had been turned upside down this way. It makes me realise how cosseted we were before George died."

He nodded. He looked as though he was going to add something but said nothing.

"What is it?" she asked.

"A confession of sorts. I'm feeling bad about the fright I gave you. You see, it wasn't just an 'obbo'."

Did she imagine a faint flush to his cheeks? "Then what was it?"

"I fancied being near to you. Just sitting outside the house and imagining you inside. Now if that isn't the daftest thing . . ."

Looking into his eyes, Moyna kept her gaze steady. She was longing to respond but her conscience warned her not to commit herself. George has only just been buried, she argued silently. You cannot be feeling anything for this man you hardly know, and even if you were he is not the kind of man . . . She couldn't go on. But she had to say something.

"It isn't daft, Mr Tanner. It's a great compliment. And very kind." She hoped that didn't sound too priggish. It was fine for him. He was a single man – or so he claimed. She was newly widowed with a son and she had no right to be falling for any man, let alone a private detective about whom she knew absolutely nothing. They could be friends, surely, but that was all. Her mother would not approve of him, that was certain, although she now pretended she had never liked George, that she had found him cold. Well, that was one epithet that could never be applied to Tanner.

She became aware that he was smiling at her. "A penny for them!"

Moyna blushed. "A penny wouldn't pay for a fraction of them!"

He gave a slight shrug. "Do you really want me around when Ginnie turns up? I can be discreet. My shoulders are broad, Mrs Ellyard."

"No, I meant it, Mr Tanner. Please stay – unless you have other work. Another case, perhaps."

"Will there be salmon paste sandwiches?"

"I'm afraid not. Only cucumber," she laughed.

He pretended to consider. "I'll stay anyway. But what say we forget business for the rest of the day? Nothing in front of Ginnie."

"Frank will want to tell her."

"Of course he will. I meant you and me – we could try and forget it. That we're only business partners, so to speak."

Before Moyna could reply there was a ring at the front door and Ginnie had arrived. To Moyna's surprise, she found the girl very easy to get along with. Despite her earlier reservations, she could see what Frank liked about her and before long they were all chatting like old friends and Frank was recounting his ordeal at the police station as no more than a hilarious interlude. Both Frank and Ginnie seemed to warm to Tanner who was enjoying himself hugely. He ate an enormous number of sandwiches, scones and cakes and Moyna found herself wondering if he fed himself properly.

The comment he had made about wanting to be near her returned again and again. Was he attracted to her in the way she was to him? It was an impossible idea. And yet he seemed to like her – unless he grew over-fond of all his lady clients. Somehow she didn't think so. He had joked about Polly and Molly and all the women in his life, so why hadn't he married one of them? Was there such a thing as man who was "not the marrying kind"? She had once asked George if he loved her.

"I married you, didn't I?"

"But do you *love* me? If you do, you don't show it."

"Perhaps I'm not the marrying kind."

"Then why did you propose?"

On and on. She had been desperate for an explanation . . .

"Mrs Ellyard?" Ginnie was looking at her expectantly.

"I'm sorry. I was miles away."

Frank grinned. "It's Douggie's birthday on Saturday and I was suggesting a picnic next weekend – for the four of us."

Moyna blinked. "The four of us?" She glanced at Tanner. "I don't think . . ."

Ginnie said, "*Our* four, he meant. Me and Frank and Douggie and Laura."

"Oh of course!" How stupid of her. "I'll do a picnic for all of you. I'm sure Mrs Wheatley will have her hands full with the guest house. I'll make a few cakes. It will be no trouble."

Frank said, "Any excuse and my mother rushes to bake cakes! It's a wonder I'm not twice the size! She even makes them for the staff at The Linen Store!"

Moyna wanted to strangle him. She loved her son dearly but he was making her sound like a dotty housewife. She was struggling for a smart reply when Tanner rescued her.

"I'm a cake man myself," he said, smiling at her. "And I'm not proud. Any surplus cakes just pop them round to the office. I'll give them a good home."

To cover her embarrassment, Moyna said, "Any more tea?" and lifted the teapot enquiringly.

Frank said, "Ginnie and I are going to have a stroll along the pier." He glanced at Moyna. "Would you mind, Mother, if we dash away?"

"By all means, do. You'll catch the last of the sunshine."

At the front door Moyna took Ginnie's hands in hers. "Please come again. It's been lovely meeting you."

Ginnie thanked her for the tea and the two young people hurried away hand in hand.

Moyna closed the door slowly and made her way back to the dining room. Now it was just her and Tanner and she felt distinctly nervous.

Twenty minutes later Eddie let himself into the house which had been his home for as long as he remembered. He had been born and raised in the flat in Hawley Square – four large rooms with access to the garden which was shared by other tenants. At one time, while he was young, there had been an empty rabbit hutch which later had been inhabited by a bad-tempered guinea pig belonging to the girl upstairs.

Today there was a sour smell in the hallway and Eddie screwed up his face in dismay.

"Dad!" He closed the front door and made his way slowly towards what had once been his parents' bedroom. His mother had left them when Eddie was twenty and the room was now the sole domain of his father.

"Eddie, is that you?" The voice was querulous.

Eddie opened the bedroom door and flinched. Always the same. Always disgusting. His father lay sprawled across the bed, his mouth agape, his eyes staring upwards. Beside him was an empty whisky bottle. He knew where his father got the money to pay for it – he stole it from Eddie's wallet. What he could never discover was where he hid the bottles.

Eddie crossed towards the bed. Was there no end to this, he thought unhappily.

"It's me, Dad."

"You're late. I wondered . . . I wondered where you were." The old man tried to sit up but fell back with a groan. "My head . . . !"

He had been sick again. Eddie bit back angry words.

"I'll get some soapy water. Sort you out."

He backed away. Outside the bedroom he closed his eyes. No wonder his mother had run away. He had never blamed her. An alcoholic husband was a burden no woman should have to face.

In the kitchen he set down the tin of cakes Moyna had given him and put the kettle on. He sat down and stared at the tin. Four scones, three iced fancies and a slice of Dundee cake. A gift from the Gods! He would share them with his father.

Poor Moyna! Such a sweet woman. Too sweet to have all those problems. He thought about Ginnie Wheatley and shivered. Thank goodness he hadn't had time to tell Moyna the name of George Ellyard's beneficiary. Ginnie's mother no less! That would have put the cat among the pigeons with a vengeance. She would know eventually but he would let the police tell her.

He said, "God Almighty!" and whistled under his breath. That would make Ginnie Frank's half-sister. It was more than likely.

"And they're ready to fall in love!" It didn't take a genius to see that. More problems for Moyna Ellyard. Problems he couldn't solve for her. He sighed heavily.

After the young people had left for their stroll Eddie had made himself scarce, unable to trust himself when they were alone. He had already made a bit of a fool of himself, saying what he had about being near to her. Whatever must she think of him?

"You overstepped the mark, my son!"

Whatever he felt for her, he had nothing to offer a woman like that. Nothing really to offer any woman. And never had had.

He had made an excuse about having to get back to the office and she had seemed relieved that he was leaving. Apart from his stupid comment he had also been afraid to face any more questions; afraid to admit the success of his research. The police, he knew, would be one step behind him. They would come to the same conclusions. All he could do was delay the fateful day when Moyna would know the full truth. It would crucify them.

The kettle steamed and he turned off the gas. He would take soapy water and a flannel in to his father and he would clean him up and change his clothes. He would make him drink strong coffee and when he was sober enough he would make him something to eat. He had dealt with the problem for years and he would go on doing it. His father was his secret. His cross. His punishment for whatever he had done wrong.

"Whatever it was!" he muttered.

Into a bowl he put hot water, a flannel and a lump of soap and made his way into his father's bedroom.

"Here we are then!" he said breezily. "Let's be having you, Dad."

It took the best part of an hour to restore to his father to something approaching normality. He had cleaned him up and changed every stitch of clothing and during the entire procedure the old man hadn't said a word.

Eddie took away the washing water and came back to him. Lifting his father from the bed, he half-carried him into the kitchen and propped him on a chair. He looked like an elderly doll. The trousers and jacket were too big for his wasted body and a small tuft of hair, prematurely white, stuck up at the front of his head.

"Special treat tonight," Eddie told him. "A slice of Dundee cake. Your favourite, eh?"

The old man watched him add hot water to the tea leaves. "Your mother used to bake," he said. "She made Dundee cakes."

"I know she did. This one's home-made."

His father gave him a crooked grin. "I knew it! I said to myself, that boy's got himself a lady friend!" he chuckled but it turned into a wheezy cough.

"Me? With a lady friend? Come off it, Dad!"

Eddie shook his head. He sometimes wondered if his father had second sight. He spent his days in an alcoholic stupor and yet very little slipped past him.

"Then who gave you the cakes?"

"A client." Eddie handed him a mug of tea and said, "Don't spill it!"

"I've seen you," his father continued. "With that daft grin on your face. I can always tell . . . Nice, is she?"

Eddie cracked eggs into a bowl and added a little milk. Scrambled eggs sobered his father faster than anything. "My client is a very nice person, yes," he admitted.

"You'll have to bring her home some time. I'd like to meet her."

"I don't think so, Dad. I told you, she's just a client!"

"Tell that to the marines!" His father peered at him with eyes that were a little too sharp. "You're ashamed of me, aren't you, son? Afraid to let anyone see your poor old soak of a father!"

"That's rubbish and you know it." It was the truth, but he would never say so.

"Course you are! And I don't blame you." He blew on his tea and sipped noisily. "So where's this cake then?"

"After you've eaten your tea. Scrambled eggs and and bread and butter. Then cake."

"You're hard, son. You know that?"

Hard? Yes I am, thought Eddie. But it was the only way. He had learned it from his mother before she gave up. "You have to be cruel to be kind," she had insisted when the drinking first started. He sighed. But his father had spoken the truth. Eddie *was* ashamed of his father and there was no way he could ever bring a woman home. Especially a woman like Moyna Ellyard.

Iris was laying the tables for supper and trying not to think about Moyna Ellyard. Which was difficult because she'd had the wretched woman at the back of her mind for nearly twenty years and it wasn't likely she could stop now. She sighed as she seized a handful of cutlery. If only Moyna hadn't had Frank – but she had. And Ginnie was getting a bit too close for comfort and Iris was going to have to put a stop to it. But how?

"Bread knife, main knife, forks and a spoon for dessert." Which was banana custard or plum tart with ice cream. She stood back and surveyed the tables with satisfaction. Clean white cloths. Good cutlery with bone handles. Shining glasses and water carafes. She sometimes thought that the first thing she'd do when she reached heaven was lay the tables for the angels' supper! The lighting pleased her too and she wondered whether Ginnie would notice it.

If she ever won the pools, she thought, she would rearrange the dining room to make the seating more intimate. She would do away with some of the larger tables and have more for two and four. The days when large families came together were more or less over.

"More's the pity."

The papers said people were going to France for their holidays. Iris couldn't think why anyone should want to cross the Channel. There was all that funny food – snails and frogs' legs and suchlike – as well as the language. Parleyvooz and silvooplate. Who in their right mind would want to put up with all that when they could come to Margate and eat proper food and speak English?

She set out the cruets and picked off a few dead heads from the daisies in the glass table centres. They'd last another day or two and then perhaps she'd buy some pansies. Not the dark brown ones but blue or yellow. Or both.

"Now . . . what else?" Ah yes. The serviettes. Ginnie usually saw to those but she was late back from Frank's place.

She was folding them into crowns when Mrs Loame drifted in waving a newspaper.

"Mrs Wheatley! Oh, I'm so glad I've found you. I've got something to show you. Something wonderful!"

Iris straightened with a smile. "Something wonderful? I could do with that and no mistake!"

The old woman waved the newspaper. "Your name's in the paper!" she cried. "I said to myself, 'That's never *our* Iris Simmons', but it is, of course!"

Iris stood stock still as a feeling of dread washed over her.

133

Her name was in the paper? It must be to do with George. Oh Lord!

"I'm Iris Wheatley," she stammered. "There must be some mistake."

"Oh no! It's in the personal column. Read it for yourself." She thrust the paper into Iris's hands and pointed to the relevant section. "Would Miss Iris Simmons, late of Margate, contact so-and-so solicitors where she will learn something to her advantage!"

Iris sat down. She didn't want to read it but something drew her eyes to the wording of the advertisement. It was exactly as the old lady had said. She, Iris Simmons, would hear "something to her advantage".

Mrs Loame hovered at her shoulder, pink with excitement. "I knew it was you, you see, because I remembered that lovely photograph in the hall. You in your young days in that pretty costume with the flowers in your hair. The one where you were a dancer! I said to myself, there can't be two Iris Simmons. Not both living in . . ." She faltered to a stop. "Are you all right, dear? You look very pale."

Iris swallowed. She tried to speak, but her throat was tight with apprehension.

Mrs Loame tried again. "That usually means money, you see. A legacy. Someone has left you money in their will. A rich aunt or someone. You might be rich! Aren't you thrilled?"

Iris nodded, her thoughts swirling dizzily. It was George. She knew it. He had left her some money to make up to her for what he had done all those years ago. It was so unexpected. So sweet and generous of him – but how could she claim it? It would get into the papers. Iris pressed trembling fingers to her mouth. Admitting who she was would mean everyone would know what had happened between her and George . . . And Ginnie would know!

"Oh George! How could you?" she whispered.

As she stared up into Mrs Loame's beaming face two large tears rolled down her face. By trying to right an ancient wrong, George Ellyard had betrayed her for a second time.

Twenty minutes later Ginnie arrived home, letting herself in at the front door with her own key. She came into the kitchen and said, "I'm back. Sorry I'm late. What's different in the dining room?"

Iris beamed. "You noticed then? It's the light. Instead of those clear bulbs I've tried pearly ones. Pearly peach it's called. I thought it would soften the room."

"It does. Fine." She had thrown her jacket on to a chair and now tied an apron round her waist. "What shall I do?"

Iris studied her for a moment. Bright eyes. A slight flush to her cheeks. She had to say something but fear made her delay. Instead she said, "We've got a young couple in the Primrose Room. At least they said they were married and she was wearing a ring but it was a cheap-looking thing. I asked where they came from and he said Bromley and she said Croydon – both at the same time and then they looked at each other and laughed."

"That's a mean trick. You shouldn't ask them such personal questions."

"I was only making conversation." She must do it. "Ginnie, I have to talk to you about something. I want you to sit down. Just for five minutes."

Her daughter paused in surprise and then sat down. "What is it Mum – I mean Mummy? Don't look at me like that. You're not ill, are you?"

This, Iris knew, was her daughter's nightmare.

"No, I'm not ill. It's . . . It's about Frank Ellyard. I want you to—" How on earth could she say this? "I don't want you to get too fond of him. He's not the right man for you, Ginnie—"

"How do you know he isn't?"

Bright spots of colour in Ginnie's cheeks warned Iris that there was trouble ahead. Was she too late with her homily? She pressed on. In the circumstances there was nothing else she could do. "I don't think you should see too much of him – and I'm sure Mrs Ellyard doesn't want you and him to—" She bit her lip. "What I mean, Ginnie, is that . . ."

Ginnie's mouth tightened. "You mean I'm not good enough for him! Because his family own the store and I'm just an assistant. Well, Mum, for your information he doesn't think like that at all. And neither does his mother. She was very nice to me actually. And sent her kind regards to you. So *that* for your opinion!" She snapped scornful fingers in front of Iris's face.

Iris sucked in her breath and counted to four. "Virginia Wheatley! Don't you dare snap your fingers at me! I never expected . . . If your father could see you now he'd be horrified. Scandalised! If I say you're to stay away from the Ellyard boy, you'll stay away!"

"No I *won't* and you can't make me. It's so damned unfair!" Ginnie's voice shook with rage and resentment. "You don't even know him but you've taken against him."

"I don't need to know him."

"Then what has he done to upset you? He must have done something. Come on! Tell me what you've got against him."

Iris stared at her daughter with a growing feeling of helplessness. Ginnie was going to defy her. For the first time in her life she was not prepared to be guided by her mother. But she had to stop the affair getting out of hand. She would have to lie. Anything was better than the alternative. She took a deep breath and said, "There are rumours around. About Frank Ellyard."

"What rumours? I know he was questioned by the police but that was nothing. A formality. Frank told me. He laughed about it."

Iris stared at her, startled. Then she saw an opportunity.
"The police think he killed his own father? Well then, there
you are!"

Ginnie's expression hardened. "It was nothing. Routine. I
was going to tell you I heard about it, but you didn't give me
the chance. Mr Tanner says they do it to every male in every
family which is connected to the crime in any way—"

"Who's Mr Tanner?

"The private detective. The one Mrs Ellyard has hired to
find out about Mr Ellyard's will. It seems he's left half the
business to a mystery woman in his will and Mrs Ellyard
is furious. She's determined to find out who she is." She
frowned. "So what rumours are *you* talking about?"

What rumours? Iris was beginning to feel rather sick. She
didn't have any rumours but she had committed herself.
Better make it as vague as possible. "You know," she
said. "Not quite what he seems. Bit of a shady character."
So Moyna Ellyard had hired a private detective to hunt
her down. Just when Iris had thought things couldn't get
any worse.

"Who told you this?" Ginnie's eyes were blazing now.
"Give me a name. Tell me, who told you that Frank was
a shady character!"

"I – I don't remember. I don't know. I must have
overheard something in the grocer's. Yes, that's it. I heard
these women talking – about Frank Ellyard. A bit of a
womaniser. That's what one of them—"

"It's not true!" Ginnie insisted. "He is *not* a womaniser.
That's a dreadful thing to say. It's libellous, I should
think. And you have no right repeating it. You don't
even know him. And I *do*! It's a lie dreamed up by some
jealous old biddy and I don't believe it." She snatched a
breath. "I shall go on seeing him whenever I please. If
you try to stop me I'll – I'll walk out! I'll find a place of
my own."

"You'll do no such thing!" Iris heard her own voice rising. "You'll stay here and you'll stop seeing—"

"And I tell you I *won't!*" Ginnie's hands were two clenched fists. "Frank's the first boy I've ever really liked and you have to spoil everything. Well, I won't let you!"

She was fighting back tears and Iris longed to rush forward and comfort her. Instead she said, "I can't explain, love. I just—"

"Don't call me 'love' when you don't mean it. Perhaps you'd like it if I *did* find somewhere else to live!"

Panic-stricken, Iris stared at her. This is it, she thought, paralysed with fright. Unable to speak. If losing a mother was a daughter's nightmare, this was a mother's. The moment all mothers dread, when their beloved son or daughter rebels and decides to leave home. Iris and Ginnie faced each other across the room like two terriers and Iris sensed that Ginnie, too, was afraid of what might be said next.

They were saved, quite literally, by the bell.

Iris lowered her gaze first. "That'll be – Oh no, she's in already."

She walked slowly along the passage to the front door, her mind heavy with dread. When she opened the door she found Michael on the step with a large cardboard box under his arm.

"You!" said Iris. "I'm afraid—"

"Me and Sukey the fifth!"

"What?" Exasperated, she glanced at the box. A faint mewing sound came from within.

He said, "A peace offering. I'm – you know – I'm really sorry about the other night."

"So you should be!" She gave him what Ginnie called "one of her looks".

"I shouldn't have said what I did. It was the drink talking."

"You should stay off it, then."

"I've said I'm sorry."

"And reading my letters. That wasn't the drink. That was nasty, sneaky . . ." She stopped abruptly as the next-door neighbour came to her doorstep to put out empty milk bottles.

Iris forced a smile. "It's been a nice day for September."

"It has indeed."

Iris said cheerily, "Come on in then, Michael," and produced another false smile. She had been tempted to send him away when he next showed his face; had planned the telling phrases she would use to let him know just how far over the line he had stepped. Her row with Michael, however, had now been topped by an even greater and more significant row, and in her present situation she felt decidedly weak and in need of support. It crossed her mind to wonder what Michael would say if she did inherit some money. He'd want to borrow some of it, that was certain. She'd have to be very firm and say "No".

"We're having a row," she whispered, closing the front door behind him. "Be careful what you say." In a louder tone she said, "Well, you'd better come in."

Ginnie was still standing in the kitchen, her face white and furious. She glared at Michael. "I suppose you've heard as well. About the police questioning Frank Ellyard. I suppose it's all round Margate by now. Well, he didn't do it."

Michael looked at Iris. "Have I missed something?"

Iris said, "Not really." To Ginnie she said, "Your uncle's brought another kitten. D'you want to have a look at it?"

He was already undoing the string.

Ginnie said, "Not 'specially. It's a waste of time. They always get run over."

Iris and Michael let the comment pass.

Michael said, "It's a half-grown cat actually. It was going to be destroyed. Carpenter at the Royal brought it in. He'd

139

had it in his basement flat but the landlord complained. Said it was digging up his prize dahlias."

As he lifted the cardboard flap a thin ginger cat peered warily over the top.

Iris said nothing. If she enthused, her daughter, in her present mood, would be sure to condemn it. The cat put two tentative paws on the edge of the box and raised itself.

Michael said, "It's a scrawny little thing."

Ginnie moved a little nearer. "Because it's half-starved."

"It was supposed to catch the mice and rats. You don't feed a cat that's supposed to hunt."

"And did it?" Iris asked.

"He didn't catch many by the look of him."

Iris, enchanted, wanted to pick up the animal and cuddle it, but more than that she wanted Ginnie to do so. The quarrel with her daughter, so uncharacteristic, had shaken her badly and it had been getting to the point of no return. The thought of Ginnie leaving home terrified her. The arrival of the cat, she thought, might have saved them from disaster.

Slowly Ginnie reached out a hand but the cat withdrew hastily into the box.

Iris said, "But Ginnie's right. It won't last long here. Bound to run out the front. The garden's full of Sukey graves."

Michael shrugged. "It won't last long at the vet's, either. One quick jab and . . ."

He broke off as the cat sprang out of the box, jumped from the table to a chair and from there to the floor.

"I'm not keen," Iris shrugged. "Ginger cats are always toms. It can't be a Sukey. I prefer 'shes'."

The cat mewed.

Michael looked at Iris, "I don't care one way or the other. You know me. I'm not a cat lover. I just thought you were missing Sukey."

Ginnie glared at Iris. "Well if you don't want it, I do!"

Michael said, "It's called Tiddles."

Iris frowned. "Because it does?"

Ginnie picked up the cat. "That's right. Find fault! Just like you do with everything. With Frank and – and me. Well, I'm keeping it, so there!" She slammed out of the kitchen, taking the cat with her.

Iris and Michael looked at each other and Iris held up crossed fingers. A moment or two later Ginnie returned, minus the cat. Without a word she filled a dish with milk and crumbled some bread into it. She paused at the door to glare at her mother. "His name's Marmalade. Ladie for short – with 'i-e' at the end. So don't remind me it's a 'he'." She withdrew in a contemptuous silence.

Iris said, "So that puts me in my place!"

Michael grinned. "We make a good team," he said. "Put it there, partner!"

They shook hands, keeping their laughter low so that Ginnie shouldn't hear them.

Iris heaved a sigh of relief. The pressure was off for the moment, but it was only a matter of time.

Eight

The following morning Moyna put out a hand and absentmindedly stroked a large tabby which sat on the counter of the stonemason's emporium.

Emily said, 'Ring again. We've been here ten minutes already.'

"Patience, Mother. They'll be along shortly."

She hoped they would. The small dusty room depressed her. A tasteful arrangement of silk lilies did little to brighten the dark panelled walls and the thick carpet muffled their footsteps. A collage of slim stone samples hung on one wall and seemed to give the lie to the whole pretence. What good was a headstone to a man who was dead? Was George going to glance down from heaven to admire the lettering or approve the stone itself?

Emily said, "I don't know why you have to change the lettering, Moyna. There's no need. But I shouldn't be surprised. You always were a difficult child."

The cat sprang on to the floor and slipped out of the door on to the forecourt.

"Because I choose to alter it, Mother." Moyna straightened her back. "And who are you to carp, anyway? I didn't tell you what to put on Father's headstone when he died."

Emily shook her head. "That was different. I can't imagine

what Mr Bell is going to think. It's so disrespectful to George's memory. It's small-minded."

Moyna tossed her head. "Disrespectful? You were quick enough to tell me that you'd never really liked George. And wasn't what George did to us small-minded? Giving half our livelihood to someone else. You think that was a decent thing to do to me and to Frank?"

The older woman remained silent.

At that moment a small, round man appeared from a black curtained recess at the back of the room. He was dressed in black except for a white shirt. Even his spectacle rims were dark tortoiseshell. "And how can I be of service, ladies?"

Moyna said, "Mr Bell? D'you remember me? I want to change the lettering on my husband's headstone – always assuming you haven't done it yet."

It was obvious he didn't remember her. "Er – what name would that be?" he asked.

"Mrs Moyna Ellyard."

His eyes widened. "Ah yes! I remember. Of course."

He had recalled the news item about George's suspicious death, thought Moyna. She said, "You expected the headstone would be ready by today but I'm rather hoping it isn't."

"Let me see now." He made a great show of searching through his book, running a stubby finger down each page. "Yes, here we are. George Bernard Ellyard . . ." He glanced up at Moyna. "I'll just check on progress, if you'll excuse me. Of course, any additional lettering will depend on how much room there is."

Emily muttered, "Whatever will people think? Changing the wording!"

"You said you wouldn't interfere," Moyna reminded her. "You said that if you came along you'd leave everything to me."

"But what was wrong with your original inscription?"

"It was too flowery, Mother." To Mr Bell she said, "I want to shorten it, actually."

"Shorten it?" He looked affronted.

Moyna nodded. He began to speak, changed his mind and disappeared the way he had come.

Emily gave her daughter a glacial stare. "Really, Moyna. I thought I'd brought you up better than this . . ."

"I think in the circumstances I'm entitled to change my mind. I don't want to be too – too sugary. Please, just leave it to me."

"You always were a wilful child."

Mr Bell returned. "Our mason was just going to apply his chisel!" he told them. "I caught him just in time." He reached for a pencil and looked at Moyna enquiringly. "So how would you like it to read, Mrs Ellyard?"

"Instead of 'Dearly beloved husband' I want to say 'Beloved husband and father'."

"Not '*Dearly* beloved'?"

"No."

The tightening of his lips revealed his disapproval without the need for words but Moyna ignored it. She watched as he wrote laboriously in capital letters with much licking of the pencil point. "Is that all you want to change?" he asked when he had finished.

Moyna could imagine him regaling his wife with the story over supper. "You'll never believe what happened this morning. This dreadful woman, Ellyard's wife! Yes, *that* Mrs Ellyard! I don't know how I held my tongue . . ."

For a moment her nerve almost failed, but she steeled herself to go on. This small action was the test she had set for herself. This was the new person she was trying to be, a stronger person who was no longer controlled by other people's opinions, a person who could think for herself. For the past eighteen years she had tried to be the wife George wanted her to be and she knew she had failed.

From now on there was no one else to please. She was on her own.

She caught sight of Mr Bell's expression and bridled. What did he know of her feelings? How would he like to be humiliated by a spiteful will left by an unkind husband? How would this silly little man like to be impoverished through no fault of his own?

She said, "The last line reads 'Remembered always with love.' I want to leave off the last two words."

He looked up. "Leave off the 'with love'?" He was trying unsuccessfully to hide his surprise and disapproval.

"Exactly."

Mr Bell glanced appealingly at Emily, but she was studying the silk lilies as though her life depended on understanding their construction. Moyna felt slightly hysterical. Her mother would never understand how she felt. She had tried to love George even when he had changed towards her. He had let their marriage go ahead, had done his best by them and had adored Frank. So why this final cruelty? Why was she left feeling unloved and unworthy of love? She didn't think she deserved such treatment, and try as she would, she couldn't fight off the bitterness that filled her heart.

"Anything else you'd like to delete?" Mr Bell asked, his tone deliberately neutral.

Yes, she thought. I'd like to delete my marriage to George Ellyard. I'd like to delete eighteen wasted years. She blinked furiously as tears threatened. I'd like to find a man to love who will love me in return.

"Is that too much to ask?" she cried.

Mr Bell and Emily stared at her, nonplussed. Damn. She had spoken the words aloud! Well, so what? Moyna stared back, giving each of them a long, defiant look, although deep down she sympathised with their outrage. In a flash of insight she realised that she must accept some of the blame for those wasted years. She should have challenged George.

But she hadn't done so because she feared what he would say. She had been afraid to face the truth. She swallowed hard. But now she was changing, finding the courage to fight back.

"Anything else to delete?" she echoed. "No thank you, Mr Bell. I think that's all."

Her mother gave a sigh of relief and Mr Bell smiled thinly.

Moyna looked him straight in the eyes. "You've been most understanding – and helpful."

Her mother looked thoroughly mortified, as though she might run out of the shop at any moment. But Moyna recalled suddenly that she hadn't finished and she was not about to allow her mother to hurry her away.

"Except the headstone itself," she said. "I'm afraid I can't afford the marble after all. An unexpected change of circumstances forces me to make economies."

He said, "I quite understand."

Emily murmured, "Moyna, do you really think this necessary?"

Moyna looked at her. "Why not, Mother? Sadly, I now need to make major changes to our lifestyle. Could George really object?"

Daunted by her daughter's expression Emily stepped back, waving a dismissive hand. "Don't ask me, Moyna. I'm sure you know best," she said, although her tone clearly suggested otherwise.

Moyna turned back to Mr Bell. "Is there much difference in the prices?"

"Oh dear me yes!" He fetched a slim brochure and pointed out the various prices. "You would make a considerable saving say, with this one – granite. That can look very attractive. Or there's reconstituted granite but that doesn't wear quite so well. A little vulnerable to the weather, shall we say."

At last it was settled. Moyna followed her mother out into the sunshine and bent to stroke the cat who began to purr noisily.

"At least the cat approves," she murmured.

Her mother straightened her hat with trembling hands. "I thought I'd die of embarrassment. I sometimes wonder about you! You were never like this as a child. Never . . . difficult."

"Not difficult enough!" Moyna murmured. Too dutiful by half. Too willing to please.

"What's that you say?"

"Nothing." She straightened up as the cat leaned lovingly against her legs. "I'm going to see Mr Tanner now, Mother. The private detective I told you about." She struggled to suppress a smile. "Would you like to meet him?"

Emily rolled her eyes heavenward. "No *thank* you, Moyna. I have had quite enough for one day!"

There was no answer when Moyna knocked on the door of Tanner's office, so she tried the handle, which turned. She went in – and smiled. Eddie Tanner was leaning back in his chair with his feet on the desk, snoring gently. She moved a little closer and stopped, watching him with undisguised curiosity. He had loosened his tie and unfastened the top button of his shirt. On the desk were a few chips in a crumpled newspaper, a salt cellar and a mug. Among the scattered papers she saw a blue-edged handkerchief, neatly folded.

Studying him, she felt both compassion for his lonely state and envy for his freedom. Nobody to worry about but himself. For a moment or two she watched him in silence. A cheerful, good-hearted man, she thought, who enjoyed his work and was content with his life. Perhaps one day she would feel that way about her own life. Not that she didn't want Frank in her life. She dreaded the day

147

he would leave home but, of course, he would. She hoped
he would make a happier marriage than she had done and
wondered whether it would be Ginnie Wheatley. Would she
mind if it *were* Ginnie? Not really, she thought. The girl was
bright and affectionate with a down-to-earth manner that was
rather appealing. And nice looking – with those green eyes
and lovely red hair. They would have handsome red-haired
children.

Without opening his eyes, Tanner said, "Well, aren't you
going to say 'Hello'?"

She jumped guiltily.

He sat up, grinning broadly.

"Mr Tanner!" she stammered. "I thought you were
asleep."

Removing his feet from the desk, he stood up and came
round to shake her hand with enthusiasm, holding it with
both hands and apparently reluctant to release it. He said,
"That's what you were meant to think! I saw you coming
from the window."

"You cheat!" she said guiltily.

"Well, I thought – I'll be the sleeping beauty and you
can wake me with a kiss!" Before she could react to
the suggestion he went on quickly. "Here, sit yourself
down, Mrs Ellyard. It's wonderful to see you again." He
removed files from the spare chair, tossed the chips into the
waste-paper basket and wiped his hands on his handkerchief.
Seeing her expression he said, "I know. It encourages the
mice, but they have to eat, don't they? Same as us." He
sat down, elbows on the desk, fingers steepled. "Very nice
cakes," he told her. "I've washed the tin out. Save you
the trouble." He nodded to where it sat on a nearby shelf.
"You're looking very spruce today, if I may say so."

Moyna said, "You may, Mr Tanner and thank you. I didn't
see your car outside my house so I realised you weren't on
an 'obbo'!" She smiled.

"I've had to stay in for a couple of phone calls. Blasted nuisance. I need to get some more pills from the chemist."

"Pills? Aren't you well, Mr Tanner?" She was surprised into the question, for he looked the picture of robust health.

He hesitated. "Oh! They're . . . just a few sleeping pills."

He didn't meet her eyes and Moyna was aware of an immediate unease. Was he telling her everything? The thought of him being ill was unbearable, but she mustn't press further. It was none of her business.

He went on. "Can't afford to miss phone calls. It's bad for business." He grinned. "Have to keep the pennies rolling in." He waved a hand to indicate his untidy surroundings. "I have this elegant office to maintain!"

Moyna nodded. "I was at a loose end . . . I thought you might need something typed up. Just for an hour or so." Please say "Yes", she thought. It was her only excuse to spend time with him – the only way to keep dark thoughts and doubts at bay.

He gave her an intent look. Almost as though he could read her mind. "That's an offer I can't refuse," he said. "Did you say you could take dictation?"

"Dictation? Good heavens!" Her first instinct was to say she couldn't but a small voice within her urged to make the attempt. "I haven't done any for eighteen years. Not since we were married, in fact, but I'll try if you don't mind going very slowly."

Moments later he was composing aloud and Moyna was thrilled to find the old skill hadn't quite deserted her.

" . . . *Further to our last conversation I am sorry—*"

"Not quite so fast, Mr Tanner." She laughed apologetically.

"My fault . . . *I am sorry to inform you that, as you suspected, your daughter has not been attending school . . .*"

149

"Has – not – been – attending – school. Go on."

" . . . *but has spent the time . . . with a young man . . . of doubtful character . . .*"

Moyna looked up. "Poor woman! Children are such a worry."

"I wouldn't know, unfortunately."

"Did you want a family?"

"Course I did. Didn't get round to it, that's all. Kids are such a good excuse to go the zoo and the Tower of London. Not to mention Madame Tussauds—"

The telephone interrupted him and he listened intently, making notes as he did so.

He asked a few questions as they talked. Gone was the relaxed, careless manner. Eddie Tanner was brisk and efficient. "Debts, I'm afraid . . . no, I can't reveal my source, but his credentials are impeccable . . . This coming Thursday? That's OK with me . . . Same place? . . . Do you think that's wise? Know what I mean? It's up to you but I don't advise it. Eyes and ears everywhere . . . Yes, I do . . . Right you are . . . Cheers!"

Moyna said, "What was the letter about – or shouldn't I ask? Confidentiality?"

"You don't know who it is so it doesn't matter. A mother, a very classy lady, has a problem with her daughter of fifteen. Bunking off school to be with a layabout man twice her age."

"You must see a lot of sad people in your line of work."

"Pretty much."

"Doesn't it depress you?"

He shrugged. "I learned long ago to remain detached. The police force taught me that. All the problems are someone else's, not mine. I just do the necessary. Find the facts and present them to the client. What they do then isn't my problem."

Moyna nodded. "But it can't be easy to stay detached.

That man, for example. Carrying on with a young girl. Don't you ever get angry? Aren't you tempted to strangle the wretch?"

"Nope. That's for the police and the courts."

She nodded. "We should finish the letter and then I can type it for you before I leave. If you need to go out I'll answer the telephone and take a message."

He regarded her through narrowed eyes. "You're up to something, Mrs Ellyard. Out with it."

She took a deep breath. "You said you had just lost a secretary. If I'd be any good, for two or three mornings a week . . ." She faltered, unable to read his expression.

"The answer's 'Yes'," he told her. He didn't appear at all surprised. "Shouldn't you ask about the wages?"

"Shouldn't you ask for a reference?"

They both laughed.

Tanner said, "But there is one condition. All my secretaries call me Eddie."

They stared at each other, both knowing that it was a lie. Moyna felt she should argue the point, but in fact she was longing to call him by his Christian name.

"And I suppose you will call me Moyna."

"Only if it's OK with you."

"It is – Eddie."

"Thank you, Moyna."

She said, "And *I* have a condition. I'll want to tidy up just a little."

"Done!"

He immediately took her up on her offer to man the telephone in his absence. She typed up the letter, unable to stop smiling. She was Eddie Tanner's secretary. She had a job – and an income, however small. It felt wonderful. Humming cheerfully to herself she addressed the envelope and fastened it to the letter with a paperclip to await Eddie's signature. She decided to make a start on the tidying, removed several crumpled cigarette packets and emptied the ash tray. In a bottom drawer she found a yellow duster and was making significant inroads into the dust when the telephone rang. Delighted she picked it up.

"Edward Tanner's office. How can I help you?" She thought she sounded very cool and professional and wished Eddie could have been in the office to hear her.

"Who are you?"

"I'm Mr Tanner's secretary. How can I help you?"

Moyna frowned. She thought she could hear suppressed anger and reached for a pad to make notes. Another client. Eddie would be pleased.

"Well, you can tell your boss that I know what he's up to and I object to being spied on. I've just come from the solicitors—"

"Perhaps you would give me your name."

"My name? It's Iris Wheatley – and I know what's in George Ellyard's will. The secret's out so he can tell Mrs bloody Ellyard she can stop having me and my daughter snooped on by your boss! You tell him to leave me and my daughter alone. For better or worse, I inherit half The Linen Store. I've earned every penny of it—"

"In what way?" Moyna's voice was hoarse. So this is what had been happening all these years. She had suspected George of having an affair with Ginnie but all the time it was her mother he was seeing.

"That's none of your business. Just pass on my message to Mr Tanner. I'm entitled to that money and there's nothing she can do to stop me having it."

The phone went dead. Moyna replaced the receiver with a trembling hand. She no longer felt cool or professional.

"Iris Wheatley," she muttered. She sat back, staring into space. "Ginnie's mother! Oh, my God!"

The same afternoon three men sat together in Margate's

police station, Sergeant Evans, Constable Budd and Detective Sergeant Fox.

The latter said, "It's not looking good. Time's passing and we're missing that vital *something*."

There was a gloomy silence. The detective sergeant had been wished on to them by those higher up and was resented as always by the local men. Now, however, the crime was still unsolved and they were glad to share the blame with him.

DS Fox said, "Read the witness statement again, Budd."

Mrs Stuckey's signed account of the quarrel was digested in silence.

Sergeant Evans said, "Why couldn't she have been a minute or two later? She'd have seen the whole bloody thing then!"

The constable said, "Crimes have been solved on less than this, sir."

His two superiors turned in unison, their expressions identical.

He mumbled, "Sorry."

The sergeant said, "Unless you've got something useful to say, Budd, keep your mouth shut."

"Yessir. Sorry, sir."

DS Fox said, "So we rule out the son."

The other two nodded.

The sergeant said, "The friend corroborated his statement. He was in France all right. Couldn't have done it . . . And the beneficiary's a widow so no avenging husband. And we don't think the daughter's the murderous type."

The constable said, "It has been known, sir. A woman, I mean. In America there was this woman—" He realised his mistake. "Sorry!"

DS Fox said wearily, "Make us some tea, lad. It's all you're good for."

"Yessir." He made a hurried exit.

Sergeant Evans said, "He's not much use but he *is* keen. I've seen worse."

The detective riffled through the file. "What in hell are we missing?" he murmured. "Somewhere there's the clue we need. But where?"

"Probably staring us in the face."

"Let's see . . . Who stands to gain? Not the son. Not the wife. Only the beneficiary, one Iris Wheatley, also a widow. Could she have done it? No. Our witness identified a male."

The sergeant said, "And anyway, Wheatley didn't know about the inheritance. The solicitor's certain of that."

DS Fox tossed the file on to the table. "This Tanner chap the Ellyard woman's hired. Above board?"

The sergeant nodded. "A hundred per cent. Ex force. I worked with him years back. I'd bet my life on him."

The constable returned with a tray on which stood three mugs of tea and a sugar bowl.

DS Fox scowled at his. "What is this – gnat's pee? For future reference, I like my tea to *look* like tea."

"Sorry, sir."

For a few moments they sipped in silence.

Sergeant Evans said, "All dead ends, if you'll pardon the expression. Where else do we look?"

Constable Budd said, "Why *did* he leave Mrs Wheatley all that money?"

The sergeant reached for another spoonful of sugar. "Good question. We don't know the answer but where would it get us if we did? All we've got is a grateful beneficiary of the female variety. We're looking for males with a grudge and we haven't got any."

The constable said, "Maybe she's got a brother. Or a cousin."

"Which 'she' are you talking about?"

"Mrs Ellyard. Or even Mrs Wheatley? Either. I mean, if we're looking for related males . . ."

There was a long silence. His superiors exchanged glances.

The sergeant said, "No harm in trying. Get yourself round there, Budd, and do the necessary. Now."

Pleased, he jumped to his feet. "Which one, sir?"

"Both."

His face fell. "But sir! I finish at—"

Two heads turned towards him.

The detective sergeant said, "It was your idea. So get on with it."

"Yessir. Sorry sir!"

In Tanner's office Moyna was still staring blankly ahead when he returned. One look at her face told him she was in shock.

"Tell me," he said at once.

"I had a phone call. A message for you. You're . . . you're to stop snooping around Mrs Wheatley. She knows what you're up to. She knows she's inherited half The Linen Store. Mrs Iris Wheatley, that is. Ginnie Wheatley's mother."

He looked uncomfortable. "Yes, I know. I'm sorry."

"You *knew*?" she said dully. "You knew and you didn't tell me. You let me find out like this." Her voice shook. "Eddie! That damned woman told me to my face! She swore at me!"

"Hey now, take it easy!" He took hold of her hand. "She didn't know it was you. How could she? She thought she was speaking to my secretary." He pulled a chair nearer to her and sat down. "I'm so sorry. I found out who she was the day I came to tea. I was sitting in the car, wondering how to tell you – I knew you'd be upset. Then you asked me in and told me about Ginnie coming to tea with Frank, and you'd gone to all that trouble. I couldn't bring myself to spoil it all."

"You sat there all through tea and – and didn't say a word?"

"I thought it was for the best, but I was wrong."

"You were. Very wrong." She couldn't keep her voice steady. She blamed him, but for what? He was only the bearer of bad news. "When were you going to tell me? When would it have been the *right* time?"

He leaned across the desk and picked up a file. From it he pulled a typed sheet.

"It's here. I thought it would be easier if you read it rather than heard it face to face. More time to—"

She snatched it from him and began to read.

He said, "I had just finished typing the report when you came in. You took me by surprise and I hid it."

"Please!" she said tersely. She was being unfair but she was fighting to stay on top of her emotions and anger was the easiest option. The report told her nothing that she didn't know already. The woman had married a man called Stanley Wheatley shortly after she, Moyna, had married George.

"So presumably . . ." She glanced up. "He must have been in love with her at some time. Sufficiently in love to want to leave her a lot of money when he died."

"But he married you."

She looked at him. There was something about his manner that puzzled her. Guilt, probably. He should have told her, but she could see that he had held back out of kindness because he didn't want to distress her. "What a mess," she muttered. "My son and her daughter."

He said, "I think a drop of something is called for." From one of his cupboards he produced a bottle. "Sherry," he told her. "Not much left." He produced two cheap glass tumblers and shared the sherry between them.

"Is this a secret vice," she asked, "or for medicinal purposes?"

"In my business many of my clients have to face unpleasant news. A little tot can sometimes help."

He watched her swallow a mouthful and when she coughed he handed her the blue-edged folded handkerchief.

Moyna said, "Is this the one I cried into?"

"The same."

"Keeping it especially for me?"

"Something like that."

She smiled faintly. "She sounded like a very nasty person, this Mrs Wheatley. Not at all like her daughter. Not at all like someone who's just had a windfall." The sherry warmed her stomach and she felt slightly better, but her mind was mulling over the ramifications of the unwelcome news. "If Frank and Ginnie marry she'll be the mother-in-law! I couldn't bear that."

He hesitated. "Moyna, there's something . . ."

"What is it?" He still had that worried frown. "Not more bad news. I think I've had all I can deal with at the moment."

It was his turn to sigh. "I shouldn't worry about the new hat just yet," he said with a poor attempt at humour. "Anything could happen. They could have a row. A lover's tiff. These childhood sweetheart things don't last."

"How would you know?" she challenged. "You've never even been married."

"Exactly!" He finished his sherry. "Drink up. Doctor's orders."

Moyna sat forward suddenly. "Suppose she somehow finds out that it was me and not your secretary? Can you imagine how she'd gloat?"

"Maybe she's not the gloating sort."

"She is! I can feel it in my bones."

She swallowed the rest of the sherry. It had helped.

He said, "She might be quite a pleasant woman. She might

have suffered all these years, seeing you and George and Frank together. Maybe George had to choose between the two of you and chose you. Think of that."

"Nice try, Mr – Eddie, but it doesn't work with me. And whose side are you on, anyway?"

"Yours, of course. I'm trying to help you. We don't know all the circumstances, do we."

Moyna put a hand to her head which was beginning to throb. "She couldn't have been very fond of him or she wouldn't have rushed off and married Stanley Wheatley. I don't suppose that pleased George." She put her hands over her face for a moment and then glanced up at him. "I'm not dealing with this at all well, am I? The classic jealous wife."

"You're doing OK. Fine. Most women would be in floods of tears by now."

"I'll save those for bed time."

After a moment he said, "Look Moyna, everything I do, I do for the best. I want you to remember that. All I want is your happiness. I mean, of course I do my job. That's what you pay me for, but how I do it—" He shook his head. "I'm not much good with words. But I do care about you and that makes it—"

"Do you? Care about me?" She was startled to hear the words from him.

"I do. Yes. You're the goods as far as I'm concerned. Lovely classy lady. Dear to my heart – isn't that what they say?"

She looked into the dark brown eyes and wanted to weep. His kindness made it so much harder. She had promised herself that she would change, be stronger altogether, less easily crushed. Now, faced with his tenderness she wanted to throw herself into his arms and let him take care of her.

She said, "That's very kind of you, Eddie. You make

me feel so much better about everything. Thank you." She leaned forward and squeezed his hands in hers.

He rolled his eyes humorously. "Anything you want to tell me is OK. Like you might care a bit for me – although I'm sure you don't . . . but if you did?"

"I do like you, Eddie. Very much. But I've so much going on in my mind I don't seem able to think about anyone but Frank and myself. It's horribly self-centred but . . ." She broke off, unable to explain the chaos of hurt and fear inside her.

"Maybe later?"

"Oh yes! I'm sure." She stood up uncertainly. "I have to go now. I need to think about how to tell Frank. When do you want me again?"

"How about forever?"

She smiled. "You're a dear man, Eddie. You deserve to be happy. But seriously. My part-time job, remember."

"What about tomorrow, ten to twelve?"

"If I can't manage it I'll ring you . . . I think I'm going to buy a puppy," she said. George had never allowed pets. "Something small that won't eat us out of house and home. Frank's always wanted a dog."

"Jack Russells are nice."

"We can find a flat with a garden."

She came out of his office, down the stairs and out into the street. Mrs Iris Wheatley. *Mrs Iris Wheatley*. As she stepped into the sunshine she came to an abrupt decision. She was going to have to confront the woman once and for all.

159

Nine

They had served and cleared the supper tables. Ginnie was washing up and Ladie was curled up in a box in the corner. Iris, folding serviettes for the next morning's breakfast, was trying to pluck up the courage to broach the subject of the legacy and the Ellyards. By way of Mr Tanner, she had struck back at Moyna Ellyard in the only way she could, but now she regretted her outburst. It was hardly ladylike and she wished she hadn't said "bloody" but she had. Too late for regrets. She could only pray that Ginnie would never get to hear about it. With any luck the secretary would forget to pass on the message.

She looked at Ginnie, standing at the sink with her hands deep in suds, and wished there was an easy way to do this. Since the row they had been treating each other with caution, polite but hardly warm. The cat had been a useful subject of conversation and Iris was allowing Ginnie to persuade her of the animal's good points.

Iris said, "I've got a surprise for you, Ginnie. A really big surprise."

Ginnie waited in silence, pretending indifference.

"It's about money. It's to do with – well, someone's left me some money."

Unable to resist, Ginnie turned. "Much?"

"Quite a lot. Yes."

160

"I didn't know we had any rich relations."

Iris could see she was interested, shaken out of her caution. "It was someone I knew before you were born. Before I married Stan."

Now she had all Ginnie's attention. She was watching her mother, hands dripping soapy water on to the floor.

Iris's hands shook slightly as she folded the last serviette and stacked them on the tray. "It was a man who was in love with me and – and I . . ." She stopped. It was proving harder than she expected. She was trying to release the facts slowly to lessen the shock. "I really loved him. Your father – Stan – wanted to marry me but I was crazy for – for the other man and I had to say 'No'."

"Poor Dad." Ginnie looked puzzled. "But you must have changed your mind because you did marry him."

"Yes. But the thing is . . ."

"What happened? Did you go off the other one?"

"Not exactly." Iris's sigh was heartfelt. There was no way this conversation could have a happy ending.

"You mean he went off you?"

"Yes . . . and no . . . There was another woman. He knew her long before he met me."

Ginnie frowned. "But why did this other man leave you the money if he'd gone off you? It doesn't make sense."

While Iris searched for a way to continue, Ginnie concentrated on the last of the washing up. Then she reached for a tea towel and dried her hands. She crossed to the table and sat down opposite Iris. "That's quite romantic, isn't it. What was his name?"

"George."

"And he's dead now?"

"Yes."

"So he was older than you." Ginnie's eyes were bright. "So you had a secret admirer – all these years!" She was

161

struggling, thought Iris, wanting to be enchanted by the story but not wishing to approve because of Stan.

Ginnie said, "You don't seem very thrilled. Aren't you pleased? Or is it because he's dead? Did Dad know anything about it? Did anyone know?"

Ladie stretched and sprang out of his box. He jumped into Ginnie's lap and curled up, purring loudly.

Iris swallowed. It had to be said sometime. "It was George Ellyard," she said.

"George *Ellyard*?" Ginnie's mouth fell open. "Not . . . not *my* Mr Ellyard? Not Frank's . . ." She blinked, confused. "Frank's father . . . was in love with *you*? I don't believe it." Her expression darkened as the ramifications surged through her mind. "Oh no!" she cried. "Not him and you? That's – that's awful!" Her eyes widened fearfully. "You mean he's left you some money? But what will Frank think? Oh Lord, Mum!"

Iris sat numbly watching her daughter's face. This was the moment she'd been dreading – or rather, it was the first moment she'd been dreading. A worse moment was to come.

Ginnie fell silent, her gaze never leaving Iris's face. "Does Frank know?" she asked.

"I expect his mother will tell him. She didn't know until today and neither did I."

"But . . . but she was so nice to me! Perhaps she doesn't know. And Frank . . ." She put a hand to her mouth. "Frank won't be very pleased, will he, if his father's left you money . . . For heaven's sake, Mum! Why did you have to mess about with Mr Ellyard, of all people?" It was an accusing cry.

"We weren't messing about," Iris said. But of course they were, she thought guiltily. Otherwise Ginnie wouldn't have been born. "We were in love."

Ginnie slumped back in the chair and began to stroke

Ladie with a trembling hand. "Can't you refuse the money?" she suggested. "Before they find out. They need never know." Her face brightened. "Or even if they do know. It would look terribly decent if you refused the money. We don't need it."

"We do! Anyway, Mrs Ellyard already knows. The solicitor told her. He had to. It was in the will."

Ginnie's eyes widened. "The will! Of course. That's why she hired the detective. And he found you!"

"Maybe not. Look, Ginnie, I know this has been a shock for you but you have to understand it was a shock for me, too. I didn't know what he was planning to—"

"Wait!" cried Ginnie. "I don't see how it works. You refused to marry him and married Dad instead. So were you more in love with Dad? And if you jilted Mr Ellyard, why did he leave you some money? It doesn't make sense, does it?"

"I didn't jilt George. He jilted me. He felt bad about it. He had been engaged to Mrs Ellyard and then he fell in love with me. But he had to marry her—"

"He could have broken off their engagement."

"Mrs Ellyard was expecting a baby. They had to get married."

"You mean . . . Frank?"

"Yes." Iris wondered if it was too soon to congratulate herself on the way she dealt with the situation. So far Ginnie hadn't thrown a tantrum – but she was still in a state of shock.

Ginnie rolled her eyes, exasperated. "How could you? How could you all make such a mess of things? Honestly! Frank's going to be furious!"

And so are you, thought Iris sadly. Everyone is going to be furious with everyone.

There was ring at the front door.

Ginnie said, "I've got Ladie. I can't go."

Iris went to see who it was and discovered a young policeman standing outside. She was tempted to shout "Go away!" but instead she said, "What is it?"

"May I come in for a moment?" he asked. "It's just routine enquiries."

"About what exactly? This isn't a very convenient time, to be honest."

"About the murder of George Ellyard."

She stared at him, surprised. "I can't tell you anything. I don't *know* anything."

"We have to widen our enquiries, madam."

"Well, if you must."

She gave in with a bad grace and led the way into the kitchen. As she went in Ginnie said, "So it's *you* that's getting half The Linen Store! That must be worth—" She stopped abruptly and jumped to her feet as the policeman followed her mother into the room. Ladie fell to the floor and fled into the passage with an indignant squeal.

"I'm Constable Budd," he told them.

"You'd better sit down," said Iris and they all did.

"We're still searching for George Ellyard's murderer," he told them. "We're now talking to any male relatives of the parties involved."

Ginnie's face went white. "My mother's not involved! Just because I'm a friend of Frank's . . . You've talked to him and you know he didn't do it."

He looked apologetic. "I'm afraid you are not the link, Miss Wheatley. Technically speaking it's the legacy that involves your family. The fact that George Ellyard left a large sum of money to your mother means there could be a link."

Mother and daughter exchanged apprehensive glances.

Iris said, "But we're just two women. No male relatives. My husband's been dead for years. Killed in the war."

"Do you have a son?" he asked. "A brother? A father?"

164

She shook her head.

He looked at Iris. "A male cousin, perhaps?"

"Only Steven. He died in an accident years ago. He was only seventeen."

Ginnie said, "I didn't know that!"

"It was before your time."

"So there's no other male in your family?" He stood up again.

"No, constable, there isn't." Iris was almost sorry to see him go. Now she was faced with telling Ginnie the rest of the story.

At that moment, however, the back door opened and Michael came in. He saw the policeman and his eyes narrowed. He said, "Ah!"

Iris said, "The constable is asking after male members of our family. I've just told him, Stan's been dead for years and Steven—"

The constable said, "And you are, sir?"

Before he could answer, Iris said, "He's my brother-in-law."

Michael had recovered. Grinning, he held up his hands and said, "Not guilty, my lud!"

Constable Budd was not amused. "On which side of the family, sir?"

Michael said, "I'm Stan's brother. Mrs Wheatley's husband's brother."

"I see, sir." He wrote something in his notebook.

Iris said, "I didn't think . . . You didn't mention in-laws."

"Right you are then. I'll be on my way." His smile reached each one in turn. "Thank you for your time."

Ginnie said, "I'll see him out. I have to find Ladie."

Iris sat down heavily. Perhaps she had said enough to Ginnie for one night. The arrival of the policeman and Michael had interrupted her story. She would finish her confession to Ginnie in the morning.

*   *   *

As soon as Mrs Cook stepped inside the door of The Linen Store, Miss Crane grabbed her arm with thin fingers. "We're to go up to the office as soon as you arrive," she told her. "Mr Dunn wants a word with us."

They looked at each other in alarm. Mrs Cook drew her cardigan closer round her matronly chest. "A word?" she echoed. Her face paled. "Oh! You don't think . . ."

"I don't know what to think – and Miss Wheatley's not come in yet but he said not to wait for her." Miss Crane pinched her lips anxiously. "We'll find out soon enough."

Inside the office, Mr Dunn was waiting for them, sitting up straight in his chair, as neat as ever. The only sign of nerves was a tell-tale muscle jumping in his right cheek. He had pulled an ancient stool alongside the chair so that they could both sit.

"I thought it only fair—" he began.

Mrs Crane said, "What about Miss Wheatley?"

He sighed heavily. "I doubt if she'll be coming in today," he said. "I thought it only fair to bring you up to date with matters concerning The Linen Store. You may or may not have read in the local paper that Mr Ellyard saw fit to leave half the business to someone other than his wife. I have now learned that that someone was Miss Wheatley's mother."

There was a long silence. Before the two women could gather their wits he went on. "I have been in touch with Mrs Ellyard—"

"Oh the poor dear!" cried Mrs Cook. "She doesn't deserve such treatment. She was kindness itself. She—"

Miss Crane tapped her ankle none too gently and Mrs Cook fell silent.

Mr Dunn continued. "Mrs Ellyard and I are hoping that Mrs Wheatley will have no interest in the business and will be prepared to sell her half to me."

The two women exchanged startled glances.

He went on. "I have spoken to my bank manager and to a solicitor and it may be possible for me to go into partnership with Mrs Ellyard. In that case, I'm pleased to say that your positions here will be safe."

"Goodness!" muttered Mrs Cook. "What a dreadful state of affairs! I don't mean that our jobs would be safe. I mean . . . What on earth was Mr Ellyard thinking of?"

Nobody answered her question.

Miss Crane said, "But suppose she won't sell? Does that mean Miss Wheatley's mother will be running the store?"

"Let's hope not," said Mrs Cook. "What does she know about the drapery business? It would be impossible. And how would poor Mrs Ellyard feel?"

Mr Dunn shrugged. "We can only assume that the poor man was a little unsound in his mind. We shouldn't speak ill of the dead but I do believe it was a wicked thing to do. But . . . he has done it and we must find a way out of the maze. Assuming that Mrs Ellyard will not wish to act in partnership with Mrs Wheatley, I imagine the business may be sold and half the proceeds passed to Mrs Wheatley."

"In which case," Miss Crane said slowly, "our jobs will *not* be secure. Oh dear!"

Mr Dunn shrugged wearily. "It's a very sad, very difficult situation. All I can do is keep you informed. We must all hope the matter can be resolved to our satisfaction. If not . . ." His expression was grim.

Mrs Cook said, "Mr Ellyard and Miss Wheatley's mother! Well I never!"

They digested the information for a moment or two and then Miss Crane frowned. "So did Miss Wheatley know about it all along?"

"That explains why he let her off Saturdays! There was something going on between him and her mother! Poor Mrs Ellyard. And to think I used to envy her with her nice house and the boy."

Mr Dunn stood up abruptly. "We can only surmise. We don't know the whole story." He glanced at the clock. "Time to open up the store." With a touch of ceremony he handed a key to Mrs Cook. "Perhaps you will do that for me. I have a couple of telephone calls to make and the rep from Courtaulds is due in shortly."

Mrs Cook nodded and took the key from him a trifle self-consciously. Mr Ellyard had always opened up the store and she considered Mr Dunn's gesture one of confidence in her ability. Miss Crane's protest died. She was the older woman but Mrs Cook had been at the store longer than she had. The two of them went downstairs. At the bottom they stood for a moment.

Miss Crane said, "New broom, eh? . . ." The vague comment covered her confusion.

"Sweeps clean!" Mrs Cook had recovered her colour and moved towards the door.

Miss Crane went to her position behind the counter with her fingers firmly crossed. "Mr Ellyard and Miss Wheatley's mother!" she muttered. "Curiouser and curiouser!"

An hour later Moyna was walking through the churchyard on her way to visit George's grave. She was almost there when she slowed her steps and then stopped. Beyond the neatly manicured bushes a woman was kneeling beside the as yet unmarked grave. At the sight of her, Moyna's heart skipped a beat then began to race. It must be her, she thought, but surely . . . Disbelief mingled with mortification and for a moment she found herself almost breathless and struggling with a desire to run away. She had intended to confront the woman, but not so soon.

"But why not?" she muttered and broke into an awkward run. The nerve of the woman!

"You!" she called. "What do you think you're doing?" It had to be Iris Wheatley.

The woman scrambled to her feet and turned to face her. She was clutching a small bunch of anemones.

Moyna was sorry to see a pleasant-faced woman with a strong resemblance to Ginnie. She had hoped for a sour-faced harridan. Belatedly her anger flared.

"You're her, aren't you?" Moyna demanded. "Iris Wheatley?"

The woman nodded. "I wanted to—" She indicated the flowers.

"You – you dare to come here . . . !" Moyna thrust out a hand, snatched the little posy from the woman's hands and hurled it into some nearby bushes. "He didn't even like anemones!"

After a moment's hesitation the woman made to retrieve them, but Moyna grabbed her arm. "No! Leave them where they are!" With difficulty she restrained herself from striking the woman. "How dare you show your face here? Haven't you done us enough harm without adding insult to injury?" She was breathing fast, frightened by the intensity of her feelings. She had never resorted to physical force in her life and this loss of control was alien to her. "After all these years you see fit to shame us in front of the whole town. They're all talking about us. I hope you're satisfied!"

"I didn't mean to. I was . . . It was just—" Stammering, her face flushed, Iris Wheatley stood her ground.

Moyna's hand crept towards her heart. "You have no right at all. This is my husband's grave and I'll thank you to respect that. *My* husband – in case you've forgotten!"

"It was just a 'thank you'." Obviously intimidated by Moyna's wrath, Iris Wheatley looked round nervously.

"A 'thank you'? *A thank you?*" Moyna mocked. "A 'thank you' to George for ruining my life and leaving me and my son in financial difficulties? Is that why you're thanking him?"

"You can't blame me for that," the woman protested.

169

Pamela Oldfield

"The will was as much a surprise to me as it must have been for you."

"I doubt that *very* much. I'm sure you had some idea of what he meant to do."

"Mrs Ellyard!" She took a step closer and raised her right hand. "I swear I didn't know. Don't you think it's been an embarrassment to me? I have had to explain to my daughter why her employer is leaving me a share of the business. Of course I'm grateful to him and I don't pretend we don't need the money, but it's put me in a very difficult position."

She took another step forward but Moyna stepped backward and said, "You keep away from me!"

She glanced round, relieved to see that there was, for the moment, no one to view the ugly scene. "And while you're here, perhaps you'll explain why he *did* leave it to you. I'd be very interested – and so would my son who should have been going up to college in London to study music and is now haunting the Labour Exchange in search of a job! I don't think he'll be quite so keen on your daughter when he knows the whole truth, and that will suit me nicely." Moyna, feeling slightly dizzy, drew in several deep breaths.

Iris Wheatley gave her a strange look. Slowly she said, "Do you want to know the whole truth? I doubt it."

"Of course I do. That's why I'm asking."

A fine sheen of perspiration was breaking out on her skin and she fought to remain calm. It would never do to show weakness in front of this awful woman.

Iris Wheatley said, "He was engaged to you when we met but he didn't tell me. We fell in love and when he did tell me he promised he would ask you to release him from the engagement. Before he got round to it you told him you were expecting a baby."

Moyna felt the colour rush into her face. All these years she had kept quiet on the subject, pretending that Frank had been born prematurely, but all the time Iris Wheatley had known. It was unbearable. Humiliating.

The woman went on. "So he did his duty by you and I was left to make the best of a bad job."

"But when you *did* know you should have left him alone. Instead you deliberately came between us. Which just goes to show the kind of woman you are!"

A deep grief was mingling with Moyna's anger. A deep grief and a growing sense of shame. George had never loved her. She had long suspected it but now she knew. Throughout their married life he had been secretly in love with Iris Wheatley.

She forced herself to ask the next question. "Did you go on meeting him – after we were married?"

"Never. We never spoke again. I was mad with him. I thought he'd simply walked away from me but now I can see that it preyed on his mind. His conscience wouldn't let him leave it at that. I've been thinking about it since I knew about the legacy. He must have—" She stopped as an elderly man walked past them. "George must have expected the will to be read many years from now. He couldn't have guessed that he would die so early."

"What difference does that make? He's still ruining my life."

"He ruined mine, too."

"Of course he didn't. You married someone else and had a child. You have a guest house. He left you money. I think he treated you very well." She was feeling very hot and faint and turned to look for somewhere to sit. There was a seat nearby but she didn't see how she could retreat to it with any dignity. Iris Wheatley would have the last laugh. She must somehow bring this conversation to an end and quickly. "Well, whatever," she said. "I'd rather you didn't put flowers on his grave."

"And if I do?" The woman's mouth tightened ominously.

"I'll throw them off again."

"How can you be so childish!"

Moyna felt herself sway and fought to stay on her feet. Before she could speak again Iris Wheatley crossed to the fallen posy and picked it up and brushed the flowers lightly with her hand. She gave Moyna a challenging look and stepped once more towards George's grave. With a cry of anger, Moyna stepped forward but as she did so everything went dark. She knew she was falling but she didn't feel herself hit the ground.

When she came to Iris Wheatley was leaning over her and so was the elderly gentleman who had passed them earlier.

He said, "She's opening her eyes. She'll be fine."

Iris Wheatley was peering into her face. "You fainted, but you're OK. Take it slowly."

Moyna blinked. Her throat felt dry. "I'm fine. Really."

The elderly man said, "Can you stand, d'you think? We'll help you."

Slowly they levered her upright. One knee was bleeding from the gravelled path and her stockings were torn. She felt sick and dazed.

They helped her to the seat and sat her down. Moyna murmured her thanks and the old man left them to it.

Moyna said, "I'm sorry. I didn't mean to faint. That was silly . . ."

"You don't have to apologise." Iris Wheatley was bending over, examining Moyna's knee. She produced a handkerchief. "You'll have to wash that when you get home."

Accepting the handkerchief, Moyna dabbed at her knee and thought how strange it was to be sitting there, with Iris Wheatley beside her. She caught sight of the anemones at the far end of the seat but it no longer seemed to matter. She said, "Ginnie's a nice girl." It seemed the least she could say.

"She's at that difficult age."

Moyna wiped her forehead with a clean corner of the handkerchief. "I must get home," she said. "I'll take it slowly."

Iris Wheatley looked at her with an unfathomable expression.

"What is it?" Moyna was aware of a frisson of alarm.

"I have to tell you something, Mrs Ellyard, before you go. Not to hurt you but because of the children. Because of Frank and Ginnie. It's about me and George . . ."

"I don't want to hear it. You've said quite enough." Moyna thought she might cry. "Just leave your flowers and go away. I won't do anything to them."

"It's about Ginnie. Please don't faint again but . . . she's George's daughter."

The words seemed to echo meaninglessly round Moyna's brain. She said, "No she's not." As though that would make it so.

Iris took a deep breath. "I was also expecting a baby, but I didn't know it. By the time I realised—"

"But that would mean he was . . ." Moyna shook her head, shocked. "Not with both of us? Not George!"

"I'm afraid so. He wasn't exactly a saint, was he!"

Moyna looked up at her. "So why didn't you say anything?"

"Not much point, was there? By the time I realised, you were already rushing to the altar with *your* baby on the way. I didn't see why you should be hurt. What we did wasn't your fault and you *were* engaged – even though I didn't know at the time. It was a terrible shock. But I wrote a letter to George and told him about the baby. I sent it to The Linen Store. I said I was keeping her and would he contribute something for her upkeep. I didn't ask for much. He didn't even answer the letter and I must admit I was very angry. I called him everything under the sun!"

She picked up the flowers and sat down. "But then I had to do something quick before my Mum and Dad found out, so I married Stan. I'd turned him down twice so he was delighted. Poor Stan. I thought I might tell him later when we had a child of our own, but nothing happened, and then the war started and he went abroad. Never came back."

Moyna was turning the facts over and over in her mind. At last she said, "So to make it up to you, George decided to leave you some money."

She nodded. "Not for me, you see, but for Ginnie. All these years I did my best to keep George and Ginnie apart. I thought he might want to see her, but then Stan might have found out the truth and he adored Ginnie. After Stan died I was afraid Ginnie would find out. One day George waited ouside the school and spoke to her. He tried to give her some toffees but my brother-in-law saw him and sent him packing. He didn't know who he was. Thought he was a nasty old man. When he told me I guessed, but I didn't dare say anything."

Moyna closed her eyes. Iris Wheatley's words held the ring of truth. George had been making love to Iris *and* to her. It was incredible, but she knew it was the truth. Now at last she understood the change in him and the reason behind it. He had made two women pregnant and could only marry one of them. She suddenly recalled with great clarity the conversation in which she had told him about the child. They were walking along the sea front and her arm was through his. For a long time neither of them spoke. He was deep in thought and she was trying to find the courage to break the news. Before she did so he stopped walking and turned to face her.

"Moyna, we have to talk. I have something important to tell you."

"And I have something to tell you, George." She took his hands in hers. "I've been waiting to be sure, but now I am.

George, I'm expecting a baby. Our baby. I know it's early days, but we have to get married."

She had expected surprise, even shock, but she hadn't bargained for the small anguished cry. Now, years later, she realised that George had never told her what that "something important" was. He had been about to tell her that he was in love with someone else.

Moyna drew a long breath, then opened her eyes and looked carefully at her companion. Strangely her anger had gone, but she felt years older. Iris Wheatley had put up with a lot over the past eighteen years. "So *you* married a man you didn't love and *I* married a man who no longer loved me!"

"All by courtesy of George Ellyard!" Iris shook her head ruefully.

Moyna sat up a little straighter. "But poor George. He married a woman he didn't want and he was never able to know his daughter – until . . ." Her eyes widened. "Until, quite by chance, Ginnie applied for the job at The Linen Store!"

Iris nodded. "He must have thought his luck had changed! I nearly had a fit when she told me, but I didn't know what to do."

"Nothing much you could do," Moyna agreed, her mind racing. "No wonder he lent her the money for the bicycle!"

"And gave her the rise!"

Moyna drew a long breath. "No wonder he was so pleased with 'his new assistant'!"

Iris nodded. "And gave her her Saturdays off! I could see it all but—"

"No! Wait! That's not it." Light was dawning. "George gave her the free Saturdays because that was the day I went into the shop. I take cakes in on Saturdays for the staff tea break. Obviously George didn't want me to meet her." As the pieces of the jigsaw fell into place they looked at each other in astonishment. Moyna said, "Incredible. All these years and I had no idea."

Iris regarded her curiously. "Did you love him?"

"At first. For a long time, in fact, but I didn't understand why he'd changed towards me. I thought it was my fault."

She fell silent, remembering the excitement when George had asked her father for permission to marry her. George was ten years older than she was and her parents had been reluctant at first.

"You're only eighteen," her father argued. "You're still a child. Wait a while, Moyna. There's no hurry."

Her mother nodded. "What's a year or two when you've got all your life ahead of you?"

"Wait until you're twenty-one," her father suggested. "Get married on your twenty-first birthday!"

But that was three years away and Moyna couldn't bear the thought of the long wait. More importantly, she knew George wasn't prepared to wait. He wanted a year's engagement, so they finally compromised on two. The longest two years of her life. As the wedding grew nearer she sensed his impatience. He wanted to take her to bed and did his best to persuade her.

"Nothing will happen, Moyna. I'll see to that."

As ignorant of sex as any other well-brought-up girl, Moyna had trusted herself to him, assuming that at his age he would be knowledgeable on such matters. The child was conceived the first time they were lovers.

She stared down at her hands and then up at Iris. "Eventually I thought there must be another woman and then . . . It's going to sound ridiculous, but I thought he was falling in love with the wonderful Miss Wheatley. He kept on about her so much."

There was another silence. Moyna covered her face with her hands and for a long time neither spoke. Then Moyna said, "So now what?"

Iris patted Moyna's uninjured knee. "You'll pull through it. You're stronger than you think. Women are. It's the children we have to worry about. George's two children."

Moyna gasped. "Of course! Oh God! How could I forget that? They're getting so fond of one another! We have to tell them."

"I started to talk to Ginnie last night but we were interrupted. I shall tell her the rest this evening."

"They'll be furious with us – or maybe with George."

Iris shook her head. "Ginnie will be furious with the entire world! She's like that. Michael says the word is 'volatile'." Seeing Moyna's expression she added, "Michael. My husband's brother. He's been a tower of strength. Ginnie adores him. After Stan was killed he tried to be a father figure. Took her out. Bought her presents. He's been a real brick."

Moyna nodded. She was beginning to feel a little stronger and stood up, testing her legs. "I'll be all right now." She looked around. "I suppose we should keep in touch. And we also have to talk about The Linen Store."

"And you must let me know how Frank takes it." Still holding the flowers, Iris stood also. She held out the flowers, a questioning look on her face.

Moyna said, "Of course. I'm so sorry. It was stupid of me," and watched as the other woman laid them gently on the grassed mound. She said, "I've arranged for a headstone," and wished she hadn't been so mean about the wording.

Iris nodded.

"And good luck with Ginnie." Moyna's eyes narrowed. "Now I come to think about it, there *is* a likeness. Don't you think? Between Frank and Ginnie. About the eyes – and the same hair. What *is* their relationship?"

"Ginnie is Frank's half-sister," Iris told her.

They walked back to the church gate and stood there awkwardly.

Moyna put a hand on Iris's arm. "I'm truly sorry about everything – the way it worked out. It was George, I suppose."

Iris smiled. "Altogether too attractive. Too persuasive!"

"But we were to blame as well. We allowed him to . . . You know what I mean. We were willing to be persuaded." She shrugged. "If you could have the time over again, would you still do it?"

Iris fiddled with the latch of the gate while she considered the question. "I've wondered that for eighteen years," she said. "And the answer's got to be 'Yes'. Because I was so in love. You do anything, don't you, to make them happy, to make them keep loving you. You think it will all end happily – and sometimes it doesn't. But I do wish I had told Stan the truth. I was trying to spare him pain, but—"

She stopped as the vicar hurried down the path towards them. He was clutching what looked like a Bible and was obviously in a hurry. He said, "Morning ladies! Another fine day. One of life's little pleasures." And swept past them in a flutter of black robes.

Iris continued. "I was wrong to keep it from him. What about you? Would you marry George again if you could go back?"

Moyna shrugged. "With hindsight, probably not. We didn't make each other happy – but there *were* some good times and there's Frank." She smiled suddenly. "Frank makes it all worthwhile. And you've got Ginnie."

Iris nodded. "Water under the bridge."

They hesitated but there was nothing more to say. Impulsively, they hugged briefly, then went their separate ways.

Frank was poring over the local paper when Moyna arrived home. He threw it down and jumped up when he saw her. "Whatever's happened? Your leg!"

178

"It was just a fall. It's nothing. You know how gravelly that path in the churchyard is."

"Mr Tanner was here. You missed him. He stayed about ten minutes in the hope you'd come back." He grinned. "I rather like the man. So enthusiastic and cheerful. Devil-may-care sort of chap. Has he got a family?"

"He's never been married. Never mentions any family."

"Bit of a loner, then. He said you were going to work for him, part-time." He frowned. "Are things as bad as that?"

"The income from the shop is halved so it does make a difference. We'll have to give up the house because we won't be able to manage the mortgage, but we can rent a nice flat. I thought a bit of extra income might be useful, although I'm sure you'll find something soon. I saw the opportunity and took it. It's interesting work."

"Ginnie's uncle's going to let me know if anything turns up at the theatre."

Moyna hesitated fractionally, then said, "That's kind of him."

Frank nodded. "So . . . have they finished Father's grave yet?"

She regarded him blankly.

"You went to the churchyard to find out."

Had she? It seemed a lifetime ago. "Oh yes. But it's still covered with dead flowers. I shall have to see the vicar. They may be waiting for the headstone."

"I'll make you a cup of tea."

"No!" She held up her hand. "In a minute, but not yet. Something's come up. Something unexpected. About Ginnie."

His expression changed. "I think I'm ahead of you," he said quietly. "Because of the legacy to Ginnie's mother. I was thinking in bed last night – about various dates."

Moyna sat hurriedly. "Dates?"

"Our birthdays. Mine and Ginnie's are so close. Seemed

179

a bit of a coincidence. I came up with a theory but I didn't know if *you* knew. I thought that Ginnie could be Father's daughter, but I didn't know how to ask you, because if you didn't know I was afraid of upsetting you."

She stared at him. He was taking the news so calmly. And thinking about her instead of himself. He really wasn't a child any more. He had suddenly grown up.

"Frank . . . I didn't know until half an hour ago. I met Iris Wheatley and I'm afraid we had a row—"

"Oh no! For heaven's sake!" He groaned theatrically. "Aren't things bad enough already without you two coming to blows?"

"It's all right. We got over it. I was so angry I couldn't breathe and I fainted. That's how I hurt my knee, and she was very kind. Contrite, maybe, because she'd been shouting at me. Then we started to talk about everything in a sensible way. I expect you've met her already."

"I haven't. Ginnie's mother was trying to discourage Ginnie from seeing me. Now I know why. She was trying to break us up. Telling lies about me to Ginnie. Of course Ginnie told me. I thought it was odd, because she'd never even met me."

Moyna let out a sigh of relief. "Ginnie's your half-sister. Can you bear it, Frank? I know you were getting fond of her."

"We were getting fond of each other, but thank goodness it hadn't gone any further. It's a blow, but we can deal with it. We can be brother and sister. Now I've got used to the idea it could be fun. I always wished that Louisa had lived."

Startled, Moyna said, "Frank! You've never said a word about her."

"I thought it would bring back unhappy memories. Poor Ginnie. She doesn't know yet, but I don't see how her mother thinks she can keep it a secret any longer. The will's blown it all into the open."

"She's going to tell her as soon as she can. Iris has always known, of course." She shook her head. "What an incredible muddle."

He grinned. "You women!" And rolled his eyes.

"You men!" She stood up carefully. "I think my leg will be very stiff tomorrow. I must have gone down like a sack of potatoes." She put a hand to her back and groaned slightly. "I could do with that tea. I'll bathe my knee while you put the kettle on."

He stood up. "What's she like, Ginnie's mother? She used to be a dancer. That's all I know."

Moyna considered carefully. "Pleasant enough, I suppose – but I can't see us ever being friends."

As she reached the door he said, "Grandmother's not going to like this!"

"Frank, please! Haven't I got enough to worry about?"

Moyna made her way to the bathroom with the beginnings of a headache. It seemed as though the problems would never end.

Ten

It was dark in the auditorium. The rows of seats were silent and still except for the cleaner who walked along each row with a broom and a cardboard box for the rubbish. She picked up empty ice cream tubs and small wooden spoons, discarded cigarette packets and chocolate wrappers. She worked methodically, taking no interest in the action on stage where the two scenery shifters were tugging painted flats into place. Overhead someone was experimenting with the spotlights, throwing pools of light on to the dimly lit stage.

Every sound echoed in the vastness of the interior but Michael didn't hear them. His eyes were on the stage plan he carried and he was deep in conversation with the stage manager, a burly man in his fifties.

He glanced up and shouted, "A bit more to the front, Harry!" and ignored the muttered curse as Harry and Eric moved the flat yet again.

He lifted an assenting thumb and the shifters relaxed.

A commotion off stage made them all turn to see Mr Biffen, the stage door keeper, bustling into view, his face red with indignation. He was a small, wiry man whose age was never disclosed, but nobody could remember a time when he wasn't around, and they put his age at around a hundred and ten.

"What is it, Biffy?" the stage manager asked testily.

"It's a policeman, Mr Laye. I can't get rid of the fellow. Can't take no for an answer. Wants to speak to Mr Wheatley."

Michael said, "Tell him I'm not here. My day off. Anything."

Mr Laye nodded. "We'll be busy here for at least another hour. Tell him to come back later."

Mr Biffen wrung his hands. "I've tried everything. He won't go. Says it's police business and I'm – I'm interfering with police procedure."

The stage manager said, "Bloody coppers! You'd better have a word, Mike."

Michael hesitated. "Tell him I've emigrated! Died! Any damned thing."

Mr Biffen said, "It won't work, sir. You'll have to come. It's the only way we'll get shot of him – if you don't mind."

"I *do* mind!" To the stage manager he said, "Back as soon as I can. Sorry about this." Heart thumping, he followed the little man back along the gloomy passage. Without further comment they made their way to the stage door keeper's den which was just inside the door to the street. Silhouetted against the light from outside a bulky man in a familiar uniform waited, his hands clasped behind his back.

"I'm Sergeant Evans and I'd like a few words, sir," he said as soon as Michael appeared.

Michael, saying nothing, fought down panic.

The man continued. "I'd be grateful if you'd accompany me to the police station to answer a few questions and—"

"A few questions?" Michael decided to try to brazen it out. "About what? I don't think I've robbed a bank recently. Or if I have, I've forgotten!"

Mr Biffen tittered obligingly but the police sergeant ignored the attempt at humour.

Pamela Oldfield

"Just routine enquiries, sir. In connection with the recent death of George Ellyard."

"George Ellyard? For heavens sake!" Michael ran his fingers through his hair. "I don't know anything about it, and I *work* for a living, in case you hadn't noticed. We're busy. Can't it wait? I could call round later when—"

"I'm afraid not, sir. Now, if you'll come with me . . ."

Michael longed desperately to bolt back the way he had come, but that would simply delay the inevitable.

Mr Biffen, his eyes like saucers, looked at Michael and shrugged helplessly.

Michael said, "I don't seem to have any option." To the stage door keeper he said, "Explain to Mr Laye, will you, Biffy. Say I'll be as quick as I can," and with a heavy heart he followed the policeman out of the theatre.

The interview room was small and smelled of sweat and cigarette smoke. The sergeant sat down on the opposite side of a small table. A constable was called in to take notes and he sat against the wall a discreet distance away.

"Would you like a glass of water, Mr Wheatley?" The sergeant eyed him closely, as thought Michael's answer to the question might be significant. What would he read into a 'Yes', Michael wondered. That he was nervous and his throat was dry?

"No thanks," he said. "Just get on with it, will you." He gave an exaggerated sigh.

"Certainly, sir. Would you be kind enough to tell me where you were around midday on September the tenth when George Ellyard was murdered?"

"God knows. I don't keep a diary. I just get on with my life."

"Can't tell or won't, Mr Wheatley?"

"Can't . . . probably on my way to work. Or *at* work."

"You don't work regular hours, then?"

184

"It varies. I'm there throughout the evenings when there's a show and sometimes in the afternoons – like today, when the scene shifters are working on something new."

"So if you were working when George Ellyard was killed, someone would be able to corroborate your story."

"I don't have a story. Just the facts. Would someone give me an alibi? That's what you mean, isn't it? The answer is that I don't know. Someone might remember, though why anyone should is a mystery to me. I couldn't tell you when Biffy was at work – or Mr Laye."

The two policemen exchanged glances. Michael recognised the pantomime. Pretend he's given himself away. Pretend the most innocent answer is somehow significant. Rattle the suspect. Without warning an image rose uninvited of the cell where he had been incarcerated all those years ago. The dark green walls with their scratched messages, the single high lightbulb, the smell of sweat and fear and violence and the interminable voices. Michael shuddered.

"So-o . . ." The sergeant was leaning closer. "But you do know the gentleman who was killed? There's a connection between your families."

"No, I don't and no there isn't."

"What? Never met him? Not even to exchange a few words?"

"Not to my knowledge."

"A few *harsh* words?"

Keep calm, Mike. Don't lose it, he told himself. "I've heard about him, obviously, from my sister-in-law."

"Your sister-in-law knows him very well, doesn't she?"

"She *did*. Apparently. She kept that very dark. An old romance that ended years ago. Long forgotten."

"Only now it seems to have re-emerged." He fingered the pages on the desk in front of him, his lips pursed, his brow furrowed.

Michael, hating him, allowed himself a small fantasy. He

would leap forward, grab the man's lapels and lift him to his feet. Then he'd rush him backwards and bang his head against the wall. He would enjoy the fear in the stupid face and relish the small cry of alarm.

"Now . . . we come to the will, Mr Wheatley. It now seems that your brother's wife has been left a tidy sum by none other than the late George Ellyard! So the way I see it, the two families *are* connected."

"If you say so."

The sergeant glanced sideways at his constable. "You getting all this?"

"Most of it, sir."

"Most of it's not good enough."

They sat in silence as the young man caught up with his notes.

Michael decided to take the offensive. "Why don't you come right out and ask me if I killed George Ellyard? That's what you think, isn't it?"

"Did you kill him?"

"No, I didn't." He leaned back in his chair. How much exactly did they know about him and Ellyard? "Can I get back to work now?"

The sergeant raised his eyebrows. "In a hurry, are we, sir?"

Michael tightened his lips without answering.

"Did you accost George Ellyard on the tenth of September – a Saturday – and quarrel with him? I think I should warn you, Mr Wheatley, that we do have a witness."

"No, I didn't." A witness?

"The description given by the witness matches you exactly, Mr Wheatley. Are you sure you don't have anything to tell us about that day? A quarrel that might have got out of hand, perhaps?"

Michael shrugged. "I wasn't there. I didn't quarrel with him. Why should I?"

"Because he was involved with your sister-in-law years ago and you might resent that. On account of your brother who was killed."

"I didn't know about the – relationship. She didn't tell me."

"You could have found out."

"Possibly, but I didn't."

"Do you think you should have a solicitor, Mr Wheatley?"

"No." He swallowed, uncomfortably aware of the movement of his Adam's apple. "I don't need one because I haven't killed George Ellyard or anyone else. Now can I get back to work?"

"We shall talk to your sister-in-law, Mr Wheatley. To see if she can corroborate any part of your story. And to your workmates."

"It isn't a story. It's the truth." He pushed back his chair. "Now, if there's nothing else . . ." He hoped he looked calmer than he felt. Calm, bored and irritated.

"Sit down, please, Mr Wheatley. I'm afraid I am going to hold you in custody until we can arrange a line-up. Then our witness will be able to look at you all and see if she recognises anyone—"

So it was a woman!

"—as the man who attacked and killed George Ellyard."

Michael found himself short of breath. "You're keeping me here? Then I do want a solicitor."

"We're not arresting you, Mr Wheatley. We're holding you in custody pending an identification parade. You're simply helping us with our enquiries. Do you really feel you need a solicitor?"

Michael hesitated. If he said "Yes" it would look bad. As though he were guilty and needed help. He mustn't give that impression. Damn and blast George Ellyard.

He shrugged. "Forget the solicitor. How long's this charade going to take?"

Pamela Oldfield

The sergeant nodded to the constable who closed his notebook and left the room.

"We'll send for the witness immediately and Constable Budd will rope in the required number of lookalikes. You should be out in about an hour, Mr Wheatley – unless you are identified, of course." He also left the room.

Michael was aware of a wrenching fear growing inside him. The police needed a suspect and they had chosen him. A shot in the dark, probably. Hoping against hope. But surely they had no real evidence. No proof. They must be clutching at straws. He folded his arms on the table and leaned his head on them as black despair settled on his shoulders like a physical weight. His shoulders were broad, he thought, but not broad enough.

Frank arrived at Ocean View at the same time as an elderly lady and stepped back to let her go up the steps ahead of him.

She gave him a vague smile as she fumbled in her bag for her key. "I'm always forgetting it," she told him. "So silly of me but – Oh! Here it is!" She held it up for him to see. "Are you wanting to see someone?"

Frank smiled. "I'm a friend of Ginnie's. I wanted to see her mother."

"A friend of Ginnie's? Oh how nice. You must come in with me then." She gave him a roguish smile. "I expect she's got lots of admirers. She's a very pretty girl. Takes after her mother. She was dancer, you know." She inserted the key and after a moment managed to open the door. "Do come in, young man. I'll tell her you're here."

She made her way along the passage towards what Frank imagined was the private part of the guest house. Frank waited in the hall, hoping his nervousness was not too obvious. Mrs Wheatley was not going to welcome him with open arms, but he had to talk to her.

188

From somewhere at the end of the passage he heard a voice raised in surprise. "A friend of Ginnie's? A young man? I hope it's not . . ." Footsteps and then Iris Wheatley appeared. She wore an apron over her dress and her hands were floury. She was followed by Mrs Loame, who passed them on her way upstairs.

"I'm Frank Ellyard. I'd like to talk to you about Ginnie. It's rather urgent actually."

Ginnie's mother hesitated. "I'm cooking supper," she said. "And I'm expecting Ginnie back at any moment. You'd better come on in."

She led the way into the kitchen where a very large pie dish full of stewed meat waited on the table.

"Cobbler's pie," she told him. "People love the old-fashioned food." She glanced at the clock and then carried on with her work, shaping the dough into flat cakes and arranging them on top of the meat. She didn't offer him a seat so he remained standing. She didn't look up and Frank wondered if this was a way of showing disapproval or because she didn't know what to say to him. While he searched for a way to start she said, "I'm sorry about what I said – about you. I had my reasons." She looked at him. "Do you understand now why I did it?"

"Yes. Mother explained, but I already knew most of it. I guessed most of it."

"It wasn't personal. I had nothing against you."

He nodded. "Does Ginnie know?"

"I'm telling her this evening. I'd rather you weren't around."

"Well, that's why I'm here, Mrs Wheatley. You see, I know how upset she'll be. We were getting very close and she's going to feel cheated – as I did. I've been thinking it over, and I think that if *I* tell her it might be easier for her."

"You?" Mrs Wheatley's surprise was obvious.

189

Frank continued, choosing his words carefully. "If the two of us were alone together and I explained and let her see how it could be as brother and sister . . . That I've accepted the idea and the fun we could have . . ."

Iris was staring at him, the pie dish in her hands.

He said, "What have I said? It was an idea, that's all."

She turned suddenly, pushed the dish into a waiting oven and closed the door with a clang. "You sound just like your father," she said. "Same voice exactly. It's uncanny! You're George's son, that's for sure."

Frank wanted to shake her. At any moment Ginnie might return and they hadn't settled anything. "So what do you think?" he asked urgently.

"About your idea?" She frowned. "I can see your thinking, but there's so much I know that you don't know. About how it all happened."

"You could fill in the gaps afterwards. After she's accepted the idea."

"But she adored her Dad. Stan, I mean." She regarded him uncertainly. "It's a very generous offer, Frank, and I don't pretend I'm looking forward to telling her but . . . Well, I know my daughter and she's got a temper. Like her mother." She reached for a damp cloth and began to wipe down the table.

Frank pushed his hands into the pocket of his jacket and searched for a convincing argument. "You see, she might lose her temper with you and say things she might regret. I don't think she would with me. If only we can persuade her that it's really not a tragedy—"

"Even if it is!"

He shrugged. "But does it have to be? If I break the news, by the time you two talk about it the worst will be over."

"I don't know what to say and that's the truth."

Frustrated, Frank cursed his lack of conviction. He was so certain that he was right, but she wouldn't accept the idea.

"I do wish you'd trust me, Mrs Wheatley," he pleaded. "I'm sure—"

She rolled her eyes. "Your father said that to me! They were his exact words. Trust me, Iris. And look where it's got us all." She rinsed the cloth. Over her shoulder she said, "Sorry. That was a bit mean. None of it's your fault. What worries me is—" She glanced towards the back door. A bicycle bell sounded and she turned to Frank. "Oh! That's her! Now what do we do?"

Frank was frozen with indecision. He could either escape out of the front door or stay and face the approaching confusion. He decided to stay.

The back door flew open and Ginnie came in carrying a ginger cat. "Poor Ladie was in the road and—" She stopped as she saw Frank.

He said, "Hello, Ginnie, I was just talking to your mother . . ." and then stopped. Had he had permission to go ahead or hadn't he? Dare he risk it?

Iris said, "Don't blame me. I called Ladie earlier but he wouldn't come in."

Ginnie pushed the door shut behind her with one foot and stood gazing from one to the other, clutching the cat so tightly that he wriggled in her arms in an attempt to get free.

She said, "What are you doing here, Frank?"

The following pause lengthened.

The cat wriggled in her arms and she tipped him on to the floor and said, "Well, get down then, silly animal!" She turned to her mother. "What's happening? Tell me."

Frank looked at Iris, who was clutching her apron with both hands.

Ginnie took a step forward. "It's bad, isn't it? Somebody's died! Is it Uncle Mike? *Tell* me!"

Still Frank waited. He wouldn't say anything without her mother's permission. If she didn't say something soon

Ginnie would be really annoyed and they would get off to a bad start. This was bad enough. This wasn't how he'd envisaged it at all. He had planned to walk together along the beach. In this atmosphere he couldn't see his plan working successfully. He had almost talked himself out of the idea when Iris said, "Frank wants to tell you something. Please don't be angry."

The cat jumped on to the draining board and Ginnie said, "No! Bad boy!" and lifted it down again.

Frank cursed inwardly. Now he was committed. He said, "Ginnie, it's about my father."

Iris said, "It was nobody's fault, Ginnie. It just happened."

"What about him?" Ginnie looked at Frank.

Frank said, "Shall we go for a walk, Ginnie? I can—"

"Tell me!" she repeated, and there were two spots of colour in her cheeks. Her expression was changing.

Frank caught Iris's gaze and she nodded.

He said, "Let's all sit down, shall we?"

Ginnie's voice shook. "Please! Just tell me!" She remained standing.

The cat rubbed itself against Frank's legs with a big show of affection, but Ginnie darted forward and snatched it up. She held it close and bent her face against its fur.

Frank said, "You know that my father had two women in his life."

She made no sign that she had heard.

Frank hesitated. She was young and very vulnerable and he hated hurting her. "Whatever else I have to tell you, Ginnie, I want you to know that I love you and I always will – although it might be . . ."

Ginnie had lifted her head and was watching him wide-eyed. Frank snatched a look at Iris, who was on the verge of tears. Please God, don't let her cry! he thought desperately. It was hard enough without complications.

192

Ginnie said, "Your father had two women. So?"

"He loved both of them very much – but sadly he loved your mother more than mine."

Ginnie stared at her mother. "And . . . did you love him?"

Iris nodded but said nothing. Her right hand covered her mouth. Perhaps she was trying to stop herself from interfering.

He said, "He had to marry my mother because she told him she was expecting a baby – me – but he really wanted to marry your mother. That's why he left her half The Linen Store."

Slowly Ginnie turned her head. "Oh, poor Mum!"

Iris simply nodded.

The cat escaped for a second time and disappeared into the passage. Frank kept his eyes on Ginnie.

She let out a long breath. "And that's what you wanted to tell me? That's the big secret?"

"Not all of it." He knew how much depended on how he broke the news. "My mother had another child – a little girl. She died very young. We were all broken-hearted, but nobody realised how much I cared because I didn't know how to tell them. I've always wanted a sister."

Ginnie's expression had changed. "She died young? Oh that's awful. You poor thing!"

Frank wanted to look at Iris but didn't dare. Instead he heard her suck in her breath.

"Now, Ginnie, I've discovered that my father *did* have another child. A girl. That girl is my half-sister and I want her very much. As a sister. Someone to share my life in – in a very special way."

He was watching her closely, trying to gauge her reaction.

She said, "So have you met this half-sister?"

"Yes . . . Her name's Ginnie Wheatley . . . It's you, Ginnie. I know it's a shock but—"

"Me?" Ginnie turned from Frank to her mother, frowning. "But that means . . . that you and Mr Ellyard . . . No! That can't be right."

Frank said quickly, "Remember how much I love you, Ginnie!"

She was still staring at her mother. "That means that you and Mr Ellyard – but he was *married!*"

Iris said, "No, Ginnie! He wasn't. Not at the time we . . . He was only . . . I mean, they were engaged but I didn't know that at the time." She looked helplessly at Frank, then sat down on the nearest chair. There were tears in her eyes, he noted.

After a moment Ginnie also sat down.

Frank ploughed on, unable to tell whether he was winning or losing. "Father was engaged to my mother but then he met and fell in love with your mother – while she was still single. You have to see it as a love match, Ginnie. Nothing sordid."

Ginnie was still looking at Iris. "But what about Dad?"

"Frank's told you that I wasn't married to your – to Stan then." She fumbled in her apron pocket and found a handkerchief. "Please be grown-up about this, Ginnie. I've wanted to tell you—" Two large tears rolled down her cheeks.

"Did Dad know that I wasn't his daughter?" Her voice was dull, her eyes dark with shock and Frank's hopes began to fade.

Dabbing at her eyes, Iris shook her head by way of answer. "Stan was so keen to marry me. And I wanted him to love you . . . I thought if he knew the truth . . . I don't expect you to understand but—"

"I'm trying to understand, but . . ." Her face crumpled suddenly and her eyes glinted with the hint of tears.

Frank said hastily, "All that's in the past, Ginnie. What matters is that you are my father's child. My half-sister.

What matters now is that I have a sister. Our friendship . . ."
He faltered, chilled by the look in her eyes. Lamely he said,
"I can bear it if you can."

Iris struggled for breath. Frank caught her eye and in a
desperate glance suggested that she leave Ginnie to him.
Without another word, Iris slipped out of the room, leaving
them alone together. For a while neither spoke. Frank was
wondering how best to deal with the problem. He didn't
want Ginnie and her mother to be at loggerheads.

At last Ginnie said, "Your father is *not* my father. I won't
have it. He's nothing to do with me, Frank. *Dad* is my
father. Stanley Wheatley. I don't want any other father! I
don't!" Her lips trembled. "He brought me up – until he
was killed. *My* father was killed in the war, fighting for his
country. George Ellyard did nothing for us. Nothing at all.
He never loved me. He didn't take care of us. The truth is
I don't *want* him as a father!"

Frank was nonplussed. Her reaction was unexpected. He
said, "Then forget about him being your father. That doesn't
matter. The thing that matters is will you have *me* as a
brother? I want you very much. Please, Ginnie. We can't
be . . . can't ever be lovers, but we can be very close.
We can be *family*." He forced a smile. "Brother and sister
against the world! Come on Ginnie. To please me. What do
you say?"

She looked up at him. "I remember when the telegram
came. Mum thinks I was too young but I wasn't. It's as
clear as day to me. The boy brought a telegram and Mum
screamed when she saw it. She wouldn't open it. She said
later that until she read it she could pretend he was still
alive. The moment she opened the envelope he was dead.
She felt that she'd killed him. She couldn't stop crying.
She had to go to bed and the doctor came and said she
was hysterical and gave her something to make her sleep.
My grandmother came round to look after her. Everything

changed then. We came to live at Ocean View with my grandparents . . ."

Frank reached out and took her hands in his. "It was a long time ago, Ginnie. Your father wouldn't want you to be unhappy. Don't you remember any good times?"

She frowned, pressing her clenched fists against her mouth. "I remember one Christmas. I was supposed to be asleep but I woke up and there was a strange man in the room. He had a red coat and a funny beard and a sack. I started to scream for Dad and he pulled off the beard and said, 'It's only me, darling. Only me, your Dad! Don't be scared,' and Mum came in and they both hugged me and then we all laughed and he put the sack against the foot of the bed and said, 'Don't open your presents until the morning. Go back to sleep,' and he kissed me . . ." She looked up at Frank. "That's my father. My one and only father."

Frank pulled her to her feet and held her tightly in his arms. "Right," he said. "You reject George Ellyard. His application to be elected 'father' has been turned down." There was an anxious moment before she giggled.

He said, "But what about poor old Frank? Due to circumstances beyond his control he has withdrawn his application to be your young man and is now applying to be your half-brother? To love and to cherish . . . in a different way."

She held him at arm's length. "Don't you *mind*?" she asked incredulously.

He was serious. "Of course I do. I mind desperately. But most of all I don't want to let you slip out of my life."

"A brother . . ." she mused. "I suppose it's better than nothing."

"It's *much* better than nothing. Just think of it. I'll be your children's favourite uncle and you'll be my children's favourite auntie. And we'll confide in each other about our

196

problems and help each other along. We'll never fall out of love like my parents did."

She said, "So nobody will be able to come between us. You should have been a salesman. Very persuasive . . . just like—" She gave him a wicked smile and raised her eyebrows.

He rolled his eyes. "Like my father before me! I know! My terrible father." Suddenly he knew that the worst of the storm was over.

Ginnie clung to him and he kissed the top of her head and smelled the sweetness of her hair. His sigh was heartfelt.

Somehow, he thought, they would have to settle for this.

Thrilled, Mrs Stuckey sat in the policeman's car, her head held high, her white-gloved hands clasped in her lap. She was doing her duty as a citizen and was very proud of the fact that the police needed her help. She had never been in a motor car before but she didn't tell the driver that. When they reached the police station she was helped from the car and gave the young constable a gracious nod of thanks. She was escorted inside the building where Sergeant Evans was waiting for her.

He hurried forward, hand outstretched to shake hers. "Thank you so much for giving up your time, Mrs Stuckey. We won't keep you longer than necessary. The line-up is almost ready. You do understand what you have to do?"

She nodded, although she wasn't at all sure.

He said, "You will walk along a line of men and I want you to look at each one in turn. They will be facing the front. Then they will turn sideways, first to the left and then to the right. That way you can see each one from several angles. It's very important that you take your time, Mrs Stuckey. Then we will ask each man in turn to speak so that you can hear his voice. This will help you in your recognition. Each man has a number for identification purposes and you don't have to say anything until we withdraw from the line-up into the next room. In fact, I don't want you to say *anything* in front of the men in the identification parade. Then you can tell us the number of the man – *if* you recognise him, that is."

She was nodding, her expression earnest and eager. "If he's there I shall recognise him."

He said, "There's no need to be nervous."

"Oh, but I'm not!" she exclaimed. "Not at all. I'm looking forward to it. If I can be of assistance to the law – if I can contribute in *any* way – I'm more than happy to participate."

A moment or two later she was led into a room where everything was as she expected. At once she saw the man who had been quarrelling with George Ellyard. He was staring straight ahead and hadn't seen her. She opened her mouth but closed it again.

He was number six. She felt herself tremble slightly as she followed the police sergeant slowly along the row. She stared diligently at each man and then passed on. Nobody spoke and she was deeply aware of the significance of the event. They were all waiting for her verdict and she was confident that the man they were looking for was within their grasp.

None of them looked at her, not even the man she was going to point out. Backward and forward along the row and then it was time for them to speak.

One after the other they stepped forward and shouted, "Don't think I don't know what you did!" It was fascinating. There was no other word for it. Mrs Stuckey loved every moment. Then they left the room. Sergeant Evans said, "Well?" She said, "It was number six. I knew him immediately, even before he spoke."

The policemen exchanged knowing glances.

"Thank you for your co-operation, Mrs Stuckey," said the

sergeant. "One of my men will take you home if you don't mind waiting a couple of minutes."

"I don't mind at all," she said. "I'm glad to have been of help."

Two hours later Michael Wheatley had confessed to the accidental killing of George Ellyard. He was red-eyed and pale, with a small muscle twitching in his face. Bent over the notepad he wrote down his account of what happened with a hand that shook. He looked up as the sergeant re-entered the room.

"Finished it?" Evans asked.

Michael nodded and handed over the statement. Constable Budd brought him a mug of tea and he sipped it slowly, holding the cup in both hands, his body cold with shock, his mind numb.

The sergeant read aloud his confession.

I found out what Ellyard had done three years after my brother was killed but I didn't know what to do about it so I didn't let on to my sister-in-law but pretended I knew nothing of their affair. I was angry that my brother had been made a fool of but I was fond of the child and fond too of Iris who did her best. I kept meaning to face her with what I knew but never quite dared because I didn't know how it would all turn out if I did. On September the 10th I had had a couple of drinks and a mate at the pub had been telling me about his daughter's affair with a married man and somehow it made what Iris and Ellyard had done seem worse and I suddenly decided he wasn't getting away with it any longer. I just meant to shake him up, not bodily but in his mind and prick his conscience so to speak and hung about near his house and waited for him then I stepped out and said don't think I don't know what you did, you bastard. He tried to push past me and I grabbed his arm and he was embarrassed and trying to get rid of me but I kept on at him, telling him I knew his nasty little secret and what a fool he'd made of my brother and he had to pay for what he'd done. He tried to push me away and called me a sad vindictive little man and that did it. I punched him three times on the face and he stumbled. I shoved him again back against the wall and he fell sideways and hit his head on the brick pillar by the gate. He went down and stayed down and I thought I'd probably knocked him out. I kicked him twice and then I ran off. I didn't know I'd killed him. I didn't mean to and I'm sorry. What he did wasn't bad enough to die for. It happens all the time and he was Ginnie's father and they'll never forgive me.

Sergeant Evans pushed it back to him and said, "Sign it please, Mr Wheatley."

In a daze, Michael took up the pen and added his signature.

"Lock him up, Budd," said Evans.

Eleven

N ext day, in the dining room at Ocean View, Iris served the breakfasts alone. The previous evening Ginnie had retired to her room in a stricken silence and refused to come out. She was still locked in her room and Iris was wondering whether to get in touch with Frank.

"Good morning, Mrs Loame," she said with a smile and held the chair while the old lady arranged herself on it. "What will it be this morning? We've got kippers or eggs and bacon."

The young couple were talking in whispers to each other across their table and another family – parents and two young boys – were arguing about the relative merits of the funfair and a trip round the bay in a boat.

Mrs Loame considered her options. "Are the kippers fresh?" she asked. It was her usual question.

"Oh yes. Very fresh."

"Hmm . . . No, I think I'll have scrambled eggs – if it's not too much trouble."

Iris wrote "S EGGS" on her notepad and said, "And your usual pot of tea?"

Mrs Loame nodded. "Where's your daughter this morning?"

"She's got a bit of a headache. I told her to have a lie in."

"You don't look too perky yourself. Is anything wrong?"

"No, no! I slept badly, that's all." That was the under-statement of the year, she thought wearily. She had hardly slept a wink. Ginnie's sobs had distracted her and she had tried three times to talk to her through the door. Cocoa with an aspirin was refused. Being the cause of her daughter's grief and being unable to offer comfort had been a great burden. Suffering for Ginnie as well as for herself, Iris had tossed and turned throughout the night, dreading, and yet longing for, the morning.

Now she longed to be finished with the meal and was aware of a growing irritation with her hapless guests. For once she wished that she had no guests so that she could concentrate on more important matters, but that was heresy, of course. She had decided to sell her share of The Linen Store and was making plans for a grand refurbishment of Ocean View. And where would they be then without the guests?

She wanted to talk to Ginnie about the future but at the moment the revelations about George had taken precedence. She wondered if they might take Michael on as a manager. It was usual in a guest house to have a man about the place.

As she turned to leave the room the young man from Bromley or Croydon caught her eye and said, "Could we have some more toast, please?"

"Of course. I'll make some at once."

"No hurry," he told her.

She envied them their youth and freedom. This generation were so much luckier than her own. Less hidebound by tradition. In the kitchen she found Ginnie, red-eyed and subdued, making toast. Taken aback, she searched for the right words but Ginnie was ahead of her.

Without facing her mother, Ginnie said, "I talked to Frank and we've agreed not to talk about his father ever again."

"Good idea." Maybe it was, maybe it wasn't. She said, "Scrambled eggs for Mrs Loame and—"

"I thought it was eggs and bacon or kippers."

Ginnie turned and Iris's heart contracted with pity for her. She looked exhausted, her face drawn and her eyes red-rimmed. She had made no attempt to comb her hair and her face had seen no soap or flannel.

Instinct told her this was not the moment to offer affection – and certainly not criticism. Instead she answered Ginnie's question. "It is, but you know what Mrs Loame's like." She cracked two eggs into a bowl and whisked them. "Stick a couple more slices under the grill, will you, love?"

Ginnie said, "Frank says we're to enjoy the money his – the money that's been left to us. To you. Forget about where it's come from and why. We could take a holiday and then spend some money on this place. He said Ocean View might be my legacy."

"Frank's full of good ideas." Iris uttered up a small prayer of thanks for Frank's good sense. Relief coursed through her. It was going to be all right. She added a splash of milk, salt and pepper and tipped the eggs into the saucepan. Outside on the windowsill, Ladie meowed to be allowed in. She said, "Haven't had time to feed him this morning," and pretended not to hear Ginnie's muttered reproach as she opened the window.

The cat hurried to his bowl and found it empty.

Iris said, "You can give him the bacon scraps for now."

As Ginnie gathered them up the front door bell rang and her mother went to answer it. A moment later Constable Budd joined them in the kitchen.

"So what is this bad news?" Iris demanded.

Ginnie turned sharply. "Bad news? Haven't we had enough?"

"I'm sorry ma'am . . . miss. It's Michael Wheatley.

We thought you should know that he's been arrested for
the—"

Ginnie cried, "Arrested? Uncle Mike?"

"For the murder of George Ellyard."

Iris felt the silence settle over them like a dark shroud.
"For George's *murder*," she stammered. "But that's ridiculous! There must be some mistake."

The constable shook his head. "I'm afraid not."

Ginnie cried, "Uncle Mike wouldn't hurt a fly! He
wouldn't! Tell him, Mummy!"

"She's right," said Iris. "You've got the wrong man!"

"I'm afraid not, ma'am. Mr Wheatley has signed a full
confession."

There was a stunned silence. Ginnie ran to her mother
and Iris held her close. "It's a mistake!" she stammered
but she no longer believed it. If Michael had signed a
confession . . .

"I'm sorry to be the bearer of bad news."

His words went unanswered. Somehow Iris saw him to
the door and made her way back into the kitchen. She looked
at Ginnie and said, "Oh God! . . . Oh *God!*"

Horror-stricken, they faced each other.

Ginnie whispered, "Not Uncle Mike! It *can't* be true."

"But the confession!" Iris's face crumpled and Ginnie ran
forward to throw her arms around her. They clung together
wordlessly while the toast turned black and the scrambled
eggs burned in the pan.

It was nearly eleven o'clock when Frank returned from a
visit to Ocean View and broke the news to Moyna. Her
expression changed from incredulity to reluctant acceptance
as Frank told her about the confession.

He stared up at her from the depth of an armchair, his
young face contorted with worry.

"Poor Ginnie! First Father and then this."

Moyna stood by the French windows, staring out across the back garden. "So Iris's brother-in-law killed your father! We seem to be living in a nightmare."

Frank shook his head wearily. "Ginnie looks about all in, poor girl. I said I'd take her out this afternoon. We'll go for a bus ride or something. Anything to try and take her mind off things."

"What did the wretch have against George? That's what I can't understand. They didn't know each other and this Michael fellow didn't know about the . . . the connection." She sat down on the steps and her gaze moved restlessly along the flower beds which George had tended so lovingly. It had been his Sunday occupation, after church and before their lunch. Golden rod, Michaelmas daisies, a row of hollyhocks – all were past their best and turning brown. The grass needed cutting but she didn't know if she could push the mower. George had insisted on a larger model and it was heavy.

She asked, "Did you ever meet this Michael?" She hated the idea that Frank might have been civil to the man who killed George.

"No, but Ginnie thought the world of him. And he said he would let me know if a job came up in the theatre. He sounded very decent."

"But he wasn't."

"Wasn't what?"

"Decent. He killed your father."

Frank said nothing.

Moyna watched a thrush with a snail. It held the snail in its beak and brought it down hard several times on the paved area beside the shed. Then it began to peck at the softness revealed among the pieces. Moyna couldn't watch the slaughter and looked away.

"I felt so sorry for them." Frank sighed. "Terrified for someone they love. Helpless. What can they do? What can anyone do?" He moved to sit beside her on the step. "This is difficult for all of us, Mother. Please don't set your heart against Ginnie and her mother because of Michael Wheatley. They're not to blame."

"*She* is – in a way. If she and George hadn't . . ." She didn't finish the sentence.

"We don't know yet that it's anything to do with what happened years ago. It might be something totally unconnected. And even if it was . . . that means Father was partly to blame also."

"You're siding with your father's murderer, Frank. You do realise that, I hope." As soon as she said it, Moyna regretted the words. They didn't truly express the way she felt, but she had to blame someone and she certainly didn't want it to be George. "I'm sorry, Frank. I didn't mean that. I know you're right." She held out her arms and said, "Pull me up, Frank. Mrs Locke will be here shortly and I have to tell her we can no longer afford her. She won't be too happy about it, but I'm trying to find someone else who will take her on. If not, I'll give her an excellent reference. I shan't say anything about – about Michael Wheatley, but she'll find out soon enough. The local paper will be full of it!"

Frank stood up and tugged Moyna to her feet. "I'm off to the Labour Exchange and then I'm meeting Douggie. Anything you want me to do?"

She hesitated. "I don't think so. The truth is I don't know if I'm coming or going! I think I'll look in on Eddie Tanner. He might be able to ferret out some more information. He's got contacts in the police. Will you look in on your grandmother? But don't tell her about the arrest. Or maybe you should just say they've arrested someone and leave out the rest."

He frowned. "Must I?"

"Somebody must, and I also have to see the bank manager and the estate agent. There's so much on my mind I'd like to go quietly mad. It would be so much easier!"

Frank smiled. "You go mad, Mother? Never. You're stronger than you think."

Startled, Moyna looked at him. "Iris Wheatley said the same thing!"

He gave her a quick hug. "Iris Wheatley's not all bad, Mother. Nobody is."

When he left the house, she ran to the window to watch him hurrying down the street and as she contemplated his future her heartache grew until it was a very real pain.

When Moyna reached the office of Edward C. Tanner the door was locked. There was a notice stuck to the inside of the glass. "*In an emergency try 41 Hawley Square.*" She knew where that was, but was that his home or was it the address of another case on which he was working? And there was no time on the notice. He might have been there and gone away again. It might be a wasted journey. Moyna hesitated. She knew she ought to go home again or else make that overdue vist to the estate agent, but still she remained indecisive.

"Go home, Moyna!" she told herself. "You don't *have* to see Eddie Tanner."

But to her surprise she found that she desperately wanted to see him again. Telling herself to give up did no good at all.

"Edward C. Tanner," she whispered, staring at the gold letters on the window. "He's nothing to you!" she reminded herself. She was using the arrest of Michael Wheatley as a convenient excuse to see him again. "Nothing!" she repeated, but suddenly, unbidden, an image rose in her mind. It was Eddie beaming at her across the table in Bert's Pie Shop. She had made him happy by just being with him. Now, the thought of him set her pulse racing.

"He's not your type, Moyna," she insisted. "You're being

totally ridiculous!" And whatever would her mother say? A smile lit her face. She would call at 41 Hawley Square.

She found it in a row of four-storied terrace houses, but there was no sign of Eddie's car. Slowly she walked past again in the opposite direction, trying to pluck up courage to approach the house. It was reached by eight steps – a substantial building in an area which had once been a great deal more prestigious. As she passed she saw the curtain move in one of the lower windows, so someone was at home. Someone had registered her passing.

"Not Eddie," she muttered, because he would have come rushing out to greet her. Unless he was in there on one of his "obbos" – in which case she might well ruin it for him. But then he would hardly have left a forwarding address for an "obbo". Common sense told her to retreat with honour, but the desire to be with him again overcame her scruples. Turning abruptly she went back to the house, up the steps and knocked on the door. From the corner of her eye she caught another movement behind the curtain and a little while later footsteps approached the front door.

Moyna drew herself up and tried to look businesslike while whoever it was tried to open the door. It was apparently proving difficult, but at last it swung open to reveal an small elderly man in a state of disarray. He was unshaven and looked unwashed. His blue eyes were rheumy and his cheeks were sunken. He had put his pullover on back to front – a pullover which he wore over blue striped pyjamas. His hair stood up in uncombed wisps and she could smell cigarette smoke and what might be whisky. He clung to the door and for a long moment they regarded one another with suspicion.

He recovered first. "What d'you want?"

Moyna forced a smile. "I'm looking for Mr Tanner," she said. "I was told I might find him here." He might live in the flat above, she thought, or even in the basement.

"You've found him, then."

He was probably deaf. "Mr *Tanner*," she repeated.

"That's me. Mr Henry Tanner – unless you want my son Eddie."

This man was Eddie's father? Dismayed, Moyna regarded him through narrowed eyes. But of course, she shouldn't be too hasty. He might be ill. She might have dragged him from his sickbed. She said, "I'm so sorry. I've obviously come at a bad time." She took a step backwards. "I assume your son isn't at home." Surprise mingled with disappointment.

"True – but he might be at any moment." He gave her a sly smile. "Come on in. I won't bite you." He chuckled at this witticism and, swaying slightly, held the door open wider. "Come in and wait for him."

Reluctantly Moyna stepped inside. If it was true that he was expected home then she would see him. A ten-minute wait would do no harm. If he didn't return she would claim a prior engagement – with the estate agent – and leave.

Mr Tanner senior led the way at a stumbling run which ended in a room at the back of the building. It was large and nicely furnished, if old-fashioned in style, and heavy net curtains made it darker than it need have been. Through a half-open door she could see a scullery and beyond that a garden. On a small table there was a whisky glass and a bottle of Bell's whisky which was almost empty.

Henry Tanner lurched towards an armchair and almost fell into it. Moyna realised with alarm that he was drunk. She realised that coming in to wait for Eddie had been a mistake, but it was too late now. Dismayed, she began to wonder how Eddie would react if he knew she was here. By implying that he had no family Eddie had deliberately hidden the existence of the old man and she could understand why. Now she had stumbled on to the truth and that might prove awkward.

He poured himself another drink, raised his glass and said, "Your good health!"

"Thank you."

Unwilling to stare at him, she turned her attention to the room. There was a sampler on the wall next to a framed portrait of an elderly woman wearing the fashion of the turn of the century. Maybe Eddie's grandmother. There was a paper calendar and a painting of Highland cattle in an ornate gilded frame. A small table supported an unhealthy-looking aspidistra with browning leaves. The easy chairs had wooden arms and had once been handsome. Each one contained a patchwork cushion, made by Eddie's mother, perhaps. Against one wall there was a bookcase and a writing desk stood in one corner.

He said, "So are you a friend of Eddie's? He hasn't mentioned you but I can always tell when there's a special lady in his life. His skip's a little lighter and he smiles a lot." This little speech was altogether too much for him. He started to wheeze. When he had recovered his breath he went on. "Whistles under his breath. Oh dear, Eddie. You don't fool me." He began to chuckle and then to cough and the hand holding the whisky shook dangerously, spilling some of the drink on to the arm of the chair. He rubbed at this with his sleeve. "So what's your name?" he demanded.

Again Moyna hesitated. "Mrs Ellyard."

"*Mrs* Ellyard? Very formal. Hmm."

Moyna wondered how soon she could leave without causing offence, although she doubted that the old man would know how long she'd been there. Before she could decide he waved a hand towards the aspidistra. "Horrid thing. I never did like it but Eddie won't get rid of it. It was his mother's pride and joy. That's why he keeps it."

Moyna, deep in thought, made no comment as he rambled on. Poor Eddie, she thought, coming home to this. But what else could he do? No self-respecting nursing home would take the man in. Presumably he wouldn't be classed as genuinely sick and admitted to hospital.

She glanced up as he struggled to his feet, still holding the glass with the last few dregs of whisky.

He made his way unsteadily towards the aspidistra. "Damned ugly thing!" He staggered on, reached the bookshelf and pulled out a book at random. "Look here! That's one of Eddie's books. He's a proper bookworm is Eddie. Always reading. Very clever lad. Always was. Top of the class, he was, but his heart was set on the police force." He tossed another book on to the floor. "Textbooks, these are. Study books. That surprises you, I bet." He steadied himself and drained the glass. Then he seemed to spin on his heel, tripped and fell. There was the sound of breaking glass and the old man screamed in pain.

"God Almighty!" He sprawled on the floor, clutching his right hand. Blood dripped on to the linoleum from a gash on the inside of his thumb. Moyna rushed to kneel beside him.

"Don't worry, Mr Tanner. It's not as bad as it looks. I'll see to it for you."

"Oh Jesus!" he muttered. "Eddie's not going to like this." He scrambled awkwardly to his knees. "Hide the bottle. Yes. Hide the bottle before he comes home."

To pacify him, Moyna pushed the whisky bottle behind one of the cushions and tried to get him up on to his feet. "Come into the scullery," she said. "There'll be some water there and I'll bathe your hand."

She half dragged him into the next room and sat him on a chair. The wound was not extensive but deep and blood flowed freely, staining his pyjama trousers and trickling along his arm. She made a note to clear up what she could of the broken glass before someone trod on it in bare feet. Examining the wound she satisfied herself that there was no sliver of glass remaining, then found some warm water in a kettle and used the edge of a tea towel to clean the cut. Throughout the operation Eddie's father said not a word but he moaned softly, his face scrunched up with pain and shock. She wondered whether an alcoholic haze lessened or worsened the effects of the accident. Unable to find anything better, she took a clean handkerchief from her handbag, folded it and tied it round his hand.

"Your son will check on it when he comes in," she told him. "Would you like me to make you some hot sweet tea? It's very good for—"

"Tea?" He shook his head in disgust. "Get me a whisky. Under the coal in the coal shed."

"I think you've had enough whisky, Mr Tanner." She tried to sound stern. "It's tea or nothing."

He mumbled something which sounded remarkably like "Miserable cow!"

"Will you be all right?" she asked him. "I have to go now. I can't wait any longer for Mr Tanner. I have to see my estate agent."

"He'll be back any time now."

"He seems to have been delayed. I really must go."

"Go then," he said gruffly.

"Look," she said. She propped his elbow on the table so that the wound was raised up. "If you keep your hand like this the bleeding will soon stop." She smiled. "I hope you'll soon feel better."

As she moved to pass him he caught at her sleeve with his uninjured hand. "I'll never feel better," he told her. "Never. That's the trouble."

"Of course you will." Firmly she detached his fingers. "I'll let myself out."

She walked home with a terrible tightness in her throat. She was trying not to think about Eddie's life and the problems with which he had to deal, day in, day out. Who cooked for them? Who cleaned the house? Not the old man. Eddie presumably did it all as well as holding a business together. And I think *I've* got problems, she reflected unhappily.

She returned home to find Mrs Locke waiting for her.

"Oh there you are, Mrs Ellyard." The familiar powdered face creased into a nervous smile. "You asked me to wait for you. You wanted to talk to me."

Moyna looked at her, dismayed. She had to tell her that she was no longer needed and that so far she had been unable to find her another employer. Suddenly it was all too much. She said, "Oh, *poor* Mrs Locke!" and burst into tears.

When the unhappy situation had been explained and Mrs Locke had gone home, Moyna decided to go round to Ocean View. Her main motive was a desire to offer support to Ginnie's mother over her brother-in-law's arrest, but she was honest enough to admit, also, to a certain curiosity. She now saw the Wheatleys as "George's other family" and wanted to see how they lived. The idea of moving closer to the family had no appeal but Frank was already very friendly with them and she was reluctant to be excluded. She had also admitted to herself that Iris Wheatley had shown courage in bringing up a daughter single-handed, as well as great restraint. It couldn't have been easy all those years, keeping such a secret.

It had been a close thing, she reminded herself, as she turned into Union Crescent. If George had known that Iris was pregnant, he would have married her instead and she, Moyna, would have been left with an illegitimate child.

She rang the bell and Iris herself came to the door in her dressing gown. To Moyna's surprise she spoke defensively. "If you've come to gloat you can turn right round—"

"Come to gloat?" Moyna, taken aback, spoke sharply. "Of course I haven't come to gloat. If you must know I—"

"Michael didn't do it!" Iris clung to the door as though for support. "He *couldn't* have done it. They must have made a mistake."

Her face was pale, her eyes sunken, her hair scraped back with a couple of hair clips.

Moyna said, "I hope so. I came because I wanted to help." For the first time she realised what a blow Michael Wheatley's arrest must have been to them, and was aware of a growing compassion. "May I come in?"

"What can you do? What can anyone do to help?"

Iris continued to glare at her and Moyna was beginning to regret the kindly impulse that had brought her.

Moyna said, "If you don't want me here—"

The door opened wider. "Do what you like! I'm past caring!" Iris walked back into the kitchen, leaving Moyna to close the door and follow.

Over her shoulder, Iris said, "I'm not sleeping very well." By the time they reached the kitchen her hostility was fading. "I was taking a quick nap. Good job we're not busy." Slumped into a chair, she pointed to a large teapot and said, "Help yourself."

"No, thank you."

"Your Frank came round. He's a lovely boy. He and Ginnie have gone to the police station to see what they can find out." She leaned forward. "Michael *couldn't* have killed George. You must believe that. They said he'd made a confession but they must have forced it out of him. They do that, you know. They keep on and on until you crack. It's called a false confession. When you're thoroughly confused and scared you'll say anything!"

Moyna sat down next to her. "The police told me it was an accident. Your brother-in-law says he lost his temper and punched him and George fell down and hit his head on a stone gatepost. That isn't murder, Iris. I'm sure it isn't. I went round to see Mr Tanner but he wasn't there. He wasn't at his house either. But he'll know." She wasn't going to mention her meeting with Eddie's father.

"They'll want to hang him. You know what they're like, the police." She rubbed her eyes tiredly. Then she looked up. "I'm so sorry, Moyna – that it was him. Somehow he found out about me and George, but I didn't know he felt so bad about it. I never dreamed he'd tackle George. He's been so good to us – Michael, I mean. I never thought . . ." Her voice shook. "I don't know what Stan would think. His own brother killing someone. Frank says they'll get him a solicitor. He's going to ask if we can take him anything – flannel and soap and pyjamas. A book to read."

Moyna thought it unlikely, but didn't say so. Michael Wheatley was in prison, not in hospital. "I could ask Ed – Mr Tanner. He'll know. He used to be a policeman."

Moyna glanced round the kitchen. The washing up waited behind the sink and soon there would be another meal to prepare and serve. It was never-ending. She felt thankful that she had never had to run a guest house. "Why don't you go upstairs and change while—"

"I'll change when I'm ready." Iris gave Moyna a sharp look.

"I thought you might need to look presentable if Michael's solicitor should call."

"Michael's solicitor? Oh lord!" Alarmed, Iris struggled to her feet.

"I'll wash up these few things for you."

Iris's eyes widened. "Wash up? Why should you?" She still sounded faintly belligerent, but Moyna understood her resentment. George's legacy had elevated her but Michael's arrest had brought her down again.

"No reason," she said lightly. "I'd like to help." Seeing Iris hesitate, she added, "No one likes to feel useless in a crisis."

"A crisis! You can say that again!" She eased her

shoulders, stretching her neck as though it was stiff. "My whole damned life's been one long crisis."

Moyna said, "Have a bath. Bath salts – everything. You'll feel much better afterwards."

"There won't be enough hot water," she protested. "That's another thing I'm going to get. A decent boiler."

Moyna made no comment as the door closed behind her, but her mind was busy digesting the information. Iris was going to instal a new boiler using George's money. And she had said that the boiler was another thing she was planning. So she obviously intended to sell her share in The Linen Store and spend the money on the guest house. That was interesting. If Mr Dunn bought it . . .

As she filled the sink with hot soapy water Moyna mulled over the possibilities. A ginger cat came into the kitchen and she gave it some milk.

She finished the washing up and wiped down the table and other work surfaces, and as she did so her thoughts returned to Eddie Tanner and his father. What had happened, she wondered, to reduce a man to such a pathetic state? No work, apparently, but enough money to drink himself silly. She tried to guess his age but found it impossible. The man was a physical wreck. He could be anywhere between fifty and seventy. Perhaps she wouldn't tell Eddie they had met – although the father might tell him. If he remembered. No wonder Eddie needed sleeping pills. He had so much on his mind.

"A penny for them!"

Iris had returned. She was wearing a smart blue dress and she had taken trouble with her hair.

Moyna smiled. "You look a lot better."

"I feel it." She looked round at the kitchen. "Thanks a lot."

Moyna said, "At least you'll be able to pay for a defence lawyer for Michael."

Iris rolled her eyes. "Pretty ironic, isn't it? Using George's money to help his—" She stopped short at the word "murderer".

Moyna said, "I'm sure he didn't mean it. He got carried away I expect. Lost his temper. It can happen to the best of us."

"He was one of the best. Michael, I mean." Iris stared round vaguely. "Supper. What are we supposed to be having?" She crossed to the dresser and pulled a small notebook from the drawer. "Ah . . . Salad with hard-boiled eggs and ham. That's not too difficult."

"Do you plan to stay here?" Moyna decided to be forthright. "What I mean is, if you want to sell your share in The Linen Store I know Mr Dunn would be willing to buy. If he can raise the money. The valuers have been in. I shall get their report any day now."

Iris nodded. "I want to improve this place. I've got lots of ideas. It'll be something for Ginnie when I'm gone. I think George – Oh! Sorry."

"It doesn't matter." Moyna wiped her hands on the towel. "I'm going to see a couple of flats. I want Frank to come with me. It will be his home, too. I don't think it will be such a wrench for him. More a bit of excitement. A change. Young people don't mind these . . . these upsets."

"You blame me, I suppose."

"Not entirely. You and George. I wish I hadn't wasted my life with him though." She looked up and her eyes glinted with tears. "We all want someone to love who will love us in return. Will you ever remarry?"

"Never. I don't want to. I'm used to my independence and I like it."

Moyna wanted to talk to someone about her feelings for Eddie Tanner but knew she dared not succumb. Her feelings were too unformed to share with anyone else. She had acknowledged to herself that she was very attracted to him but didn't know whether to let matters take their own course or to stop it right here. Eddie Tanner was so different from George – or any other man she had known – but he was warm and cheerful and hard-working. She had tried imagining what it would be like to awake in the morning beside him. And she had found it exciting. Eddie obviously liked her. The question was, how much? He had said he wanted to be Prince Charming, awakened with a kiss. He had said, "What about forever?" But perhaps he was that way with all women. A bit of flattery offered in fun. Perhaps he made the same remarks to all his secretaries.

She sighed. If he hadn't married then he didn't want to. She was being ridiculous even to consider the man – and she had only just been widowed. Guilt flooded her and she was glad Iris couldn't read her thoughts. With an effort she forced her mind back to what Iris was saying.

"—and even if it was an accident he'll be sent to prison because he did kill him, in a way. Not with malice aforethought, though, and that's what matters. I mean George would be here now if it wasn't for Michael. Everything would have been the same as it was a month ago . . ." She sighed heavily. "Instead of which it never will be the same. What about you? Will you marry again?"

Moyna shook her head quickly. "I very much doubt it, although—"

"Although?"

"I like being with someone. Sharing. I'm not used to being on my own." The longing to confide overcame her and she was on the point of mentioning Eddie Tanner when Iris spoke again.

"Poor Michael. I bet he's terrified in there with all those criminals. Burglars and what have you. And he does like his food. They say it's awful in prison. Cabbage soup and stuff like that."

"Still, he won't be hanged. That's the main thing, isn't it? He'll do his time and then come out."

"But then what?" Iris was determined to look on the black side. "He'll be an ex-con. A jailbird or whatever they're called. Nobody'll give him a job." She shuddered.

"You could give him one. Make him your manager. Let everyone see that you still have confidence in him." Moyna didn't know where the idea came from – she was simply being positive – but as soon as she had made the suggestion the two women regarded each other seriously.

Iris said slowly, "That's not a bad idea. It might work." She narrowed her eyes. "But then again it might not. He fancied me once upon a time, and if he was living here . . . No. Better not to chance it. I think he'll have to move away where nobody knows him. Start again."

Moyna stood up. "Well, I want to see Mr Tanner. If I can catch him I'll mention Michael and see what he knows. Will you be all right now?"

Iris nodded. "As all right as I ever will be!" She shrugged. "Have I said how sorry I am – that it was Michael?"

"I know. It's one of life's little ironies."

"A rather big irony if you ask me!"

Iris went with her to the front door. "Thanks for everything."

Moyna flashed her a quick smile and hurried away. George's other family, she reflected. She was beginning to like them.

Twelve

After Mrs Ellyard's departure, Henry Tanner sat for a long time thinking about her. She obviously liked Eddie. A nice woman. A bit toffee-nosed, maybe, but that wasn't her fault. She had been brought up that way. Lovely eyes and a soft voice. He liked a woman to have a soft voice. Very feminine . . .

He said, "Mrs Ellyard. Are you fond of my son? You could do a lot worse. Straight as a die, Eddie is."

Henry tottered to the sideboard and searched inside the cupboard and both drawers. He had drunk the whisky from the bottle hidden in the coal shed and that seemed to be it. A tour of the kitchen produced the same results. Nothing.

He went into the front room and collapsed into an armchair. "Nothing to bloody drink!" he muttered. He didn't want much, he told himself. Just one more glassful. That would see him through. Until when, he wasn't sure, but he lived for the moment.

Dozing in his chair, the best part of an hour passed and he woke feeling terrible. Almost sober. He could see everything too clearly and he didn't like what he saw. He also recalled his visitor.

"Mrs Ellyard," he muttered. "Nice lady. And my Eddie fancies his chances." He smiled faintly.

He'd be a good catch for any woman. He had a decent

job, a home, a friendly nature. And a drunken father. Oh well.

"Life's never perfect."

He struggled to his feet and made his way to the lavatory which was outside next to the coal shed. He managed to unbutton his flies but his aim was a little unsteady and he knew there was a mop somewhere. He looked for it half-heartedly, then gave up and stumbled back to the kitchen. He lit the gas under the kettle but didn't refill it. Ten minutes later the kitchen was full of smoke and he had to open the back door and flap a tea towel around to clear the air. Unable to clear the air, he decided to take a nap and hauled himself along the passage. He passed the bathroom and wondered if he had left any whisky around. Opening the bathroom cabinet he found a small bottle full of tablets. His heart lurched with sudden fear. Eddie was ill and hadn't told him. The thought sobered him even more and he stood peering at the label with blurred vision.

"Spectacles, Henry!" he told himself and found his way to the bedside table. He put on his spectacles and tried to read the label. To his surprise he saw his own name and the words "*Sleeping pills. One or two with liquid*".

"Sleeping pills?" he muttered. "Not me . . . Not unless . . ." His mind moved slowly, but at last he understood. Eddie gave him sleeping pills. That's why he slept so heavily.

"Gordon Bennett!" he whispered. Had it come to that? His son and the doctor conspiring against him?

He stared at the bottle of pills, struggling with a deep shame. Eddie had been forced to ask the doctor for help. He recalled the steaming cups of cocoa he had been talked into drinking. Foul stuff laced with sugar. Cocoa spiked with sleeping pills to keep him quiet for a few hours; to keep him off the whisky for as long as possible.

Painfully he confronted the facts of life. Of his son's life. Or lack of a life.

"Eddie!" he murmured. *"Eddie!"* No wife, no children. Just a drunken father. He was filled with shame and two tears rolled down his cheeks.

He sat there for a long time and then he unscrewed the bottle and emptied the pills into his trembling hand.

Eddie was waiting outside Moyna's house in the car and he jumped out when he saw her. A broad smile lit his face as he hurried towards her. At the sight of him Moyna's spirits lifted and by the time they met up, her smile was as broad as his. They clasped hands awkwardly, as though wanting to do more.

"I've been enjoying a bit of Mozart," he told her. "At least, I think it was. Must be your Frank."

Moyna glanced towards the house. "Yes it is. He's probably entertaining Ginnie. She's been nagging him to play something for her." Reluctantly she withdrew her hands from his. "I was looking for you!" she told him. "Have you heard about Michael Wheatley?"

She led the way into the house and Moyna noticed that he followed without an actual invitation, as though it was the most natural thing in the world. She said nothing, although it pleased her immensely.

Frank and Ginnie were in the sitting room and after a brief greeting, Moyna left them together, explaining that she intended to consult Eddie about the arrest.

"They don't know how lucky they are," she said, "being allowed to spend so much time unchaperoned. We had to get up to all kinds of tricks to find any time to be alone together."

Eddie laughed. "He plays beautifully."

"Thank you. It's a shame about the music but he doesn't seem to mind. Ginnie suggested that they buy a piano for Ocean View and Frank play it as an accompaniment to the Saturday tea. All very genteel."

"She's a nice girl."

"She is. But now I don't know what to say to the poor creature. Frank said she idolised her uncle. A sort of father figure. And now her uncle's killed their father. It's terrible."

As they moved into the kitchen Moyna was wondering how best to approach the subject of Eddie's father. She was going to have to say something about her visit and she didn't want to risk Frank or Ginnie overhearing the conversation.

"Come and admire my garden," she suggested. "It's not looking its best, but I want to talk to you."

It was not a large garden but it had a chestnut tree and a few rhododendrons. The lawn was a little overgrown and the circular flower beds needed weeding. A small terrace was dotted with geraniums in pots.

"Very nice," he said.

"I shall be sorry to part with the garden," she told him. "But I could never manage all this on my own. George was the one with green fingers . . ." She had a sudden vision of her husband leaning into the lawn mower or kneeling to plant daffodil bulbs. George had spent hours in the garden and she had wondered whether it was his escape from her. Now she wondered if that was the time he thought about Iris and Ginnie. With an effort she forced the unhappy thought from her mind.

She pointed to the far end of the garden. "That was Frank's swing. I couldn't bring myself to take it down so George renewed the rope last year. It was well made, like everything George did. He was a bit of a perfectionist."

"I always wanted a swing when I was a kid!"

"It's never too late. Have a go!" She led the way. "It will take your weight. I used to use it if no one was looking!"

He settled himself on the wooden seat and grasped the ropes. "Aren't you going to push me?"

"Eddie, really!" Laughing, she took up her place behind

him and gave the swing a few pushes and Eddie began to scream and waggle his feet.

"Higher! I want to go higher!"

"Stop it, you great baby!" she laughed, hoping the neighbours weren't watching. Eddie allowed it to slow down. He remained sitting and for a moment she studied his sturdy back and the way his hair curled over his collar. She imagined a small boy on the swing – a smaller version of Eddie – and felt her heart contract with longing. Shaken by the intensity of her feelings, she leaned against the trunk of the tree. Eddie's child. It was suddenly clear to her. That was what she wanted. Eddie Tanner and another child. He turned and caught her expression and for a moment they were both transfixed.

Confused, Moyna began to gabble. "See that poor dead tree next to the fence? It was a gorgeous lilac but it died last winter. A lovely deep purple. An anniversary present from George's parents years ago. At least, it looked dead but George said, 'We'll give it a chance. It might revive itself,' but it didn't and . . . and it died." She swallowed hard and drew a long breath.

Eddie also took the coward's way out. "Our back hedge doesn't look so nifty either," he informed her. "I think the extreme cold got down to the roots."

Recovering her composure, Moyna recalled the reason for their exploration of the garden and tried to think of a subtle way to mention her visit to his home. Finally she gave up.

"I called at your house, Eddie," she said. "I was trying to find you." She raked the toe of her shoe across the grass, pretending to dislodge a small weed.

He said, "Ah!" and turned away briefly. Then he faced her again. "You met Dad, then. He loves to have visitors."

Moyna nodded, still trying to find suitable phrases.

"How was he?"

"A little shaky and a little drunk – but very polite."

"Bit of a shock for someone like you, I should think." He abandoned the swing and stood up. If he was disconcerted he didn't show it.

"Yes it was." She looked him squarely in the eye. "I felt very sorry for him and for you – although knowing you, I'm sure you deal with the problem."

"I do the best I can." His expression was bleak. "I can't get any help for him. All the doctor says is, 'Keep him away from alcohol.' It's not very helpful. Dad can be so blooming crafty."

"Surely there's something he could give him?"

"He's given me sleeping pills for him. If he sleeps through the night he's not roaming the house looking for drink. I crush one up in his cocoa. If he's had a bad day I give him two. He doesn't know."

She said, "He's very proud of you. Gave you a wonderful reference!" He rolled his eyes but she could see he was pleased. She chose her next words carefully. "He had a bit of an accident. Fell on to his glass and cut his hand. I washed it and tied it up. I didn't think it needed stitches but you'd better have a look at it when you get home."

"You got more than you bargained for, then! I'm sorry."

"I was glad to help."

"So he was drunk." He sighed. "Where on earth does he hide it? I checked all the usual places before I left for work."

"He said there was another bottle under the coal."

"Under the coal! Well, that's a novel idea." He stood up. "I'll push you now."

Moyna didn't like to refuse so she sat down gingerly. A little self-consciously she grasped the ropes and then Eddie moved behind her and set the swing in motion.

"Not too high!" she warned.

"Scaredy cat!"

It came to her abruptly that this way she could not see his

expression. Talking about his father was obviously difficult for him.

Eddie said, "Dad doesn't eat enough – that's half the trouble. If he ate more the drink wouldn't work so quickly or have such an effect."

"Who cooks for you?"

"I do. At least I can do a fry-up. And I buy fish and chips. Stuff like that – and we go to the pie and mash shop when he's sober enough."

"I could bring you a casserole once or twice a week. I always make at least one. A casserole is very filling – or I do a pie or dumplings."

The swing slowed. "I couldn't let you. It's not your problem. We manage, Moyna. Have done for years. I don't know how he's lived this long with what he drinks. Should have ruined his liver ages ago."

He had come round to stand in front of the swing and now pulled her gently to her feet. Then, before she realised what was happening, he had pulled her closer and his arms were round her. He was pressing his face against her hair.

She dare not speak. If she said anything he would release her and this moment was the one she'd been waiting for since the first moment in his office.

"You smell wonderful," he whispered.

Still she couldn't speak. She wondered if Frank and Ginnie could see them – but hopefully Frank was still playing the piano at the front of the house. Slowly she allowed her head to rest against his and they stood there for a long time, close and comfortable.

At last she drew back and they looked at each other.

"Was I wrong to do that?" he asked, his voice low.

"No. I loved every moment."

She hoped he would repeat the embrace but he didn't. Disappointed, Moyna said brightly, "Rhododendrons. We had a lovely show this year. They're at their best in June, of course." She remembered guiltily that George had been dead less than three weeks; that he had planted them years ago on a cold April day, fussing with the soil and a special mulch while a fine drizzle soaked his clothes.

"Come in, George, for heaven's sake!" she had told him. "You'll catch a chill out there."

"Don't fuss, dear. I've survived worse."

"But you're soaked! You'll get pneumonia!"

"We all have to die sometime."

How horribly prophetic. Here he was, dead before his time, killed in the space of a few random moments. Had she fussed too much? George had called it fussing. She had thought she was caring. Aware of a lengthening silence she asked quickly, "Do you like gardening?"

Eddie shrugged. "Don't have time for it. But if I did I don't think I'd take to it. So slow, isn't it? You plant something and wait months or even years for a few blooms. Then the frost gets it or something!" He gave her a crooked grin. "I'm the impatient type."

She said, "I was coming to you to ask about Michael Wheatley. When the police came to say they'd caught him, they said he'd confessed to it but it just happened. It wasn't planned. Does that mean it wasn't murder?"

They began to walk back to the house.

Eddie nodded. "Manslaughter. Almost certainly. He was responsible for your husband's death but he hadn't intended to do him any harm. At least that's his story, and it sounds genuine. He'll go down, though. He won't get off scot-free."

"I didn't want him to hang . . . because of Ginnie and Iris . . . and because the initial fault was with George. If he hadn't . . . Well, you know what I mean."

He nodded. "They won't hang him but he'll be punished for what he did. And so he should be. Can't go round killing people in a fit of temper. Life's a bit too precious for that."

They watched two sparrows fighting over a scrap of bread on the bird table.

Eddie said, "Who killed cock robin!"

"Sometimes it seems as though the whole animal kingdom is intent on killing. *Homo sapiens* included." She sighed. "I'm going to look at a flat this afternoon. If it seems suitable I'll take Frank along. It's not too far from your office. If I did work for you – a few more hours – I could walk it. It would save bus fares."

His face brightened. "I like the flat already!"

"My mother's horrified that we're having to move, but in a way I don't mind. It's a way of making a fresh start. There'll be no memories of my life with George – although I know that's going to be hard for Frank because he was born here."

"You worry too much. Young people are more adaptable than you think. Everything's an adventure to them. That's how it should be."

They were nearing the house. "I did a very mean thing, Eddie. Mother was appalled." She told him about the headstone and waited for his condemnation. Instead he laughed.

"Hitting back at life, most probably, for all the knocks and disappointments. You're allowed to hit back, Moyna. You're only human. You don't have to be perfect."

She nodded gratefully and changed the subject. "Will they let Iris talk to her brother-in-law?"

"I doubt it. But she could write and he can write to her."

"They've found a solicitor for him but he might not be any good."

"Apparently it's Dan Saunders. He's OK. Tell Iris not to worry."

They paused outside the back door and Eddie took hold of her hand. "Will I ever be able to kiss you?" he whispered urgently.

After the smallest hesitation, Moyna leaned forward and kissed his cheek.

He smiled but made no effort to return the kiss. "I can wait," he told her.

The flat was on the ground floor, approached by four curved steps. Moyna waited outside an oak door that was in need of a good oiling. She stood there for some time before the estate agent turned up with a key. During the wait she had time to assess the road and was disappointed. There were no trees and the pavement was uneven with a broken paving stone here and there. No one had swept it and bus tickets and scraps of paper rolled along the gutter whenever the breeze gusted strongly enough.

A small stout man hurried towards her, his hand raised in greeting. From his rather self-confident manner, she guessed this would be the assistant manager, Mr Bundy. He looked about fifty, she thought, judging by the amount of grey in his thinning hair.

"So sorry!" he said breathlessly. "So very sorry to keep you waiting. The previous business took longer than expected." Smiling expansively, Mr Bundy shook her hand, still apologising for his lateness, then took a bunch of keys from his pocket and consulted the various labels. "Ah, here we are. In we go!" He gave her a triumphant smile and opened the door. "Great potential."

"I'll follow you," Moyna suggested.

He closed the door and stared round. "A spacious hall-way," he said.

It was large but gloomy. The anaglypta on the walls had been painted a dark brown and a single light bulb swung in the draught from the open door. Mr Bundy tried to switch on the light but nothing happened.

"I expect the bulb's gone," he muttered.

Trying to be positive, Moyna wondered if a glass-fronted

door would improve the area. She wanted it to be suitable because it was near Eddie's office, but first impressions were not favourable.

"Leading into a sunny sitting room," Mr Bundy smiled, throwing open a door. Moyna saw a drab box of a room with a cracked mirror screwed above the fireplace. "What my dear old mother would call the parlour!" Seeing Moyna's dismay he added, "All it needs is a dab of paint and some bright wallpaper. You look like a lady with a creative bent. I'm sure you could transform it in two shakes of a lamb's tail!"

It *was* a sunny room, Moyna conceded. There was a large bow window which she could drape with satin curtains. "It *could* be very pleasant." But trying to see it through Frank's eyes, Moyna's dismay deepened.

Moments later she found herself in a living room which smelled faintly of some kind of liniment. Seeing Moyna wrinkle her nose, Mr Bundy said, "An elderly couple had it. It just needs a dose of fresh air. Open the door and window . . ." He left the rest to her imagination. "And there's the kitchen through here."

The room contained a free-standing gas stove and a deep sink with draining boards. A window looked out on to a small neglected garden.

Mr Bundy was trying hard to be enthusiastic. "Sad when people let a place go. Such marvellous potential here. They want a three-year lease. Very reasonable. Renewable, of course. I dare say if you wanted to make a few improvements, the landlord would consider an adjustment to the rent."

"I was thinking of getting a dog," Moyna told him doubtfully. "Would there be any problem?"

"None at all, Mrs Ellyard. At least, I wouldn't expect any difficulty. A dog, eh? Bit of company for you. That's it, I expect."

He knew the background to her situation, thought Moyna,

and must surely be comparing this awful flat with their elegant house in Ethelbert Road. Mortified, she was aware of a moment's bitterness towards her late husband. This is your fault, George, she thought. This is what you've brought us to.

Mr Bundy babbled on, unaware that he had lost his audience. "They *are* good company. We've got a poodle. My wife dotes on it. I think she loves it more than she loves me!" He laughed to show how unlikely this was.

Moyna wondered if George's spirit was hovering nearby, watching. If so, he must be feeling ashamed of himself.

" . . . and the bedroom's through here . . ." Mr Bundy pushed open another door.

"Bedroom?" Moyna was startled out of her reverie. "You don't mean there is only one, do you?"

He looked flustered. "Why yes! I believe so."

"But there are two of us, Mr Bundy." Moyna fought back growing irritation. "I distinctly told your young lady—"

"No no! It says one bedroom . . ." He brought a folded sheet from his pocket and studied it. "One bedroom!"

"I have a son of eighteen, Mr Bundy!" Moyna spoke more sharply than she had intended. He had wasted her time but, more significantly, he had demonstrated how different her life was going to be without financial security. "Why should I say that one bedroom is enough? Of course I said two."

Mr Bundy tutted. "Silly girl! I'll have a word with her when I get back. I'm so sorry. What a shame. It's a nice little flat. Just a mite too small." Refolding the paper he stuffed it into his pocket. He stared round despondently then his face brightened. "Would you consider a put-you-up?"

Moyna looked at him. Why on earth was she pretending, she asked herself. It seemed to her, at that moment, that she had spent too many years of her life hiding her true feelings. It was time to stop.

She said firmly, "No, I wouldn't consider a put-you-up.

And you've misled me, Mr Bundy. This *isn't* a particularly nice little flat, is it? It's a horribly depressing flat which would need a lot of money spent on it. Quite unsuitable, in fact."

His expression was reproachful. "Mrs Ellyard! I hardly think you can blame me. The property is within the budget you gave us."

Moyna took a deep breath. "I'm not blaming you for the flat, Mr Bundy. I'm blaming you for . . . for the . . ."

She glanced round in desperation. What was she blaming him for? Tears sprang into her eyes, but she blinked them back. Mr Bundy's secretary had made a mistake. That was all she could blame him for. She couldn't blame him for a dead husband who had never loved her and who had left her in financial difficulties. Nor could she hold him responsible for her own weakness. She had stopped loving George a long time ago but had been unwilling to admit it even to herself. "You're right," she told him. "I'm not thinking straight today."

Immediately Mr Bundy patted her arm. "No offence taken, Mrs Ellyard, I assure you." He smiled reassuringly. "You pop into our office tomorrow and I'll have sorted this out. We'll find you a nice little – I mean a suitable flat, Mrs Ellyard. I promise you."

Moyna thanked him and they let themselves out. Shaken by the abortive encounter, Moyna watched him hurry away to his next appointment. She didn't think she could face him again. Perhaps she would find herself another agent.

It was quarter to seven on the evening of the same day when Eddie Tanner opened the front door to his doctor. In silence he led the way into the bedroom where Henry Tanner lay on the bed, apparently asleep.

"This is how I found him," Eddie said. "I thought he was sleeping it off and I didn't disturb him. When I brought him a cup of tea just before six I realised he hadn't moved. Look in his right hand."

The doctor moved forward, put down his bag and bent over the still figure. He looked at his right hand and saw that the fingers were tightly clasped round a small brown glass bottle. Carefully he prised it free and read the label.

"The sleeping pills," he said. "Oh dear! Poor Henry."

Eddie said, "I didn't know he knew they were there. Dad never goes near the bathroom cupboard – not to my knowledge, anyway. The bottle was nearly full. He's taken all of them." He sank down on to a nearby chair and rested his head in his hands. "He meant to . . ." He faltered. "It means he wanted to die. Jesus Christ!"

The doctor felt the old man's wrist, shook his head and sighed. He laid his fingers against the face. "Cold," he said. From his bag he took a stethoscope and, opening the buttons of the pyjama top, listened for a heartbeat.

"He's gone, hasn't he," said Eddie. "Poor old Dad. If only I'd been here. I should have come home earlier."

The doctor put away his stethoscope and closed his bag. Eddie watched, white-faced, his chest heaving with unexpressed grief.

"There's nothing we can do for him," the doctor told him. He rested a hand on his shoulder and said, "Come along into the kitchen. We need to talk."

Eddie wiped his eyes and blew his nose. If only he had guessed what was in his father's mind he might have done something to prevent the tragedy. If *only* he had come home earlier . . .

Back in the kitchen Eddie put the kettle on. "You have to notify the police – I know the procedure." Then his father would have to undergo the indignity of a post mortem and would be buried in an unmarked grave. Suicides were considered unworthy. He shuddered.

He said, "I should have done something. I should have

guessed somehow . . . but he didn't seem any worse than usual when I left home this morning."

The doctor said, "Was there a note? Did he write a goodbye note?"

"No. I've looked. Nothing . . . But it couldn't have been an accident. No one can take all those pills—"

The doctor handed him the pill bottle. He said, "Listen to me carefully, Eddie. I didn't see this bottle and neither did you. I should put it in the dustbin – now."

Eddie stared at him. "But it's evidence. It shows he . . ."

The doctor was shaking his head. "It's only evidence if we saw it. If we found it nearby. We didn't, did we?"

"We didn't?"

The doctor sat down. "Who are we to judge him?" he asked softly. "He wanted to go – for whatever reason. He wasn't a happy man and he felt his time was up. And let's face it, we both know that he was never going to beat the drink. It was slowly killing him and he knew that also. Least said, soonest mended. Don't you agree?"

Eddie hesitated. For a moment his police training and his natural honesty struggled with the desire to go along with the doctor's suggestion. "What would you put then, on the death certificate?" he asked nervously.

"Death by natural causes accelerated by excessive alcohol. I think that would cover it, don't you? He died in his sleep, didn't he?"

Eddie nodded, overwhelmed with gratitude. He glanced down at the bottle in his hand then hurried outside to drop it in the dustbin.

The doctor said, "No need to notify the police. Just the undertaker. And remember. It's just between the two of us. For his sake. Henry and I have been friends for years and I'm not prepared to put him through all those indignities. I always have thought the law on suicides was a bit harsh. Your father deserves a decent burial."

Eddie was lost for words.

The doctor went on. "I'm sure you're sensible enough to keep this to yourself. You would cause me some serious problems if you spoke about it to anyone else."

"I don't know how to thank you . . ." Eddie began.

The doctor drew a pad of forms from his bag and wrote rapidly, asking only for full name and his patient's date of birth. He handed it to Eddie. "You will have to register the death." He smiled sadly. "Don't take it too hard, Eddie. You did all you could for him and you mustn't reproach yourself for what's happened. And don't blame your father." He shook his head. "I knew Henry long before he started drinking."

"I don't know what started it. Was it something to do with my mother? He never talked about his past."

"Your mother? No, no. It started long before they were married. It was an accident. He was friendly with the Knott brothers. Bill and Alan. They were a couple of tearaways. They bought an old fishing boat and patched it up. They asked Henry if he wanted to go fishing with them. The 'maiden voyage' they called it. It grew dark and they turned to come back but it had started to leak. Of course they didn't know what to do. Bailed like mad but the water kept coming in and they panicked. Somehow the boat turned over and, of course, they couldn't right it. They clung to the upturned hull for hours but one by one the other two lost consciousness and drifted away. Your father was the only survivor. He blamed himself for not being able to save them."

"Jesus! Poor old devil!"

"I was called to certify the bodies when they washed ashore. I was in my first year here in my father's practice. I met your father at the inquest. Afterwards he was haunted by the accident. He started drinking and lost his job and drank more. Your mother married him against all the advice. She thought she could save him, I suppose. She did what she could but she gave up in the end. There was no other man in her life, if that's what you thought."

"I didn't know. Dad refused to talk about it."

"She told my wife that she wanted to take you with her when she left, but she didn't want to leave Henry with nothing. You were the light of his life. Maybe she thought he'd come off the drink when he had you to cope with, but he didn't. He did his best, but he wasn't up to it. He was a fool to himself, but too good for an unconsecrated grave."

He walked to the front door with Eddie trailing behind him.

The doctor said, "Goodbye for now, Mr Tanner." He lowered his voice. "Put it behind you and get on with your life. That's what he would have wished for you."

Eddie could only nod. Stunned by the shock and the revelations, his mind was in turmoil.

He closed the door and stood in the hall, trying to make some sense of what had happened. Then slowly he went into his father's room and knelt beside the still figure. He looked at the lined face and greying hair and tried to see him as a young man, full of life and eager for adventure, setting off in a rickety boat for a disastrous fishing trip that was going to ruin his life.

"I'm so sorry, Dad," he whispered. "Whatever went wrong, you didn't have to do this, but I think I understand." He leaned forward and kissed his father's cold cheek.

He sat there for twenty minutes, unwilling to leave him on his own. Then he said a short prayer and struggled to his feet.

In the kitchen he stood in the middle of the room, listening to the silence, and realised that, for the first time in his life, he was completely alone.

In The Linen Store Miss Crane and Mrs Cook were tidying up and hoping that they had seen the last customer of the day. Stanley Dunn was standing by the till checking the day's takings, his forehead wrinkled, his lips pursed as he added up the numbers in his head. The till was a recent and expensive innovation, but he had never fully trusted it so he liked to see that it tallied with the receipt books.

"Ten, thirteen, twenty-one, twenty-four – that's a nought and two shillings . . . two and nine, that's eleven, twelve and seven is nineteen and three more is twenty-two. That's one pound and two shillings . . ." He wrote a two in the shillings column and carried a one into the pounds column. When he was satisfied, he turned his attention to the receipts, but from time to time he glanced towards the door as though he was expecting someone.

He glanced up. "Miss Crane! A moment, please."

She dropped the pile of pillow slips and hurried across to him. "Mr Dunn?"

"This receipt is in your handwriting? This is your signature?"

"Yes, it is."

"I can't read it. I've told you several times about clarity."

"I'm sorry, Mr Dunn. I expect we were rushed. That's—" She pointed. "One pair flannelette sheets."

He said, "Hmm. You have made flannelette look like two words. No wonder I couldn't decipher it."

"I'm sorry, Mr—" She broke off as the bell over the shop door jangled. "Oh, it's Mrs Ellyard!"

All three stared at the visitor and Stanley breathed a sigh of relief. He had waited patiently all day for this moment.

Mrs Ellyard smiled at each one of them. "Mr Dunn . . . Miss Crane . . . Mrs Cook. I have something to tell you. That is, Mr Dunn and I have something to tell you, but . . ." She glanced at the clock above the main counter. "Yes, it is just five-thirty. Do please lock the door, Mr Dunn, so that we won't be interrupted."

237

Miss Crane and Mrs Cook exchanged glances. This was certainly a departure. They watched in silence while the manager locked the shop door and turned the card so that the word CLOSED faced outward. Mrs Cook seized the last tape measure, rolled it up and slipped it into the appropriate drawer. The tray of cotton reels received a perfunctory shake and then she moved cautiously forward to stand beside Miss Crane. Mrs Ellyard smiled at them. Stanley positively beamed. This was exactly as he had imagined the moment.

Mrs Ellyard straightened self-consciously and cleared her throat. "This is a very special occasion," she said, "and we – that is Mr Dunn and I – thought you should share it. I know you've all been anxious about the fate of The Linen Store, since the unfortunate will left by my husband. Half the value of the store was left to Mrs Wheatley for reasons I need not go into. After some discussion it is now clear that Mrs Wheatley has no interest in the store and is very keen to sell her share to Mr Dunn."

She smiled at Stanley who nodded modestly. Only Mrs Ellyard knew what a large loan he had taken out. It was certainly no business of the two assistants.

Mrs Ellyard went on, "In other words, Mr Dunn and I are now partners, owning half each of the business. Mr Dunn has managed the business under my husband's leadership for many years and I know that the store will be safe in our hands."

Mrs Cook began to clap her hands, but stopped as she realised that Moyna had not finished.

"We would like both of you to stay with us under your usual terms. If there are any questions we'd be pleased to answer them."

Miss Crane said, "Wonderful! Oh that's marvellous news!"

Mrs Cook said, "What about Miss Wheatley?"

"I'm afraid Miss Wheatley won't be returning," she said. "Her mother intends to refurbish and develop her guest house and Ginnie – that is, Miss Wheatley – will assist her full-time."

Stanley noticed that the two women exchanged relieved glances.

He said, "There has been a lot of gossip in the local paper, but in a week or two that will die a death. We shall carry on as we did before – before the unfortunate demise of Mr Ellyard. We will need another pair of hands and I will – *we* will advertise for someone full-time. Without Mr Ellyard's contribution we shall be hard pressed, but we can manage if we all pull together."

Mrs Ellyard said, "I shan't interfere in the day-to-day running of the store, but I will consult with Mr Dunn on matters of policy."

Miss Crane said, "Why doesn't young Frank come into the firm? Or is he still going to college?"

Stanley gave her a warning look – the woman was too presumptuous by half – but she was staring at Mrs Ellyard, who hesitated.

"That is a possibility at a later stage," she said, "but for the moment he has other plans. If he did come into the firm he would be replacing me. Mr Dunn is a fixture!"

They all laughed.

Stanley said, "Frank Ellyard is only eighteen. At that age the world beckons, as they say!" Moyna nodded. He continued. "As a small token of our appreciation for all your hard work in the past, Mrs Ellyard and I have decided to add a pound extra to your wages this week."

There were delighted cries of surprise and thanks.

Mrs Ellyard said, "Now I have a lot of things to attend to, so I'll leave you." She shook hands with all of them and turned to go. "Oh by the way," she said, turning back. "I shall be in on Saturdays as usual with some cakes." And she exited to the sound of appreciative laughter.

Stanley waited for the women to collect their handbags from the office and leave the shop. He couldn't wait to get home and tell his wife all about it, but first he stood in the middle of the store, savouring the feeling of power. With a flourish of his pen he would become a partner. As he stood there, he became aware that the feeling of power was mixed with the burden of responsibility and an exciting dash of fear.

Thirteen

Iris walked through the room towards Michael. She had been to visit him three times during the three months he had been in prison and the memory of the trial was beginning to fade from her mind. The charge had been manslaughter and he had put up no defence. For a week the case had been front-page news locally, but it was quickly overtaken by a scandal concerning a local bigwig. Today Iris no longer felt the overwhelming dread which the prison had first inspired in her. It was still a place where all hope seemed to be missing, but she reminded herself that the inmates had each committed a crime against society and presumably deserved to be where they were. Her brother-in-law was no exception and though she grieved for him she felt it only right that he should pay for taking away George's life. To his credit he had never complained about the seven-year sentence.

Catching Michael's gaze, she raised a hand in greeting as he half rose to his feet, smiling a welcome. He had nobody else and Iris knew how much the visits meant to him and couldn't bring herself to abandon him entirely. In her heart she felt that indirectly she and George were responsible for him being locked up. Partly responsible. The rest was his own temper.

"Hello, Michael." She leaned across the table and kissed

him briefly. "How are things?" She didn't enquire too closely because she didn't want to know.

"So-so!" It was his usual answer. "Still sewing mail-bags."

She nodded. If he was hoping for sympathy he would be disappointed. "Ginnie sends her love."

"She won't come, then?"

"No. Why should she? I asked her, but she says she doesn't want to see you here."

"She means because I killed her father. I can't blame her."

"She doesn't talk about George as her father, but she knows he is . . . was." She frowned. "You're losing weight. Face has gone thin."

"The food's terrible." He shrugged. "Except for the macaroni cheese. That's not too bad. Not like your cooking, though." He smiled faintly.

"Ginnie and Frank—" she said. "They're doing well. They've found a way to be friends. Brother and sister. You have to admire them, the way they've come through all this. Frank's been wonderful. Very sensible lad."

"How's he doing at the theatre?"

She brightened. "Very well, according to Moyna. Taken to it like a duck to water. She's very grateful that you suggested it."

"I promised to look out for a job for him. I didn't think it would be *my* job!"

"Mr Laye said he was very artistic, so that's nice . . ." She searched for some news. "Oh yes, the contract's been signed and everything. Stanley Dunn's the proud owner of half the shop. I've got the money safely in the bank and I've started on the improvements. I've ordered a bigger boiler and there'll be radiators. You won't recognise the place when you – when you come out."

Michael glanced away uncomfortably.

That was so tactless, she told herself. Think before you

say things like that. There was an awkward silence. Iris glanced around her. At the next table there was a young mother with two toddlers and Iris was thankful that Michael had no family to worry about. On the other side a burly man with grey hair was talking earnestly to a very elderly woman who repeatedly dabbed at her eyes. Probably his mother. Poor woman. Iris sighed. She'd be glad to get out of the place, but she always gave Michael twenty minutes.

"How's business?" he asked at last.

"Two couples and a single man. Elderly. Very reserved."

"You'll have to watch the men now!" he joked. "Rich widow and all that!"

She gave him a straight look. "They'll be unlucky," she told him. "I'm quite happy on my own." Let him know how things stand, she thought. She certainly didn't want him getting any romantic ideas. "Moyna's found a flat she likes. She's waiting for Frank to see it."

"You two getting pally, then."

She considered, her head on one side. "You could say that," she conceded. "We get along very well when you think what's happened . . . when you look back over the years. Funny old world." She laughed and he smiled with her. "She works part-time now for the private detective. Not that he can afford to pay much. A bit of a one-man band, our Mr Tanner. But he's very taken with her. I can tell. Funny because they're so different and he's not a bit like George."

He glanced round, waved his hand and nodded to a burly man sitting two tables away. "Donald Pratt," he explained. "We stick together. He's my minder, if you know what I mean. No one leans on me and that's because of Donald. He's not one for words, though, so I write all his letters for him. He's trying to get a pardon. He never will, but it keeps him hopeful. He's got another ten years. Armed robbery. He stuck up a bank with a real gun. No bullets but they weren't to know that."

They fell silent again.

Iris said, "They're waiting outside for me. Ginnie and Frank. It's my birthday and Ginnie—"

He slapped his forehead in dismay. "Your birthday? Oh God! I clean forgot. Happy birthday."

"Thanks, Michael. I didn't expect you to remember. I expect all the days are the same in here." She reached across and briefly covered his hand with her own. "Ginnie has made a cake and we're having a party!" She grinned. "Eddie and Moyna are coming when they've closed up the office."

"Sorry I can't be with you, but—"

Neither of them stated the obvious – that his presence would make them all uncomfortable.

He said, "I've come to a decision, Iris. About becoming your manager at Ocean View. It was very generous, but it won't work. I think we both know that. It's going to be Ginnie's one day and she ought to be in on it with you. And anyway, I won't be around. I've made up my mind. Fresh start. I'm going away, back to Dorset."

Iris said nothing. This was exactly what she'd hoped for, although she could never have told him so. Whatever his behaviour in the future, he would always carry the stigma with him and there was no way he could contribute to the success of a guest house. Moving away was the best thing he could do.

He went on. "I like it down there. I'll make a fresh start."

She nodded, hiding her relief. "Whatever you think's best, Michael. It's your life."

He said, "Once upon a time I thought . . . you and me . . ."

"No." She shook her head. "Not then. Not ever. I'm sorry."

They were struggling for words when the bell rang loud and long and Iris rose thankfully to her feet.

She leaned over to kiss him again. "Take care of yourself. I'll see you soon."

Moyna muttered under her breath, pulled the sheet from the typewriter and screwed it up. She reached for a fresh sheet of paper, hoping that Eddie hadn't noticed the waste. She began again and as she did so the telephone rang and he answered it.

"The Tanner Agency. How can I help you?"

A long silence followed, broken only by the tapping she made as her letter advanced slowly down the page.

He said, "Twenty-one? I'm afraid he's . . . Yes, but at twenty-one he's entitled to . . . No, no. I'm simply saying . . ." Catching Moyna's gaze, he rolled his eyes and she smiled.

It was strange, she thought, how easily they had slipped into this relationship. Employer and employee. And she loved the work. Gradually she realised that he was teaching her more and more, involving her more and more in the work itself. Sometimes it helped to have a woman who could ask the questions. A more sympathetic tone, he'd told her. A woman would reveal things to another woman where she would shrink from confiding in a man. Moyna felt useful, and she relished the satisfaction.

Dragging her attention from Eddie's telephone conversation, she regarded the finished letter with pride. She typed the envelope and fastened it to the letter with a paper clip.

Eddie returned the receiver to the hook and asked, "How're you doing?"

"I've just finished," she told him and carried the three letters to his desk for his signature.

"And the invoice?"

"You've got it there." She pointed to it.

"Right. Thanks."

He signed and while he did so she reached for her coat.

They were due at Ocean View in a quarter of an hour for Iris's birthday party.

Eddie sat up in his chair and fiddled with his fountain pen, sliding the cap on and off. He said, "I've had an idea. How would it be if you moved in with me for the time being? You and Frank?" Seeing her expression he went on hastily. "I don't mean *with* me exactly. You could have a couple of bedrooms. Call them bed-sitters if you like. Since Dad died I just rattle around. It's a very big flat. Much too big for one. You'd be doing me a favour. I get lonely, if you must know."

"I – I don't know," she stammered, although her heart was beginning to thump delightfully. "I was going to take Frank to see the flat in—"

"I know. That's why I'm asking you. It's on two floors. You and Frank could have the ground floor and I'd be upstairs. You could pay me a bit of rent or you could have it instead of your wages. You'd still have the money from The Linen Store."

"We-ell. I'd have to talk to Frank, of course, but . . ." She wanted to say, "Yes." She wanted anything that would bring them closer together. The last few months had made her realise that there could be a future for her and Eddie. But she mustn't be too hasty. There might be snags that she hadn't had time to consider.

He said, "The garden could be nice if we stick in a few plants. You said Frank wants a dog. If you don't like the wallpaper I'll change it . . ." His voice trailed off. She still didn't speak, and he pressed the cap on to the pen and laid it down. "OK. Bad idea. You don't want to. I shouldn't have said anything. It's just that when you did the food for Dad's funeral it was so – so great to have you bustling about in my kitchen. Being so – so womanly . . . I couldn't help imagining how it would be if you and me – and Frank – that we made a good team . . ."

246

He swallowed, not daring to look at her. Afraid, thought Moyna, that he would see a rejection. She wasn't sure exactly what he was proposing and she didn't think he knew either.

She said, "I like the idea, Eddie. Of the flat. We could move in, as you say, and see how we all get on. I could cook for you, too, sometimes. Such as Sundays. I always do a roast." She thought how wonderful it would be to be in love with someone who loved and appreciated her.

He stood up and crossed to the window. Staring out, he said, "So is that a 'Yes'?"

She crossed the room to stand beside him. "It's a definite 'Yes'. I'm sure Frank will love the idea. He thinks a lot of you already." She turned him slowly so that he was facing her. "The only problem is that later on, pretty soon actually, you and I . . . we might fall in love. We might want to stay together forever. Would that matter, Eddie, do you think?"

He pulled her into his arms, hugged her until she was breathless and then kissed her. Holding her at arm's length, his dark eyes shone with delight.

"It might well happen," he told her. "And it won't matter at all!"